The Seafarer's Bride

by

Laura Strickland

Viking Brides, Book 3

The Seafarer's Bride

Cover Art by *Diana Carlile*

The Wild Rose Press, Inc.
PO Box 708
Adams Basin, NY 14410-0708
Visit us at www.thewildrosepress.com

Publishing History
First Edition, 2023
Trade Paperback ISBN 978-1-5092-4731-8
Digital ISBN 978-1-5092-4732-5

Viking Brides, Book 3
Published in the United States of America

He paused before the great hall. Last night, Mistress Embra had sent a messenger—an older servant—bidding him to meet her here early.

Well, early it was, and—

The door swung open before him. "Come in."

Not the servant but the lady herself.

Tall she was, this daughter of Friti Gunnarsson, though she might only reach Magnus's ear. He outstripped his own father in height. This morning she wore her dull-gold hair only half braided, with the rest of it spilling all the way down to her—well. As Magnus saw when she turned to lead him inside, she had a very nice bottom indeed.

Suddenly a vision flashed upon him—that of her standing naked before him, wrapped in naught but that curtain of hair.

By Odin's eye, he dared not entertain such thoughts. Not now.

"I thought it best we meet early, Master Magnus, before any others of my siblings are astir. None of them tends to leave his or her bed early."

"Ah."

"And I wished the two of us to speak together as plainly as possible."

She turned to face him. She wore a simple woolen dress like Modir usually wore, pale green with a white overdress. The fabric clung to her long limbs and emphasized her narrow waist. And a pair of breasts that—nei, they were not lush and heavy, like her sister Vanja's. But ja, they would fill both his hands generously.

He had to make sure this woman did not prove a distraction.

Praise for Laura Strickland and...

The Berserker's Bride:

"Cleverly written, emotionally satisfying, I highly recommend this entertaining read."

~*Author L. J. Vickery*

The Shaman's Bride:

"Beautifully written with amazing descriptions, the reader finds they practically live on the island within the settlement. This book has everything a fan of a Viking romance could want. There is action, magic, and intrigue. The book becomes a page-turner as you can't wait to see what happens next."

~*N. N. Light's Book Heaven*

Mrs. Claus and the Viking Ship:

"If you are looking for a heart-warming tale of the power of love with excellent historical detail, then this is one Christmas story you will not want to miss."

~*Reader Lady*

Chapter One

Sorvagur, The Faroe Islands—Summer 931

The evening light hung like liquid silver above the bay that footed the headland, covering both sky and water in a hush. Not so much as a breath of wind stirred the hair or clothing of the two men who stood together on the clifftop.

Magnus Tolljursson did not need anyone to tell him that such moments as this held a wide and binding magic. He'd known that all his life, from first he'd understood the stories his mother told him beside their family's hearth. Since long before he comprehended what powers came to transform his father into a berserker warrior.

He glanced at the man beside him, who appeared as transfixed as he by the approaching evening. Magnus had never expected his sister Gyda's new husband to become his closest friend. They were far too different, Lodvar being a shaman who thought in terms of dreams, and the bending of reality. No warrior like Magnus, who had trained at arms most his life.

Yet over the past year, since Lodvar and Gyda had wed, so it had come to be. For he and Lodvar had much that was alike about them, beneath the surface.

They both adored Gyda. Both of them had been fathered by Norsemen upon Gaelic slaves. And both of them believed in a power that could push a man along through life—to his destiny.

Much to Magnus's surprise, they understood one another. And Magnus, who tended to consider consequences before taking any course of action, had come to rely upon Lodvar's spiritual acuity and vision.

Apart from when Lodvar looked at Gyda, it was difficult to tell what he was thinking at any given moment. A harsh upbringing in the Norse settlement at Husavik, back in Iceland, had trained him to disguise his emotions. Tall and slender, with long brown hair twisted into braids and threaded with sigils, he held himself with a natural dignity more suited to a jarl than a slave.

He returned Magnus's look now with a certain gravity. "My brodir, are you still certain you wish to undertake this?"

"Ja." Magnus eyed the two longships riding upon the silver water of the bay below. One of them stood readied for departure come morning. Magnus had not gone viking very often. His father, who had founded the settlement of Sorvagur, kept his people much at home.

But ach, ja, they'd been on voyages enough for trading and some just for pleasure. Magnus loved the heady freedom of the open sea, and could scarcely wait for the morrow.

The business to which he must attend in Husavik, ja, that might prove touchy and dangerous. Were he honest, he looked forward to that far less than the voyage itself.

Lodvar stirred. "I fully intended to make this venture on my own."

That made Magnus glance at him. "I know you

did."

Magnus's father, Tolljur Magnussen, might rarely go raiding, but when trouble came to him or his, he fought like the bear that so often possessed him. That had happened just a year ago, when Lodvar had arrived in the guise of shaman to the jarl Gunnar Fritisson, from Husavik.

Old scores had been settled the hard way. And Lodvar had bonded with Gyda, a bond of passion and spirit that reached deep.

"You cannot possibly leave Gyda, not now," he said.

Gyda was due, any day, to deliver her first child. In truth, the midwife insisted it was a set of twins. It had not been an easy pregnancy and Gyda, a warrior to the heart, did not like being ordered off her feet. Indeed, she made a terrible patient, fretful and restless, and listened to no one but her husband.

"She is afraid," Lodvar had once confided to Magnus with uncommon perception. "And she is a woman not used to fearing anything."

Knowing his sister, Magnus could only agree.

"Nei," Lodvar said now. "Yet this mission you undertake is mine alone."

"Is it?" Magnus, his eyes back on the vista of silver, tipped his head.

"My mother, and my promise concerning her, are my responsibility."

A year ago when Lodvar had accompanied Gunnar from Iceland, bent on attacking the settlement here at Sorvagur, he'd left his mother, a Gaelic slave, behind. He'd vowed to rescue her as soon as he could and bring her here to safety, a freedom over a score of years overdue.

When he'd planned the voyage last winter, they'd had no idea Gyda's pregnancy would be so risky. And the journey could not wait. Summers were short, and this was the time to sail.

Magnus clapped Lodvar on the back. "I always planned to accompany you, anyway." Whatever miracles Lodvar might command, he was no warrior, though Magnus had seen him fight with powers that required no axe. At Husavik, Odin alone knew what sort of contests might arise.

"Ja, but now the trouble and danger of it is all your own."

"Will there be trouble?" Magnus gave his slow smile.

"We do not know who is in charge at Husavik since Jarl Friti's death, and Gunnar's."

"Friti had other children, did he not? There will be a scramble for power."

Lodvar nodded. "There will. Husavik is a wealthy settlement."

"I hope they are busy quarreling among themselves. I will step in, inform them of what befell the crew sent here to attack us last summer—"

"As if they will not have figured that out already."

"—and offer to buy your mother."

Lodvar nodded still more somberly.

Magnus tried to imagine that scene and did not need to stretch his mind far. Lodvar's mother, Catrin, was trapped in Husavik just as his own mother, Eadha, had once been. Both women had been captured during Norse raids in the southern Gaelic isles. Magnus's mother had gained her freedom when she wed his father.

Catrin still awaited rescue.

Sorvagur could not be considered a wealthy settlement like Husavik. But Lodvar had scraped together a price. Kaddi, the former shaman of the settlement, had left everything he owned to Lodvar when he died last year, including his place among these Norse folk. Lodvar would spend it all for his mother's sake.

"If you go into battle," Lodvar began.

"I enjoy a battle." Magnus grinned. "My axe has not been wetted in some time."

"Still—"

"Please, brodir. I cannot call off the voyage now. My crew would rise up in violent protest." He took with him select members of his contemporaries, young men of Norse blood over-anxious for adventure. Especially his good friend Apsel. "They will attack me, if I disappoint them."

"I suppose you cannot allow that to happen."

"Do not worry, Lodvar. It will be well. I can play at the diplomat when I need to."

Lodvar shot him a sharp look. "Have you spoken to Astrid?"

Astrid was Gyda's best friend. For some time, she had followed Magnus around with her heart in her eyes, and offered him what he could not quite resist. Did they have an understanding? Nei, and nei. Astrid might well have expectations. She might suppose they would one day wed. But Magnus, an honest man to the heart, admitted he did not love her as he should.

He wanted a love like his parents shared, all-consuming and unbreakable as iron bonds. He wanted what Lodvar and Gyda had, a connection that reached beyond the physical to the spirit. How could he settle for a woman of whom he was merely very fond?

"Nei," he said aloud.

"Do you mean to speak with her before you sail?"

In truth, Magnus had hoped to avoid it. While willing to face most any warrior in battle with his axe in his hands, he shrank from the very idea of that particular encounter.

He shrugged.

Rueful amusement invaded Lodvar's eyes—another reason the two of them got on. They shared an appreciation for wry understatement.

But Lodvar said, "You know it is the right thing to do." He turned his gaze back to the silver water. "Gyda says Astrid speaks of you all the time. She awaits the day you will ask her to wed."

By Odin's eye! That wasn't what Magnus needed to hear.

A figure moved on the green sward behind them, stirring the shadows that had formed from the gathering night. Magnus turned his head. Was it Modir? She sometimes liked to walk, to commune with the sea and her gods. Southern gods they were, brought with her from home. Yet they somehow managed to get along with the Norse gods Fadir followed.

But nei, this was not Modir.

Alerted by something beyond ordinary senses, Lodvar turned. He swore softly.

She came leaning on a staff, not unlike the one Lodvar habitually used, and she moved slowly enough to fool Magnus into thinking she was someone else. She wore a loose-fitting cloak and her hair hung all around her shoulders.

Lodvar hurried to her and took her arm. Every graceful line of him became one of concerned devotion, and Magnus's throat tightened.

He should have known his sister would come. Wherever Lodvar might be, she would soon appear also.

Lodvar murmured, "My heart, you should not be on your feet."

"Rubbish."

"You know what the midwife said. You risk delivering our babies too soon, and if they are too small—"

"If, *if*." Gyda sounded disagreeable, yet she reached up and caressed her husband's face with infinite tenderness before coming on to join her brother.

She looked wild and beautiful in her pregnancy. Gyda took after their father, with the same ashen blond hair and grey eyes, though she had inherited a measure of Modir's second sight. Part Seer and part fierce warrior. Magnus adored her, but he did not envy Lodvar the task of trying to reason with her.

Magnus, so Modir said, took after her bloodline. He'd never met any of his relatives in the Alban Islands, but Modir insisted he looked much like her father, also a warrior and a chief there. Whatever the case, he shared Modir's reddish-brown hair, hazel eyes, and freckled skin.

Gyda gazed out over the bay. "Beautiful, and well worth the walk up here."

"Ja." Magnus could only agree. On both sides, their ancestors had been seafarers. The ocean ran in their blood.

Gyda slanted a look at him. "Anxious, Brodir?"

He thought about it. "I want to see this accomplished." Lodvar's mother had languished in servitude too long. On the other hand, he had no idea what sort of reception he and his warriors would receive in Husavik, having slain the settlement's jarl and his heir, right here on this shore.

Who would he find in charge there, with both Friti and Gunnar dead? With whom would he have to deal when he landed?

"I wish I were sailing with you," Gyda said. "What an adventure! But I could not leave this one here. What would he do without me?"

"What, indeed?" Lodvar raised her hand to his lips.

"To say naught of the fact you would likely deliver those babes of yours half way to Husavik."

"No matter." She tossed her head. "I do not doubt I could still hold a sword, with a babe at each breast."

Magnus snorted, but not in derision. He did not doubt it either.

"Come, wife. Away to our bed. You should not be on your feet."

"Very well." She gazed into Lodvar's eyes and became compliant. "You know I cannot sleep without you there."

"I know."

They moved off slowly and left Magnus aching.

Ach, for such a love.

Chapter Two

"Wait. Wait!"

Astrid's voice sounded like the cry of a gull there on the shore. Morning had dawned soft and gray with clouds moving in from the southwest. The air felt heavy, and Magnus could smell rain in the offing.

He hadn't slept more than a wink last night. After parting with Lodvar and Gyda, he'd tramped the cliffs and tried to calm his mind. To speak to his gods.

If ever a man should do that, it seemed, it must be before embarking upon a voyage into the unknown. He'd been brought up in the knowledge of gods both Norse and Gaelic. Modir spoke to her god, the shining Lugh of the south, much as she spoke to Fadir. And Fadir, though a quiet man, called upon Odin in times of duress.

All Magnus's life, he'd shared the company of Kaddi, the old shaman who guided the folk of the settlement and who seemed to know his gods intimately. But they'd lost Kaddi last year during the fight Friti and Gunnar had brought to their shores.

Lodvar had taken his place.

Lodvar's belief, like Kaddi's, appeared deep and personal. But then, Lodvar being a shaman, could even speak to Gyda in his mind.

Tramping the cliffs in the dark, Magnus thought about the fact that while he believed in something real and powerful, he had chosen no personal god and called upon no one. As a warrior, he should call upon Tyr. Or some other, Gaelic god he could not name.

Now, upon the bustling shore, with the whole settlement come to see them off, he had to put such thoughts aside.

"Magnus!"

Not the cry of a gull, nei, but Astrid calling his name. Dismay seized him, and he strove to disguise it as he turned to face her. She'd caught him on the very verge of leaving.

Breathless, she paused in front of him.

A tiny thing was Astrid, delicately made, with fair hair and a face full of sweetness rather than beauty. They'd known each other all their lives, and folk expected them to end up together. In fact there were indulgent smiles now when she joined him.

"I am late." She looked up into his face in that way she had—hopeful and adoring. It never failed to make Magnus feel like a man about to swat a kitten. Not that he ever would.

"I have something for you, Magnus."

"Do you?"

"Ja. I made it. 'Tis a charm and will keep you safe on your voyage."

"Ah." Magnus did not know what else to say. He stood awkwardly watching while she fished out a stone she had threaded onto a leather cord.

"It is a hag stone. I found it myself, on the shore, and have purified it in moonlight, and blessed it also."

Women's magic. Magnus would never scoff at it. His mother's magic had strength enough.

"Here, bend down so I may put it on you."

Magnus bent his head, which brought his face very close to her earnest one.

He had made love to her in the past—not once but three times, though he'd been careful not to leave her his seed. They were too young, and he too unsure, to tie himself to her with a babe. Her willingness had seduced him. The choice of partners here at Sorvagur was not wide.

But now, beholding the look in her eyes as she placed the cord around his neck, he regretted it.

Her fingers lingered in the hair at the back of his neck, and her blue eyes brimmed with emotion. For a moment, one terrible moment, Magnus feared she would speak the words, *I love you.*

She kissed him instead, a hard kiss, there before all the company. "There. Promise you'll come back to me."

Could he do that? Would not such an utterance be a pledge of belonging? He murmured instead, "I have every intention of coming home again."

His heart lay here, in this green place between worlds, half Norse and half Gael just like him. Though his spirit might long for adventure and answer the call of the sea, it would always be rooted here.

"Good. I—"

A fortuitous interruption occurred then. Fadir stepped up and placed his hand on Magnus's shoulder.

"Son, a word before you embark."

Magnus turned to his father with some relief.

Those who did not know Tolljur Magnusson might take him for a fearsome brute. And ja, he was fearsome in battle, especially when he succumbed to the berserker's trance. He wore the scars of many battles, as well as the clawed furrows of the bear, which marked him on his cheeks.

Beneath it all, though, lay a gentle spirit, one that loved deeply. Tolljur loved his family and this land. He adored his wife.

"Fadir." Magnus's lips quirked. "Any advice for me?"

"Ja. You go with a good ship and a good crew." Half a score of men, all young and well-versed at arms. Fadir himself had trained them, and none better. Magnus had drilled them and had known them all his life. Excitable, perhaps, this being their first independent voyage. But sound.

He nodded.

"Your danger lies not at sea but once you arrive at Husavik." Fadir shook his head. "It is a dangerous place full of treacherous folk. We have nothing here to prepare you for it."

Society here in Sorvagur under Fadir remained easy, casual. No politics, no deceit.

He pointed out, "Friti and Gunnar are gone."

"Ja, and that gives me pause. The enemy you know is sometimes better than the one you do not know. We have no idea who has seized power in Husavik. Only that someone has. It is an unsavory stew, and Friti—and that bitch of a wife of his, Anaborg—had a number of other children besides Gunnar."

"Ja. They will have fought it out amongst them."

"They will have slit one another's throats. Whoever is left will be ruthless."

"I will have a care." Magnus gazed into his father's gray eyes and beheld the worry there. All Magnus's life, his father's love had been a shield protecting him.

Now, Tolljur must let him step out from behind that shield.

How difficult that must be.

"Husband, let the boy go." Modir stepped up to Fadir's side. In the morning light, her freckled face looked stark, and the brown birthmark on her cheek stood out. The mark of the gods, some called it. Magnus bore a similar mark on his left thigh.

If he'd been marked by the gods, they so far remained silent about their claiming.

She pulled Magnus into her arms for a hug as fierce as her nature. Her love flowed over him like a soothing balm. She kissed both his cheeks.

"Go safely, my son."

"I will."

"Now, let Lodvar speak a prayer. Get your crew aboard."

Was it fitting that Modir and not Fadir spoke those final orders? Unlike many Norsemen, Fadir let Modir speak as she chose. Would that also hold true at Husavik?

He met his father's gaze, which danced with quiet amusement, and called to his men. "Aboard! Let us catch the tide."

He did not see the expression in Astrid's eyes as he turned away, because he did not look.

****

"How many days before we reach landfall at Husavik?"

Magnus turned when Apsel posed the mischievous query. Apsel was black-haired, reliable, and strong in spirit, and Magnus's next-in-command. Nearly of an age, they'd grown up together, and Magnus counted him among his closest friends.

He waved an arm aft. "We just left Sorvagur and already your patience has worn thin? You are like a child."

Apsel grinned broadly. He had a chipped tooth gotten during youthful sparring, and it made him look like a boy when he smiled.

"Just eager to wet my blade. We are all of us half starved for adventure."

Magnus nodded. Viking blood ran strong in all of them, but they'd had little opportunity to go raiding. Most of them, ja, had been on trading expeditions. They knew how to sail and how to fight. But Tolljur rarely made war on anyone.

Indeed, much of their summers were spent tilling fields, which agreed with few of them.

"You may not wet your blade in Husavik," he cautioned his friend. "We do not know what we will find."

"Precisely." Apsel wagged his eyebrows. "We may find battle."

Magnus hoped not. Though he was not loath to raise the axe he favored in combat, he'd experienced the full horrors of that last summer and, in fact, had fallen victim for the first time to his father's curse—the berserker's fit.

Both he and Gyda had.

He did not want to experience that again.

"In any case," Apsel's gaze sobered, "I wanted to thank you for including me in your crew."

"As if I would go without you."

Apsel laughed softly and ran his gaze down the length of the ship, where their excited mates tended the steerage.

"We have had a wealth of adventures together in the past. Remember the time you got stuck on the face of the cliff, collecting birds' eggs?"

"How could I forget?" Magnus had been about five or six. "Modir came and screamed at me until I decided it was better to risk falling than continue having my ears flayed."

Apsel chuckled.

"And remember the time all the maids caught us skinny-dipping in the pool?"

"Ja." Much later. They'd been about sixteen then. Magnus still felt the strange combination of emotions that had filled him when he realized they were being watched. Intense embarrassment, overshadowed by an unprecedented pride in his body.

"This," Apsel declared, "will be the greatest adventure yet."

"Ja, no doubt." A brief silence fell while only the breaking of waves against the prow and the fitful breeze in the sails could be heard.

"You do realize, Apsel, not all of us may make it home again."

"I do, ja."

Another silence, briefer this time.

"My mother says Norse men cannot count on a long life." Like Magnus's, Apsel's mother had been taken captive in Alba. "My father says no man worthy of his Norse blood would want to."

Magnus laughed softly.

"We will return, Magnus. I feel it in my water. As you have business at Husavik, there is unfinished business here also."

"Ach, ja?"

Apsel slid his gaze to Magnus. "Did you speak to Astrid before we left?"

"Speak to her?"

"Ja, I saw the two of you there on the shore. Did you tell her you would come back and marry her?"

Magnus stared at his friend before he shook his head. "Nei. Why do you ask?"

Apsel pursed his lips and stared away into the far distance. "Rain coming."

"Ja, it will soon cross our path. But, Apsel, what do you say about Astrid?"

"Only that I think she expects marriage from you."

Magnus's heart sank.

"If that is not what you want—" Apsel let the words hang.

"It is not."

"Then you should make yourself clear to her."

Ja. Ja, he should.

"And, friend, if you mean to cast her away, pray consider casting her in my direction."

Chapter Three

"They are fighting again, and have drawn blood. I fear there will be a murder if you do not do something about it."

Embra Fritisdottir heaved a sigh and turned from her mirror to eye her companion with a scowl.

The mirror, a treasure, had been brought from the east long ago by her father, one Friti Gunnarsson. He'd presented it as a gift for Embra's mother, and when Embra was small, visiting Modir's rooms, she had loved to peer into it. In those days, she'd believed it held magic that allowed her to see herself, just like in a pool of water.

Ja, and the mirror must possess a measure of magic to have survived her mother's fits of madness and her parents' many arguments. Not much else had survived those days of upheaval. Not even the girl she, Embra, had once been.

Now Modir was locked away, raving much of the time. And Fadir was—well, presumed lost on that voyage to the Faroe Islands last year, along with Embra's oldest brother, Gunnar.

Their absence, and its accompanying uncertainties, had unleashed a chaos that endured this whole year past.

Now her gaze met that of her servant, Kennach. A slave captured in Erin long ago, Kennach had been with her most her life. No longer a young man, she acknowledged he was still important to her. She'd had a succession of nurses when young, but Modir invariably ordered them off in one of her rages.

Kennach, being in essence a furnishing, could not be ordered off. He'd become the one consistency in Embra's life.

She looked him in the eye and gestured to the mirror. "I was just girding myself for battle." She never used the mirror out of vanity. Though she'd been told all her life she was beautiful, the compliment meant nothing. Modir was beautiful—the most beautiful woman in Husavik, it was said. Only look what that beauty had done for her.

Nei, Embra used the mirror in order to make certain she looked formidable, nothing more.

"Which of them is it this time?"

Kennach grimaced. A man of ordinary height and girth, he had what Embra considered a typically Gaelic face, with a broad forehead and wide-set eyes. Those eyes had been her touchstones so many times—when she wept, when she felt loneliness, or despair. But when had his hair gone from brown to gray? Ach, how much time had passed.

"Your sisters, Mistress."

Ach, Freya, not that. Embra possessed a brood of brothers and sisters. One thing her parents had done well was breed. Gunnar, now missing, was the oldest and named after his grandfather, the former jarl. Another son, Runi, had inherited a measure of Modir's madness and become a reclusive schemer. Embra had been born next, the eldest of the girls, followed by two more boys and three more girls. All, miraculously, had survived and would yet, if they did not kill each other over the succession.

"I have three sisters. Which of them?"

"Mistress Vanja and Mistress Dagmar. There has been spitting and name-calling. Slaps and clawing. When it became violent, I came for you."

Embra abandoned the mirror. Her chamber was very small, but it was her own. She had traded space for privacy, but that failed to protect her when things like this occurred. And lately, they seemed to happen more and more often.

Who had named her peacemaker?

"Kennach, come."

He followed her, a steadying presence, as she strode out from her chamber and through the great hall, which lay beyond. A gray day, she saw, with rain in the offing. From the doorway of the hall she could gaze straight down to the sea.

A thriving settlement, was Husavik, and a prize any number of men here longed to seize. At the moment, only Fadir's name kept them at bay. That, and Embra's iron insistence. Incidents like this one did not help her maintain an illusion of family stability.

"Where are they?"

Kennach pointed half way down the slope toward the sea, where Embra picked out a knot of people gathered, like a scab on a wound.

Or perhaps more accurately like a writhing pile of maggots.

She swore softly and started down, wishing she carried a sword. A sword lent impact. She could holler only so loud.

If her sisters wanted to argue, there was little she

could do about it. Though born only a year apart, they differed wildly in their temperaments, and their opinions. She had told them a thousand times to argue in private, not out here where the whole settlement could see.

Even before she reached them, she heard the shouting. Screeching, more like. Curses and the sound of blows—more like two cats fighting than young women.

The crowd parted when she arrived, and she saw that Runi was there. Ja he would be, with a look of sly enjoyment on his face. Embra was surprised, though, to see her younger brother, Ulrik, just standing and watching the melee.

Ja, and Ulrik would not mind seeing some of his siblings eliminated, to improve his own chances of seizing power.

Embra did not know how this quarrel had started. With name-calling, most likely. It had degenerated to the physical. Embra's sisters writhed on the ground like, indeed, two scrappy felines. Whatever words they had for one another had become yowls and hisses.

Embra waded into the thick of it, taking her life in her hands. Vanja had gained the advantage for the moment and crouched over her sister, who lay on her back, blood oozing from scratches on her face. Embra seized the back of Vanja's dress, for she wore no cloak, and hauled her off.

It took all her strength. Not a petite woman, Vanja had inherited strength of her own from their father, though rumor said she welcomed men to her bed as Modir once had.

"By Freya's heart!" Embra cried. "What is all

this?"

Vanja jerked out of her grasp, bristled and turned on her. Madness filled her blue eyes, and Embra had only an instant to prepare for attack.

A slap came. Embra blocked it with one forearm, dodged a solid punch from her sister's left hand, and seized hold of her again. She shook, hard.

"What is the matter with you?" A foolish question. Embra knew a vein of madness ran through all the children of Anaborg Helmsdottir.

Vanja spat, a crude gesture that sadly failed to shock Embra, though she did experience a rush of disgust.

"She," Vanja panted dramatically, "says Fadir is dead. Gunnar also!"

Embra looked at Dagmar, who had now scrambled up from the ground, furious. Blood still oozed from the scratches on her pretty face. Ja, Dagmar was beautiful, looking much like Modir. She had Fadir's temper, though.

Embra cast another look at her two brothers who stood by. Runi clearly enjoyed the scene, his face tight with sly mirth and his eyes narrowed to slits. Ulrik stood expressionless. Freya alone knew what he thought.

Over the past year, they—as a family—had discussed many times what might have happened to Fadir and their eldest brother Gunnar. A year ago, the two had sailed away with a stout crew, ostensibly to go viking.

Embra knew better. Fadir wanted to settle old scores with a former fellow warrior, a berserker called Tolljur Magnusson. Magnusson had established himself as jarl in the Faroe Islands. Fadir wished to attack and humble him.

Among other things.

Fadir and Gunnar had not returned home from that voyage, nor had any message been sent. The family had debated endlessly over what that meant and had split more or less down two sides—those who believed Fadir had seized the settlement at Sorvagur, slain the berserker, and now reigned there with Gunnar at his side, and those who believed their father and brother were either imprisoned by the berserker or dead.

Embra had started out on the former side. Knowing her father and brother well, she could not imagine them defeated.

As time crept past, though, she had come to accept the other theory. She could not conceive of Fadir failing to return home and boast of his victory. If he could.

Talk ran rife of sending another expedition, now that the season had come, to find out. The only thing standing in the way of that was Embra herself, and the fragile control she had seized.

Now her anger stirred. She did not mind how her sisters and brothers disagreed in private. But even these two madwomen should know better than to display the cracks in the family to the whole settlement.

It argued vulnerability. A vulnerable man or woman in Husavik might as well be a lamb tied out, waiting for the wolves to come.

She wanted to shout. She wanted to scold them. She longed to ask her brothers why they hadn't put a stop to such a disgraceful scene. But one did not chastise adults before the underlings.

Instead she barked, "All of you, come." Her

scathing look touched each of her siblings in turn. Vanja, still in the throes of mad anger, bristled. Embra silenced her with a fierce glare.

The crowd muttered and broke up as Embra marched off with all four of her siblings and Kennach in tow. Embra was not deceived. Folk would be talking about this for the next fortnight.

And if she wanted to keep any semblance of control, an illusion that Friti Gunnarsson's house still stood strong, she could show no weakness, not even to her brothers and sisters.

Thus she swept into the great hall, which stood cool and empty at this time of day, and turned on them.

"You fools!" she began scathingly.

They all bristled, if for different reasons. Runi hated to think himself as anything but clever. Ulrik, with an eye for his ambitions, tended to challenge her position of power on general principle. The sisters, still angry, longed to strike out.

Before they could speak, Embra barreled on. "What sort of image do you suppose that scene back there creates for our enemies?"

Talk of enemies always snared their attention. The only time they ever stood together was when they opposed someone else.

"I did not begin it!" Vanja flared. "I was peacefully enjoying looking out over the harbor when this one"— she jerked a thumb at Dagmar—"came along and picked a fight."

"She was keeping watch for Fadir's ship," Dagmar sneered. "Again." She dabbed at the scratches on her face and told Vanja, "You better not have marked me."

"Or what?" Vanja turned to face her. "You won't

be able to lure men to your bed? Sostir, they do not come for your face but for your overused—"

"Enough!" Embra bellowed.

Runi chuckled. "Sostir, she has a point. Our dear Dagmar has ambitions to lay more men than Modir in her prime."

Embra leaned toward her brother. Runi outstripped her in height by quite a measure, though she was not a petite woman. He had sea-blue eyes, his mother's golden hair, and a face that could change from innocent to dangerous in an instant.

"Shut. Up." She told him.

He raised a long finger and poked it at her. "You feel threatened," he pronounced.

She did, horrendously so. She would never admit it to him.

"Fadir," she said through gritted teeth, "left us to look after this holding while he was away viking. How do you think you are doing at that, eh?"

The question made them shift their gazes to one another.

Deliberately, she went on, "We do not know where Fadir is. What he is doing. It does not matter."

Vanja fired up. "How can you say—"

Swiftly, Embra turned on her. "It does not matter what we believe, or whether we agree. Do you not see that? We must behave as if Fadir will be coming back once he consolidates his power in the Faroes. Anything else will allow his enemies, those who have been waiting for years to seize power here, to step in. And what will happen to us then?"

She watched as each of them contemplated it. They were not stupid, nei. Hasty, reckless, and often dangerous, but not stupid.

Predictably it was Vanja, Fadir's champion, who—so rumor had it—had shared more than a father-daughter relationship with him, that challenged her. "What do you think has happened to them, eh, Embra?"

"I think Fadir and Gunnar are both dead, or imprisoned. But until we know the truth of it, I will never—never!—let on to the rest of Husavik. Because, my dear ones, if Fadir is dead, we will have a vicious fight indeed on our hands."

Chapter Four

"A ship. A ship!"

The call set Embra back on her heels and sent a jolt through her blood that had her instantly on her feet.

Her gaze met that of her sister, Dagmar, with whom she'd been sharing a supper in an effort to— well, civilize her.

"Fadir," Dagmar voiced Embra's own immediate thought.

She looked at Ulla, her youngest sister at only twelve, who had run with the message. "Is it?"

Ulla shook her head. "Too far away to see. It is a longboat, though."

"Let us go and see," Embra said, but Dagmar had already dashed off.

Embra followed with Ulla, breathless, on her heels. The call had gone out, and most the settlement streamed to the bay, where a number of stout boats lay at anchor. A fine harbor was Husavik's, deep and wide.

Embra paused, the blood singing in her ears. "Where?"

"Way out, just coming round the headland. Ulrik spotted it."

Ulrik must have vision like an osprey. Embra squinted against the afternoon glare and shaded her eyes with her hand.

There. A dark speck in movement. Heading in. Ja,

it had the dimensions of a longboat, lengthy and slender.

Did she catch the glint of weapons in the sun?

Ulrik shouldered up beside her. She slanted a look at him. "Fadir?" Part of her hoped so. Friti Gunnarsson might be a difficult man, an arrogant and violent one. But he possessed the ability to keep order here in Husavik, an ability she began to suspect she lacked.

Runi didn't want that authority, and passing it to Ulrik would be pure folly.

Another part of her, her heart possibly, hoped she would never see her father or brother again.

In the past when one of their ships came home from raid or trading expeditions, celebrations always ensued. There would be plunder, goods, and maybe slaves, pretty baubles for the women and stolen weapons for the men. The instinct now was to swarm the harbor, to fete the returning warriors and their ability to prosper.

Or should they raise a defense?

She elbowed Ulrik. "Well, is it Fadir?" she asked again.

He shrugged, his face inscrutable.

"Or Gunnar?" Their eldest brother might make it home without Fadir, in a pinch. If so, he would seize the title of jarl.

The gods help them all.

A shiver ran down Embra's spine. Gunnar, a handsome man with Modir's golden hair and bright blue eyes, equated deception on two feet. What he could not gain through charm he would take by force.

Could anyone in the far-off Faroes, even a berserker, defeat two such men?

Someone down at the harbor blew a horn. If it were Fadir on that boat, or any of his crew, a horn would resound in reply.

They all stood straining their ears.

Nothing.

The watcher at the harbor squalled again. The longboat now grew near enough to see more clearly. Its crew rowed hard. No horn blew.

Runi came up and joined them, his eyes narrowed with enjoyment. "What do you think?" he asked.

Embra caught her breath. Nearer, and she could just pick out the shields hung over the side of the ship.

She did not recognize the emblems on them.

A cold knot formed in her stomach. "Ulrik, mount a defense."

Ulrik glared at her. "Who are you to give me orders?"

"Your sister."

"You are not the eldest, not even with Gunnar away."

"Runi, tell him."

"Do as your sister says," Runi bade Ulrik carelessly. "We may be under attack, if only by a single ship."

Embra made an impatient sound as Ulrik pelted off. Runi slid his gaze to her. "They will be traders."

"We do not know that."

"A single ship, heading in so casually? Traders. Either that, or someone with balls the size of Odin's head."

****

So this was Husavik. Magnus stared avidly from his place at the prow as the longboat headed in. All his life he'd wondered about this place. It held half his heritage. His and a good measure of the crew now onboard with him.

He glanced at his men before turning his gaze back to the settlement, which sprawled above the semicircular bay. Many of his men were the sons of warriors who had emigrated from this place along with the berserker, Tolljur Magnusson, when relationships here had broken, and of the former Gaelic slaves they had taken for brides.

It made for a particular breed of men, as different perhaps from these Norse who lived here as bronze from iron.

When Magnus had been small, he had asked his parents about Husavik, being unendingly curious. Fadir had been willing to say little, and the pain that invaded his gray eyes gave Magnus pause.

Modir had been a little more forthcoming, telling him when she grew impatient with his questions, "It is a terrible place full of violence and treachery. I was happy to see the last of it."

A terrible place? He wanted to say, "But I am half made from it." The stark expression on her face kept him from saying anything of the kind.

Now he had an excuse to see for himself, for Lodvar's benefit. And from the looks of his companions, their curiosity matched his own.

"Take us in," he called to Knut, at the rudder.

It appeared the entire settlement had gathered at the harbor and on the slope above. Perhaps they expected his arrival to bring word of Friti and Gunnar, now both dead. He brought news, ja, but probably not what they wished to hear.

Ah, but what did they expect when they sent men to attack the berserker's settlement at Sorvagur?

He felt a tingle as he called to his men. "Ready your weapons. We are not certain how we will be received."

"We will have kin here," said Jorg, coming up beside him. Like Magnus, Jorg looked more Gael than Norse, with rich brown hair and dark eyes that had seduced many a Norse woman. A demon with a sword, Magnus counted him a good friend.

"Ja," Magnus agreed. "Not that it will do us any good if they decide to take our heads."

Jorg grinned. "I am ready for a fight, after that idle journey."

"You call that idle?"

"Ja. A little rowing always sets me up for a brawl."

Magnus snorted. They were now inshore far enough to see individual faces in the crowd.

"Drop anchor!"

The men shipped their oars and took up their shields, all in one movement.

Magnus told himself to remain calm. Ja, this was a big moment, one his demeanor could make or break. He needed to be confident but not aggressive.

A man strode out on the fine pier that faced them. Of middle years, with a balding head and beard streaked with gray, he appeared neither hostile nor friendly.

"Identify yourselves!" he called out.

Magnus drew a breath that expanded his chest. His entire mission here rested on the next few moments.

Lifting his head, he bellowed, "I am Magnus Tolljursson from Sorvagur."

Tolljursson. *Tolljursson!* The name traveled like a scrounging crow on a battlefield, and the crowd pressed closer. Wanting to get a better look at him, no doubt.

The berserker's son.

The man who had addressed them appeared nonplussed. He glanced over his shoulder at the crowd, then farther up the slope.

Turning back to Magnus, he demanded, "What is your business in Husavik?"

"I bring word of Friti Gunnarsson."

The reaction this time passed through the crowd the way a wave might, causing a tremor that reached up the slope behind. Magnus let his gaze follow it and saw an additional stir in a knot of people gathered half way up, just his side of a large structure that must be the jarl's hall.

For an instant his eyes widened. They had nothing like that hall back in Sorvagur, and it argued great wealth. Ja, Fadir had his dwelling, but most gatherings were held outdoors. The cost of timber was dear—he could not easily estimate the voyages and raids it must have taken to gain what was needed to build what he now saw on display.

At Sorvagur, no one lived better than anyone else. Not so here, it appeared.

"Wait!" the man called.

A lad went pelting off up the slope to the very knot of people Magnus had noticed. Ach, so someone of importance lingered there. Someone with whom he would have to deal.

A reasonable man, he hoped. One whose first instinct was not to draw his sword, no matter the news Magnus brought.

He observed the conference that followed. It took a while. Those gathered in the knot appeared to argue among themselves.

"What is this?" Apsel worried in Magnus's ear. The rest of the crew shifted uneasily.

"They do not know what to do with us," Jorg proposed.

Perhaps not. But Magnus's words would assure them a reception. They must have wondered, all this time, what had happened to their jarl, Friti Gunnarsson, and his son Gunnar.

Ja, they might decide to slay them all later, but they'd listen first.

Their argument finished, the knot broke apart, some of the members heading for the large structure and some for the pier.

"Get ready," he told his men. "They have decided."

Indeed, another hurried conference took place on the pier. The balding man waved them in.

"Come ashore, son of Tolljur Magnusson. Welcome to Husavik."

Chapter Five

The doors of the great hall stood open as Embra
had left them, the late afternoon light streaming in. Had
Embra believed in omens, she might consider this a
good one, that the seafarers had arrived with fair
weather. But it had been quite some time since she'd
entertained childish beliefs.

News of Fadir. And Gunnar. It made her heart
pound. And brought by the berserker's son.

She'd heard of Tolljur Magnusson. Everyone
had—even here in Husavik where he was generally
detested, the man was a legend. Never defeated in
battle, and affected only by magic, he had broken with
the community here and gone off to found the
settlement at Sorvagur, taking many of their youngest
and best warriors with him.

Embra did not know many of the details. People
either gossiped, repeating things she couldn't believe,
or refused to speak at all. The break had something to
do with Tolljur's wife, a Gael and a slave. And with
Embra's own mother.

She could not worry about that now, with the
seafarers on their way to the great hall. She glanced at
Runi, who stood beside her chair—Fadir's chair, and
his father's before that. The jarl's throne, a seat with a
high back carved all over with leaves from the tree of
life.

If Ulrik were here, he would never let her seat herself in the place of power. But Ulrik had gone down to the shore to escort the seafarers in.

And Runi—Runi did not care. Only he did. Embra could tell by the gleam in his eyes, one of enjoyment. Runi loved events like this, loved turning things on their heads.

"What do you think?" she asked him.

"Interesting. I'm betting Fadir is dead."

Embra, too.

"Else he would have come himself."

"They could be holding him prisoner."

"Why not bring a ransom demand last autumn?"

"Why wait this long in any case?"

Ulla stood on the other side of Embra's chair. She looked troubled. "What will you do, Embra?"

"Hear him out, like a reasonable person."

That made Ulla stare. "Are you reasonable?"

"Sometimes."

Runi laughed.

"Hush, here they come."

They did, with half the settlement trailing them.

Ulrik entered first, looking arrogant and aggressive. Sven the harbormaster came next, and then—

And then.

He entered the hall with all the light behind him, a big man with a halo of brown hair lit to red. Embra could not at once see his face, nei, but he moved with casual grace and confidence, as if he owned the world.

Embra grasped the arms of her chair. She could not allow this man to intimidate her, even if, as Runi said, he had balls the size of Odin's head.

Torches burned just behind the chair. Their light caught the seafarer as he moved into their radiance and paused some five paces from Embra.

He wore only light armor, another mark of confidence, that left bare arms and shoulders burnished by the sun. A strong figure clad in ordinary seafarer's clothes but, ach, at a glance Embra could see there was naught ordinary about him.

A handsome face it was, foreign-looking, all angles, with a pair of bright, discerning eyes set beneath level brows. He wore no beard and needed none to announce his masculinity. The cloud of red-brown hair, which served to soften his hard aspect, spilled in a riot over his shoulders and back, secured only by the copper band he wore on his brow.

Ach, Freya. Ach, holy goddess!

Several other men followed him in, all well-armed, but Embra, wholly captivated, could barely spare a glance for them.

Could barely look away from *him*.

He inspected her in turn before his gaze moved to Runi, and back again. He showed no surprise. Impossible to tell what he thought.

Embra loosened her grasp on the arms of the chair which she gripped so tightly her fingers hurt. She must act. She must say something.

"Greetings. You come from Sorvagur?"

He inclined his head. The way he moved fascinated Embra. The fall of that hair over his shoulders. The quiet confidence.

"I am Magnus Tolljursson."

"Embra Fritisdottir." She too inclined her head. They would keep this civil, if they could. Murder could follow after, if necessary.

"Ah." Again, he inspected her.

She indicated Runi, who stood silent.

"My brother, Runi. You have met this, my other brother, Ulrik."

Magnus Tolljursson exchanged barbed glances with Ulrik, who looked angry enough to spit. Did he resent Magnus's presence? Or was he angry at Embra for seizing the seat of power?

"You bring word of our father?"

"I do. And of your brother, Gunnar. Both of them died last summer at Sorvagur."

Embra struggled not to react. Despite her mixed feelings for her father and her brother, the news hit her like a blow to the gut. Fadir dead. On a foreign shore. And Gunnar—his cruel, sharp brightness quieted forever.

Ulrik started forward. "You—"

Embra held up a hand which, somewhat to her surprise, halted him.

To Magnus she said, "How did they die?"

"In battle."

Was that all he would give her? No softening, no declarations of bravery, no details. Ja, men died in battle, especially Norsemen. Yet Fadir had planned that campaign—one of revenge against the berserker—for years. And Fadir so rarely suffered defeat.

"I see," she said. "And you could not bring word sooner?"

"Lodvar intended to come. Lodvar Haraldsson, I mean. Your brother's shaman."

"Ah, ja." She had wondered about Lodvar. "He lives?"

"He does, and has decided to take up residence with us in Sorvagur. As I say, he meant to return with word. Circumstances prevented that."

"Circumstances."

"Ja. I come on his behalf."

Well. And so, he came for Lodvar, not to inform a slain enemy's family of his demise. True, he owed them nothing. Still.

She tipped her head. "And what might this business be?""

"That, I seek to discuss with you privately." He glanced at Ulrik. "Or with whoever might be in charge."

A fraught moment ensued. Embra had parted her lips to say, "I am in charge," when an interruption occurred. Vanja came charging into the hall, pushing folks out of the way, a sword in her hand.

Ach, by Freya's heart, this was just what Embra needed.

Vanja looked—insane. Her fair hair had escaped its plaits and her eyes were wild. She came with words pouring from her.

"Where is he? Where is he?" Focusing on Magnus Tolljursson the way a wounded cat might focus on its rival, she demanded, "Are you the one? The one who's brought word of my father?"

Magnus Tolljursson stared, as did the handful of men he'd brought up from the boat with him.

He sounded calm, though, when he replied, "I am."

"Where is he?" Vanja repeated and waved her weapon in Magnus Tolljursson's face. Any man might be expected to back off. He did not, but held up his hands, empty of weapons.

Perhaps he did have balls the size of Odin's head.

"Dead." Magnus shot one inquiring look at Embra.

"My sis—" she began, only to have Vanja speak over her.

"Who killed him?" It was a howl of pain. "You?" Again she waved the sword. "Was it you?"

Still, he did not step back, though all of his men had their hands on their weapons, and had pressed up behind him.

Beside Embra, Runi chuckled.

"He died in battle on our shore, in Sorvagur."

"By whose hand?"

"Does it matter?" Magnus spoke to Vanja as directly as she spoke to him, ignoring the pain that infused her voice. "Men who come to our shores seeking to defeat us must be prepared to die."

Vanja blinked at him. "My brother, Gunnar?"

"He too breathed his last at Sorvagur."

"Ach, by Tyr's whiskers! I will avenge them. I swear to avenge them!"

Magnus's men stirred, and he narrowed his eyes, giving Vanja a dangerous look. "Mistress," he bowed slightly, "as you wish."

"Did you kill them?" She waved her sword in a wild arc. "Need I slay you?"

"I represent Sorvagur here. If you have scores to settle with anyone there, you must take it up with me."

Ah, Embra thought upon a thrill of rare admiration. He knew not of what he spoke. No one in his right mind would take Vanja on. She was by turns heedless, cunning, and treacherous.

A worthy daughter, in fact, of Friti Gunnarsson.

Chapter Six

A mad place entirely was Husavik, Magnus thought as the wild woman at last withdrew her sword from his face. He had barely arrived, yet already he understood why his parents—and so many others—had chosen to leave.

A handsome settlement, ja. And the women he'd seen so far were—well, no man could deny they were attractive. The one who had first faced him, with the eyes like twin war shields—singularly lovely, she was. Tall, with strong, slender limbs and a fall of yellow hair, there was something about her that immediately stirred him.

Her sister, however beautiful she might be, carried the same stain as Gunnar Fritisson. Ja—plain to see he had been her brother. They even looked alike. Fair of hair with flowing golden locks, and intensely blue eyes. Full of ready charm that could deceive, right until the moment the knife went in.

About the brothers, he could not tell. The one standing beside Mistress Embra wore a mask of ironic enjoyment. The other, whom they'd met down at the shore, was aggressive, though not so much as his mad sister.

If he wanted to conduct Lodvar's business successfully, it would have to be with Mistress Embra. She appeared to be the only reasonable person among them.

He shot a speaking look at Apsel, who stood staunch at his shoulder.

Apsel's fingers hovered above the hilt of his sword, but Magnus hoped it did not come to blows here and now. It would not bode well for future negotiations.

Thoughts moved in the wide, mad eyes of Friti Gunnarsson's daughter. She might have lowered her blade, but she had not finished with him.

"There is treachery in it," she accused. "No one ever defeated Fadir in battle. There must have been treachery."

Ja, so there had been—and all on Friti's and Gunnar's parts. Magnus would not bring up the fact that Lodvar had switched loyalties for the love of Gyda. That would help no one.

"Let us discuss this privately," Embra declared, and Magnus looked at her gratefully. "It is not for the ears of the whole settlement."

Magnus acknowledged her with a bow. "Are my men and I then to be given safe conduct, as your guests?"

She hesitated and the aggressive brother immediately cried out, "Nei! These men, Sostir, killed Fadir and Gunnar! They are our enemies."

"Vengeance, Embra! I will have vengeance!" the mad sister wailed.

The tall man beside Embra laughed again.

Embra spoke first to her sister and then to Magnus. "Are we savages that cannot forego violence? Ja, Master Magnus, while here you may consider yourself under my protection."

****

Embra Fritisdottir had sent most of the onlookers away, keeping at hand only her siblings, which included a young girl of no more than twelve or so. She'd even called for refreshments.

Introductions were made. Magnus struggled to keep track of everyone, not helped by the fact that still more family members arrived.

At home, there were only the two of them, him and Gyda. Fadir had never wanted children, being afraid of passing on the berserker's curse. Despite his caution he had done just that—to both Magnus and Gyda.

No one had ever heard of a female berserker before Gyda fell into the battle madness, or a form of it. And though it came to him but rarely, Magnus never wanted to experience that again.

He was a calm man, a measured man, one who thought things through. Having control taken from him did not sit well.

But, he thought now, battle-madness must be better than the kind that beset these children of Friti Gunnarsson.

Seven of them there were. Gunnar would have been the eighth—and the eldest. There was Embra, who clearly did not know what to do with him, the mad sister called Vanja, and the young girl, Ulla. Another sister, Dagmar, stared at him as if he'd just crawled out from beneath a rock.

The angry, aggressive brother, Ulrik, had done little so far but glare. Yet another brother, not much older than Ulla, was named Orve.

And then there was the tall fellow, Runi, who seemed to find everything so amusing. He troubled Magnus. A lot.

How would he keep track of them all? It might well be fatal not to do so.

He would prefer to deal with Mistress Embra alone, just the two of them. If he had any hope of sensible discussion, it would have to lie with her.

Yet even after they all sat down with mead and honey cakes at hand, the madwoman shot questions at him.

"When did Fadir die?"

"Last summer, Mistress."

"Why did you not bring word sooner? Did you not know we would be wondering? Grieving? Wondering and grieving!"

"I regret the delay, Mistress. As I explained to Mistress Embra, your brother's shaman, Lodvar Haraldsson, intended to return with word. He was prevented."

"Lodvar Haraldsson! The whelp of a slave. Worthless!"

Magnus's men stirred. They were nearly all the sons of slaves, women once held at this very settlement.

Vanja's eyes flashed. "Who prevented Lodvar from returning? You?"

Not giving Magnus a chance to answer, she turned her head and looked at Runi. "Remember how Gunnar used to torment Lodvar? Call him names and spit upon him? He said Lodvar should have been culled when he slipped from his mother's womb."

Runi nodded, his blue eyes glinting. "And then, Lodvar proved his worth."

"Or did he?" Ulrik asked. "If Lodvar lives, if he did not spend himself in defense of Fadir and Gunnar, there must be some treachery in it."

The others nodded, all but Embra. They fixed their malevolent gazes upon Magnus, making him feel like a goat surrounded by wolves.

Ulrik leaned forward. "Did Lodvar Haraldsson betray our father?"

Magnus's thoughts flailed. If he gave them the truth, here and now, it could only harm his chances of gaining possession of Lodvar's mother.

They would not like the truth.

"Your father, as I say, perished in hard combat. You may take pride in that." If they had any pride in such a man, who oozed cruelty and hate.

Clearly, the belligerent Vanja did.

"There is a story in it," Embra declared.

"Ja, Mistress."

"One we will wish to hear. But at a later time, perhaps, once we have had a chance to master our grief."

Magnus gazed at her thoughtfully. She did not appear grief-stricken, this Embra Fritisdottir.

She returned his look with interest. "And your other business?"

"I do have some things to return to you—your father's sword, and an amulet your brother, Gunnar, wore."

At that, the children of Friti stirred.

"I want Fadir's sword," declared Vanja with a scowl that argued she would then slaughter Magnus with it.

"What about Fadir's ship, and Gunnar's?" asked the young brother who'd barely spoken, Orve.

"The first is ours to keep," Magnus said smoothly. "The other was destroyed during a … storm."

"And their goods?" Runi asked. "Fadir never went anywhere without a measure of wealth."

"Confiscated."

"Well, you have a nerve, I will give you that."

There had been a measure of gold aboard the ship. Rather than spending the wealth Lodvar had inherited from Kaddi, Magnus hoped to buy the freedom of Lodvar's mother with it.

Justice, he called that.

"We are traders. Raiders," he said shortly. "Vikings. Would you return what you won in battle?"

They had no answer for that.

"As for the other part of my business, I will discuss that only with whoever is in charge here." He looked at Embra pointedly. "You?"

That had them stealing looks at one another again.

"No one is in charge," Dagmar declared, "save Fadir. We were waiting for him to come home and take his place. Or failing that, Gunnar."

"You understand," Orve said, "this news you bring changes everything."

Embra got to her feet. "I am in charge."

Ulrik faced her. "You are not." He fairly spat, "You were not appointed, nor named."

"I have been in charge since Fadir and Gunnar left.

"If anyone, it should be Runi. He is eldest and not a woman."

Vanja bristled. "What is wrong with being a woman, Ulrik? I could best you in single combat if I chose."

Magnus would wager she could.

"Try it," Ulrik sneered.

Embra broke through their bickering by raising her

voice. "Runi, do you want the place?"

The tall man with the handsome, dangerous face stirred. "Me?" He gestured to the door. "You think I wish to keep peace out there? Or try to discipline this lot?"

"No. but I need you to tell them, particularly Ulrik."

"Brodir, I do not want the place. If you do," he jerked his head at Embra, "take it from her."

"Do not argue in front of the strangers!" Vanja screeched. "It does not look well."

Suddenly Magnus wanted to laugh and, indeed, he heard a chuckle from Apsel, beside him.

By Odin's eye, what an obnoxious stew pot. Perhaps he needed to stir it a little.

Chapter Seven

"I swear, they are all mad," Jorg said as the group of them walked back to the harbor. The other members of their small group nodded.

"Politics," Apsel grumbled. "We are not used to such, back home."

True enough. As jarl, Magnus's father led fairly, listening to all that was said and making reasoned decisions, usually with input from Modir. He lived simply. In Sorvagur, no one was better than anyone else.

Here in this complicated place, that could not be said. Wealth abounded, and even among the jarl's offspring, they contested as to worthiness.

The crew Magnus had brought here with him, young men all, had never lived in this environment and were ill prepared for it.

"That shrieking banshee, Vanja, is maddest of all," declared Knut.

They all nodded agreement.

"But what a body, eh?" asked Apsel. "And a face to match."

Magnus gave him a stare. "Do not so much as think about it."

The other three men nodded.

"Like bedding a lynx," said Rojd.

"Therein lies the challenge."

"Nei, but we must be careful," Magnus warned.

"There are traps everywhere in this place. If we step wrong, we are caught." He glared at Apsel again. "Use your head."

"Ja, I know that." Apsel feigned insult. "But have you looked around? Beautiful women on all sides. Back home—well, we know them all, do we not?"

Knut nodded. "You have bedded them all."

Apsel ignored that. "We grew up with them. Where is the challenge, the mystery?"

"Apsel, you are as mad as these women here."

"The challenge, with yon Vanja," declared Rojd, "would be to finish your rut before she cut your throat."

"With her father's sword." Knut snorted.

"Ja." Apsel reflected upon it. "Mayhap you are right."

"Keep your tackle where it belongs," Magnus said. "All of you. As for the beautiful women here"—and ja, they were beautiful—"just remember, many of them are quite likely slaves."

That had them muttering more darkly.

"All I know," Jorg said, "I am sleeping safe on the boat tonight."

"With a strong guard," Rojd agreed.

"Ja, with a strong guard."

"I would not put it past that Ulrik to board us during the night and put us all to the sword."

"Let him try."

Magnus would prefer not to. He had seen both Friti and Gunnar fight, and did not like the glint he'd seen in Ulrik's eye.

"What a brood of asps, eh?" Jorg asked.

They all reflected on that.

"Ja," they agreed in turn.

"Grand mead, though," Knut offered, and they all laughed.

****

"Well, what do you think?" Ulrik asked as soon as the seafarers left. "I do not trust them. There is treachery."

"There is always treachery." Runi smiled.

"I say we kill them all," Vanja declared. "Just as they killed Fadir. And Gunnar. Tit for tat."

"You hated Gunnar," Orve pointed out, and it was true. "You were jealous because Fadir favored him."

"Did he? That is what you know."

A moment of silence fell. They'd all heard the whispers saying Vanja had spent some of her nights in Fadir's bed. Even they did not know if it was true.

"I want his sword, when that bastard of a seafarer brings it," Vanja declared. "It should come to me."

"It should come to whoever takes the place of jarl. And," Ulrik concluded smoothly, "that will be me."

"Nei," Embra objected. If Ulrik took the place of jarl, they would never stop raiding and shedding blood. In fact, that might be a good way to get rid of him—send him off viking.

"Ja," he returned swiftly. "If Runi does not want the place—I am next eldest," he added before Embra could speak, "son."

Embra drew herself up and stiffened her spine. "And what is wrong with a female jarl, eh?"

"Everything. It has never been done."

"If we gave things up because they'd never been done, our ancestors would not have left Norway. The coolest head among us should lead here. And, Ulrik, that is not you."

Ulrik scowled.

Embra went on, "For the last year I have held the reins."

"That was because we believed it temporary, that Fadir or at least Gunnar would come home." Ulrik tossed his head. "Who will pay respect to a settlement led by a woman?"

"Everyone who pays respect to us now." If Embra let control slip away, at worst into Ulrik's hands, chaos would ensue.

"The place should belong to Runi."

They all turned to the tall man who stood in silence.

"Runi, do you not want the place of jarl?" Dagmar demanded.

He considered it, his gaze moving among them. It rested last on Embra, and she held her breath. Capricious—ja, that was a word that suited her brother. He could say anything.

"One thing is certain," he spoke at last. "We cannot allow control to slip beyond the family. Now that word has come saying Fadir is dead, his enemies will step forward. Some of them have been waiting years for this opportunity."

"Ja," Orve agreed.

"We must present a united front. Or—appear to."

Dagmar snorted.

"Especially in front of this seafarer. So I say we decide it here and now, who will be the face of this family."

Clever was Runi, whatever else might be said of him. Embra's heart quivered. Would he, as so often, do the unexpected and step forward to seize leadership?

The gods help them all.

Ulrik, ever impatient, asked again, "Runi, do you want the place?"

"Nei. But I will advise whichever of you takes it."

Ach, and taking advice from Runi would be as risky as walking a blade's edge.

Ulrik bristled. "Then who—"

Runi spoke darkly. "Decide it among you. But I say, whoever is jarl has to go tell Modir."

"Tell Modir—"

"That Fadir is dead."

A spear of horror went through Embra, and set her back on her heels. They all looked at one another uneasily.

Said Ulrik, who feared nothing, "Nei."

"Surely," Runi purred, "it would make a fitting test of worth and mettle."

Their mother, Anaborg, lived in a small dwelling shut away from the rest of the settlement, and had for years. Indeed, Embra could not remember a time when it had been different, or she had lived among them as part of their family. Instead she'd had a succession of women to look after her. And guards.

Fadir had often said she wanted for nothing. When they were younger, he might take them to visit her. Just the memory of those visits made Embra shudder. She might greet them with a measure of fondness and call them by name. Or they might find her raving.

To Fadir's credit, though he slept with whatever other women he pleased, he never forsook Modir. And, obviously, he'd continued visiting her—often enough to get from her all eight of them.

How would she react to news of his death? Embra

dreaded to think.

"Ach, nei," Dagmar muttered.

"Ja," Runi insisted. "She must be told."

"She hated Fadir," Vanja asserted.

"She loved him," Ulrik averred. "That is what made her so—crazy."

They all contemplated it then, the fact that their mother was a madwoman. That she may well have bequeathed a streak of that madness to any or all of them.

"I say whoever has the balls—forgive me, Sostir," Runi nodded at Embra, "to go to Modir and tell her Fadir is dead will have earned the place of jarl. Brodir?" he looked pointedly at Ulrik.

Embra could see that Ulrik was tempted. He gnawed on his lip, glared at Embra, and contemplated the matter. At last he shook his head.

Runi looked next at Vanja. "Sostir?"

Vanja, impulsive as ever, answered swiftly. "I do not want to see that woman. Not ever."

"Sostir?" Runi's eyes glinted as he turned to Embra.

She drew a breath. So much rested on this. The very existence of Husavik, perhaps. "I will go," she said and tried not to regret it.

"There you are, Ulrik." Runi smiled. "Your sister has bigger balls than you have."

Angry, Ulrik stalked out. One by one the others followed him, even Ulla, until the two of them—Embra and Runi—remained alone.

"Well, Sostir. I hope you are happy."

She was and she wasn't. She looked at him. "Perhaps you will come with me, to tell Modir?"

He laughed darkly. "Not me, Sostir. I am not the one who wants the place of jarl."

Chapter Eight

Anaborg Helmsdottir had once been beautiful, and she held fast to the remnants of that beauty still. Embra had, of course, heard the stories about her. That she'd once had the ambition of bedding every warrior in Husavik, and had very nearly achieved it. That she had no shame, and no conscience. That she had once tried to commit murder, and failed only because thwarted by magic.

Embra believed that last part. On more than one occasion, in the past, Modir had fooled her handlers and got her hands on a weapon—once a knife. She'd killed her serving woman then—it had been the talk of Husavik for some time. Like all else, the talk had died down.

Even without a weapon she could attack, using her nails like claws to do dire damage. Once, when Embra had been ten or so, she'd encountered Fadir coming from Modir's quarters early one morning. He'd had a trail of ragged scratches down one cheek.

When Embra exclaimed, he'd told her, not without relish, *Your Modir was a wild woman last night.*

As if he enjoyed it. He probably had. It was said of Fadir also, he took whatever slave women he wanted, whether they were willing or no.

Such a man, she thought as she made her way to Modir's dwelling early the next day, to lie dead on a cold, distant shore. If she found it difficult to believe, how would she convince Modir?

Before heading to her mother's quarters, she'd stood long outside the great hall, eyeing Magnus Tolljursson's boat in the harbor, convincing herself it was all real. Since Runi would not, she'd pressed Kennach into accompanying her. He walked behind her now, and when she paused at her mother's door, he edged up to her.

"Mistress? I will wait outside, aye? Your mother does not like me."

True enough. Modir abhorred slaves.

But what support would Kennach be, outside the door?

"Where is the other guard?" There were supposed to be two of them, always. Now but one man lounged there. When she came up, he stared at her in alarm.

Not awaiting an answer from Kennach, she stepped up to the guard. "Where is your fellow?"

"Ach, Mistress—" The man, one of Fadir's junior warriors, came to attention and stole a telling look at the door behind him.

An instant later, the second guard stepped through from inside, still adjusting his breeches. When he beheld Embra, he flushed red.

"What were you doing in there?" she challenged. "Surely not—"

His fellow answered earnestly. "Our instructions are to protect Mistress Anaborg, and give her whatever she wants. She wanted—"

"Did she!"

They both nodded.

Even as Kennach slunk away, Embra stepped up to

the guard, anger and dismay warring inside her. "How often does this occur? Do you take turns?"

"Mistress, only when she calls to us. Someone is always on guard."

"Do you bring her the news?" the red-faced man whispered. Ja, the whole settlement would have heard that Friti Gunnarsson was dead—all but the woman inside.

"Out of my way."

She did not want to go in. But she must. Disgust warred with reluctance as she stepped inside.

A fire burned low on a small hearth, the only radiance. Embra's gaze moved around the chamber, measuring the luxuries of this prison. Fine rugs covered the floor and trinkets abounded, including a metal tub and golden comb. A large bed dominated the space. Embra's mother lounged upon it. Naked.

Touching herself.

Had the attentions of the guards not been enough?

She sat up when Embra came in, not bothering to cover her heaving breasts, or the rest of her.

"Who are you?"

"Do you not know me, Modir? It is Embra, your dottir." She deserved more than a jarldom for this. Curse Runi, anyway.

"My dottir?"

"Your eldest dottir," Embra reiterated. She should be happy the woman seemed calm. Perhaps it had been fortunate she arrived so soon after the guard exercised her passions.

"Ah." Anaborg arose from the bed.

She must once have had a body like Vanja's, lush and fulsome. Her breasts were still heavy, but the rest of her had thickened, no longer lithe. She wore her hair loose, gold streaked with silver. In the dim light she still looked beautiful.

"Modir, please cover yourself."

Anaborg caught up a robe from the foot of the bed and flung it around her body, continuing to approach Embra.

"My dottir, you say? Embra."

"Ja."

"What is the name of that young man, the one who was just in here?"

Embra fished for it in her mind. "Kettel."

Anaborg's lips curled like a cat who had just had cream. "He is pleasing."

Embra did not know what to say. The air in the chamber smelled stale. It smelled of sex. Her skin crawled.

"Let us sit down, Modir. I have something to tell you."

How would the woman react? Would she wail in grief? Turn violent?

Embra scanned the room for possible weapons. But nei, Anaborg needed none. Her nails had grown long and sharp.

Freya, protect me.

Anaborg deposited herself gracefully on a rug beside the hearth. Embra followed suit.

"Why are you here? My children never come to see me. They are an ungrateful lot." She leaned toward Embra confidingly. "I should have slit all their throats at birth."

Horror touched Embra. She went cold.

"How many of them were there?" Anaborg asked

herself the question and answered it. "Eight. I endured that agony eight times. I tell you, girl," she wagged a finger, "what goes in so easily does not come out the same."

"Nei."

"Nei. But he came back to me time after time, and I could not say nei to him. No woman says nei to Friti Gunnarsson."

"Modir—"

"I should have slit their throats. Such trouble, infants are. He would not let me kill them. He said we would need them some day to continue the—the"—she waved a hand—"dynasty."

She studied Embra from wide, blue, once-beautiful eyes. "Which one are you, again? Not very pretty, are you? Are you sure you're mine?"

"I am Embra." Would Anaborg even comprehend what Embra had come to tell? "Modir, I have grave news."

"By all means, share it."

"You know that Fadir has been away."

"He has not come to see me in some time. He was always a good lover." She leaned toward Embra confidingly. "Do you like it rough? I do. He never disappointed me."

"I—uh—I do not wish to discuss that with you."

Anaborg eyed her pityingly. "Plain as you are, you have likely never been with a man."

Embra did not consider herself plain. She might not possess Vanja's beauty or Dagmar's. Even young Ulla looked to grow into a beauty. But she caught her share of speculative glances from men.

Had the seafarer looked at her that way? Nei,

surely not.

"Modir, Fadir has been away on a voyage."

Anaborg's face brightened. "Ach, will he bring silver? Amber from the east? Will he bring slaves?" Her face crumpled abruptly. "I hope not."

"Modir, Fadir will not be returning. He has perished in battle."

"Perished?"

"Died, Modir. He died." Embra held her breath. Now it would come. The screaming, the wailing. An attack?

Anaborg seemed to think about the news Embra had given her. Thoughts moved in her eyes, but no emotions.

"Ah, he will not return then."

"Nei, Modir, he will not."

"Pity." She glanced at the bed as if imagining Friti there. "We had an understanding, he and I. Did you know that?"

Embra shook her head.

"An old understanding."

"Modir, nothing will change for you. Your life here will go on." Embra would not mention the likely upheaval beyond this chamber or the arrival of the seafarer. The berserker, Tolljur Magnusson, remained one of Modir's trip wires, as Embra understood it.

"So I will not see Friti, my husband, again."

"You will not."

"Except in my dreams."

By Freya's heart, of what did this woman dream?

Anaborg stretched like a cat. "Tell me but one thing."

"Ja?"

"Do I get to keep the robust young guard?"

****

"She took it—well," Embra told Kennach when she stepped into his waiting gaze outside. Both guards now looked impassive, though they followed Embra with their eyes.

"No screaming?"

"As you heard."

"No threats? No violence?"

"Not as yet." Embra reflected upon it. "It may take some time to sink in."

"Then I suggest you distance yourself."

"As swiftly as possible."

"So, Mistress." He spoke from her shoulder as they moved off. "The way I understand it, this secures for you the place of jarl."

"For the moment. I doubt Ulrik is done with challenging me. He will think of ways, challenges at which he thinks I cannot succeed." She glanced at her companion. "My brother is an aggressive little troll, but he is not stupid."

"And Master Runi? Is he on your side?"

Embra reflected upon it. Were there sides now? Perhaps there always had been. They could never be considered a family united. Or perhaps there had been a jumble of sides like a structure about to fall down. Now, ja, the schism appeared, wide and gaping.

"Who knows, with Runi? He plays at supporting me now. He does not want the place of jarl." Yet could she be sure of that?

"Hmm," Kennach mused. "With Master Runi on your side, Master Ulrik will not make a move."

"Not unless his temper gets the better of him. You

have seen his temper on display." She sighed. "And then there is Vanja."

Kennach twitched, a full body movement. "Mistress, if I might speak plainly—"

She shot him a sidewise glance. "You always do." And a great comfort to her it was.

"Mistress Vanja frightens me most of all."

Chapter Nine

"I still say you should not venture to meet with this woman on your own." Apsel huffed the words, deadly earnest. Magnus so seldom saw his friend entirely serious, it made an impression.

Another night had passed, and his men, confined to their vessel, were becoming—well, restless. So far their great adventure had consisted of a gathering with a hall full of mad folk, and a good deal of waiting. Rain had moved through, further worsening their moods.

Nor, Magnus suspected, had the attitude clearly prevalent at Husavik, that those who carried the blood of Gaels were somehow *less*, helped much. Since that included nearly all of them, it had rather soured their enthusiasm.

"I do not trust anyone here," Apsel added sweepingly, and Knut, also present for this discussion, nodded.

"At least take Apsel," Knut urged, "as a body guard."

"And admit I need one?" Magnus shook his head. "Nei. If I take a companion, Mistress Embra will demand one. And I want this discussion to be private, just the two of us, with no shouting or arguing."

His friends exchanged glances.

"She is the only sane one, from what I can see," Magnus answered their unspoken question. "The only reasonable person in the whole accursed family. If I cannot deal with her, I do not know how we are to succeed."

How could he return to Lodvar without having rescued his mother?

"What a place, eh?" Knut muttered. "No wonder our fathers left."

They all rolled their eyes.

"I will take my axe with me for companion. But, by all means, wish me luck."

The walk to the great hall displayed Husavik's splendor in full. The rain had cleared, and new light slid in from the east—the direction of home—lighting the fine buildings. Such wealth displayed here! They knew nothing like it in Sorvagur.

As he went, he tried to calculate the number of raids it might have taken to amass such a fortune. The voyages launched. The lives spent.

Fadir traded. Their settlement had to, if they wanted to survive. Magnus had accompanied him on voyages and, ja, loved it. And things had become sticky a few times when deals had gone bad. But Fadir was an honest man.

Magnus feared he would have to employ a measure of deception here, if he wished to accomplish his aim.

He paused before the great hall. Last night, Mistress Embra had sent a messenger—an older servant—bidding him to meet her here early.

Well, early it was, and—

The door swung open before him. "Come in."

Not the servant but the lady herself.

Tall she was, this daughter of Friti Gunnarsson, though she might only reach Magnus's ear. He outstripped his own father in height. This morning she wore her dull-gold hair only half braided, with the rest of it spilling all the way down to her—well. As Magnus saw when she turned to lead him inside, she had a very nice bottom indeed.

Suddenly a vision flashed upon him—that of her standing naked before him, wrapped in naught but that curtain of hair.

By Odin's eye, he dared not entertain such thoughts. Not now.

"I thought it best we meet early, Master Magnus, before any others of my siblings are astir. None of them tends to leave his or her bed early."

"Ah."

"And I wished the two of us to speak together as plainly as possible."

She turned to face him. She wore a simple woolen dress like Modir usually wore, pale green with a white overdress. The fabric clung to her long limbs and emphasized her narrow waist. And a pair of breasts that—nei, they were not lush and heavy, like her sister Vanja's. But ja, they would fill both his hands generously.

He had to make sure this woman did not prove a distraction.

And yet—as she stood there facing him, did she not eye him with similar interest? With speculation? Ja, sure, her gaze lingered on his shoulders and at other, more intimate places.

"I appreciate the audience, Mistress Embra."

"Sit. May I offer you some breakfast? There are cakes and some broth."

"Thank you." One did not refuse hospitality.

63

They sat near the hearth, facing one another across a short distance. The hall, utterly empty of anyone else, seemed overly large around them, and the morning light sent dust motes dancing in streams.

"I must apologize for your reception yesterday. My brothers and sisters can be…challenging."

That was one word for it.

"The news I brought was difficult to hear." Magnus spread his hands.

"Indeed." He pale blue gaze came up and seared him. "We speculated much among us about Fadir's failure to return. Some of us felt certain he had conquered the settlement at Sorvagur and moved on to still richer prizes, perhaps wintering over. There are those among us, you see, who could not imagine him losing at anything."

Did she number one of them?

"Others of us supposed him imprisoned by the famed and dreaded berserker." She tipped her head. "He is your father."

"Ja."

"And are you berserker also?"

"Not all berserkers beget berserkers, though I understand it is a popular belief."

She considered him. "I admit, you do not look the part. You are very—calm."

So was Fadir, until the fit took him. Magnus tossed his head. "I am only half Norse, you understand. Half Gael."

"Your mother—"

"A Gaelic slave from Lewis. You do not know the story?"

"Only that there was very bad blood between your

father and mine, and that it involved her somehow. Except when drunk, Fadir did not speak of it to anyone save Gunnar."

"I see."

"Gunnar was in his confidence. They would sit together and talk like old warriors. Hatching schemes."

Like the one they had launched upon Sorvagur. Magnus did not voice that. He knew nothing of this woman or what she understood about the treachery her father and brother had unleashed.

She might have been in on it, and could be playing a part now.

"Old jealousies and old wrongs," he said instead.

"So, Magnus Tolljursson, son of the berserker, who may or may not himself be a berserker, why have you come to Husavik? And what do you seek?"

Magnus had thought long about this and how best to frame his request. He sat back a bit. "I and my men have come for several reasons besides informing those here of Friti's and Gunnar's deaths. Curiosity, first of all. We wanted to see this place from whence stems half our blood."

Her brows lifted. "You are all half-slaves?"

Half slaves? What a way to put it. Not half Norse or even half Gael, or half-blood. The label of *slave* came easily in this place. Just as for Lodvar, growing up here. Despite what he had achieved, the place of shaman and the favor of the very gods, he remained half-slave.

"Most of us, ja. When my fadir and modir left, they took with them all the enslaved women they could rescue, women captured like Modir in Alba. Many later wed the warriors who also came away with them."

"Ah." Once more her gaze moved over him, thoughtful and discerning. "That is why you look so—"

"So, Mistress?"

"Different."

Magnus narrowed his eyes at her.

"Forgive me. You will think that rude, but we tend to say what comes into our heads, here. And believe it or not, I am the most tactful member of the family."

"Those who feel themselves superior to everyone else tend to say what comes into their heads."

Her brows lifted still higher.

Magnus nodded. "But perhaps that is rude, also, of me to say."

"Master Magnus, I like to think of myself as an honest woman. I am striving to be forthright with you and prevent what bloodshed I can during your visit, despite the news you have brought."

To Magnus's surprise, anger built within him. "Whereas, were you not being so *tactful*, you would put a boatload of intrusive slaves to the sword?"

"I think that would be difficult, do you not? You are well-armed and undoubtedly well-versed at warfare. I have guaranteed your safety while you are here. But you can see I sit atop a boiling cauldron. Do not push me too far."

Magnus got to his feet. "We are finished here."

She rose also, an emotion that might be alarm filling her eyes. "You have not stated your business."

"Nei, I have not." And would not until she showed him some courtesy. But what of Lodvar's mother?

"Master Magnus—" She laid her fingers on the bare skin of his arm. "You are best off dealing with me. And the sooner you conclude that business and leave

66

Husavik, the better."

Magnus stared at her hand. A delightful warmth rose from the place where she touched him, as if her fingers seared his skin. He'd never felt the like, and it drew him just like a wasp to honey. He wanted to step closer, longed to touch her in turn. To cup her cheek in his palm, lean in and capture her lips. Devour them without heed, without regard for who or what she was.

Instead he took a decided step backward. "We may speak again, anon. Or we may not."

"I have offended you." Her nostrils flared as she drew a breath. "I did not intend it."

He gave her a hard nod and withdrew from the hall. Not because she had offended him or even as a ploy, but because he wanted, with all his being, to take her down on the floor and ravish her.

His own thoughts shocked him.

Chapter Ten

What curious eyes the man had, like the flicker of sunlight upon a pool of water, light and shade. During the few moments they'd spent talking together, Embra had seen his thoughts moving there, and longed to plumb them. Not the same emotions she saw in the eyes of other men. Anger. Greed. Spite or cruelty.

She did not know what to make of Magnus Tolljursson, that was truth. She'd meant what she said—she wished to deal honestly with him if she could, avoid trouble, and send him on his way as soon as possible. Did she not have enough trouble already?

Quite possibly, she could not handle this. But she had seen Ulrik when he flew into one of his unreasoning rages and figured it was but a matter of time before his extremely limited patience wore thin.

Then there was Vanja.

So, Magnus Tolljursson had wanted to see Husavik, the settlement from whence his father came, had he? No need to ask what he thought of it. Not much. She'd seen the disparagement in his eyes.

Or had that all been aimed at her?

Several reasons, he'd said he had for coming. But he'd voiced only the one.

If he sought to engage in some sort of power struggle with them, he would lose. She could guarantee that. It did not matter which of her siblings he took on.

Not one offspring of Friti Gunnarsson would relinquish power, ever.

Did that include her? She took a turn around the empty hall after Magnus had gone, the carved pillars soaring above her head, and thought about that. She would not have said so. Now the seething mass of emotions inside made her less than certain. She understood few of them.

Ulrik would attack Magnus Tolljursson as soon as he could. Runi? Who could tell what Runi might do. Vanja would want vengeance. Dagmar and Orve would throw their weight, at least temporarily, behind whoever looked to be most successful. All she, Embra, wanted was peace.

And perhaps to touch Magnus Tolljursson again.

She dismissed that thought hastily. Impossible. She must keep her mind on the dangers at hand. She would like to know what precisely had happened to Fadir and Gunnar, at Sorvagur. Two sublimely fierce warriors, defeated. Were these men of Sorvagur so very impressive?

Magnus looked it. That sun-browned, freckled skin with the muscles rippling beneath. The way he moved. The air of quiet competence.

And that hair—rarely had she seen such a mane on a man. Confined only by the bronze ring he wore on his brow, it spilled in a wild cloud of reddish brown, all the way down his back.

Ach, by Freya's heart!

"How went the meeting?"

Embra's whole body started when Runi spoke. Her brother had let himself into the hall quietly and approached her, his tall body moving gracefully.

"Not well. He walked out on me."

That caused one of Runi's brows to rise. "Perhaps he does not like negotiating with a woman."

"I do not think that was it."

"It takes temerity to walk out on you."

"He must have very large balls, to come sailing into our harbor with but a single boat load of warriors."

Runi laughed softly. "My sostir to be talking of the size of a man's balls! And you with so little experience at comparison."

She darted a glare at him.

"If it were Dagmar, now—"

"She takes after Modir in that regard. Did you know Modir is having her way with her guards?"

Runi shrugged. "So long as the men do not object. Good luck to them."

"She will eat them alive."

Runi sat beside the fire. "Then we will get new guards." He slanted a look at Embra. "I thought you should know, Ulrik is plotting revenge against the seafarers. He was up all night drinking and bragging about it to anyone who would listen."

"Including you?"

"I listened. You should be glad. I may not want to play at being jarl, but I am willing to be your eyes and ears."

Embra grunted.

"Our brother talks of exacting a price from the visitors, for Fadir's death, by setting fire to their boat in the middle of the night. He did not say anything about revenge for Gunnar's death." Runi reflected. "I think he is glad to have Gunnar out of his way."

"Magnus Tolljursson might have something to say

about it. Runi, have you given any thought to what class of warrior could have killed Gunnar? And Fadir."

"There may have been a berserker's fit involved."

"Or there may not."

Runi gave her a long, cool look. "I hope you will not lose your perspective in this."

"Whyever would I?"

"I saw the way you looked at him."

"At—"

"Magnus Tolljursson. As if you'd never seen food before, and were starving."

"I did not."

"Ach, Sostir! Even more interesting, I could not help but notice how he looked back at you."

A slow thrill started at Embra's toes and worked its way upward. *He did not*. She wanted to speak the words aloud but would not give Runi the satisfaction.

"A fiery attraction," he pronounced.

"Do not be a fool."

"Nei, Sostir." He wagged a finger at her. "Do you not be the fool. That is what I came to tell you. Men are plentiful here in Husavik. If you want one for your bed, you have only to snap your fingers. Leave the seafarer alone. Naught but trouble can come of it."

"I do not want a man for my bed."

Runi laughed softly. "You want *that* man there. It would complicate things, perhaps fatally."

"I have no intention of taking Magnus Tolljursson to my bed." But the very thought started a fire in her belly that sped downward, intensifying as it went.

How would he look there, sprawled naked across the furs beneath which she slept? How would he taste?

"Did he tell you why he came—other than to bring

us our grave news?"

She shook her head. "Just some nonsense about wanting to lay eyes on the settlement from whence his father came."

"You think it nonsense?"

"He clearly does not think much of the place, or of us."

"So he does have some sense in his head."

****

"Magnus!" Apsel called. "You have a visitor."

Magnus looked to the front of the boat, his heart leaping in his chest. Had she come? Might he see her again so soon?

He'd regretted the huff that had taken him from her presence ever since he'd stalked out of the hall this morning. It was not like him to lose his patience, or his temper. He should have been more forbearing and placed his request.

Then again, maybe he'd been right to show her what he would and would not tolerate. Fool. She didn't even comprehend how she had offended him. So ingrained was she to injustice by being raised in this place, she could not see that her casual disdain outraged him.

The woman was poison. A shame she was so accursedly attractive.

He'd like to satisfy himself with her, a night or two. Or a month of nights.

Of course she was likely a madwoman. She merely hid it better than the rest of them.

Yet when his eyes fell not on her but her servant— the Gael—he felt disappointment.

"Master Magnus." The man bowed, clothes

dripping from his wade out to the boat. Of middle years, with brown hair and a mild expression, the fellow was obviously a slave, though well enough dressed. Another reason to scorn Mistress Embra.

"What is it?"

"I have a message from my mistress."

Magnus grunted.

"She requests another meeting where you might discuss your reasons for traveling to Husavik."

She did, did she?

The men gathered around, openly curious.

"And to show her good faith, she sends a warning. Her brother is planning to fire your vessel during the night."

"Is he, then?" Him and what army? "Which brother is this? Nei, let me guess. Ulrik, is it?"

"Ja, Master Magnus."

"And she warns me of this in good faith, you say?" Magnus huffed. "Why else?"

"She has guaranteed your safety while you are here."

Knut said, "She'd do better to let that brother of hers slay us, and be rid of the problem."

"Let him try," Rojd muttered.

Magnus eyed the Gael. "You are a slave here, are you?"

"Aye, Master."

"How long?"

"I have been here eighteen years, since I was twenty."

"Would you not like to go home? To Erin, is it?" Magnus hazarded a guess.

The man eyed Magnus with caution. "For years, I

dreamed of nothing else."

"Well then, come away with us when we sail. Return to Sorvagur with us. We often trade in Erin. When next we sail there, we will take you home." And would that not enrage the fine Mistress Embra? Stir her anger, and her passions, perhaps.

Thoughts moved visibly through the man's wide eyes. "I could not."

"Why not?" Jorg clapped Magnus on the shoulder. "You can trust his word. He'll see you home."

"I could not leave Mistress Embra."

"You're her slave, man!"

"You do not understand. She is like a daughter to me. And she has no one else."

No one else? She had that whole, mad family.

"Sir, when may I tell Mistress Embra you will meet with her again?"

"Tell her I am thinking on it. And you think on it also. If you decide you want your freedom—"

"I will not change my mind."

"Curse me," Apsel muttered. "If I were being held here in chains, I would not care whom I had to leave."

"Master, I am not in chains."

Knut shook his head. "Do you not think she would trade or betray you, if it met her need?"

"Nei, master, I do not."

"Fool." Knut waved his arm at the shore. "They are all fools here. I do not know why we came."

"A fool's errand," Jorg agreed, much to Magnus's surprise.

Apsel's gaze met his.

Ach, by Odin's eye, maybe he would have to meet with the woman again.

****

"Keep good watch." Magnus squeezed Jorg's shoulder. "If they mean to attack, it will be in the dark."

Jorg muttered, "If they mean to fire the boat, we will see the torches coming."

"Ja. Ulrik may be smarter than that. More—devious. They may come under water. Try to damage and sink us."

"Curse me," Knut said. "I do not wish to be stranded here with no way home. No matter how beautiful the women."

"Agreed. I too want to get home as soon as possible."

"Then talk to the bitch."

"I will."

Knut muttered, "I almost hope that Ulrik does mount an attack this night. It would soothe me to exercise my sword."

"You do realize," Magnus waved an arm at the shore, "we are immensely outnumbered."

"My blade does not care."

Magnus grunted his acknowledgement.

What the men of Husavik perhaps forgot was that he and his crew descended from warriors—on both sides. The sons of slave women, ja. But those women were the daughters of Gaelic warriors who had fought to defend their own lands.

As Modir had told him, her father was a clan chief in Lewis. He had battled to the death to prevent her seizure. "You come of strong men on both sides," she'd told him. "And you look like him, my da."

Da. The cadence of the Gaelic tongue came to her readily when she spoke of her past. "Tall and strong he was, just like you. Gunnar Fritisson cut him down there on the shore, before taking me captive."

Magnus wished he could have met his Grandda, known him, trained with him. Ja, Fadir had raised him well. And like any good Norseman, Magnus preferred fighting with the axe above the sword. But when it came to combat, a man could not have too many mentors.

"We will take turns sleeping," he told the men. "Have a crew on watch at all times. We will see what the night brings."

Chapter Eleven

"Mistress? Mistress, you must come. An attack in the harbor!"

"Eh?" Embra stirred reluctantly. It had taken her overlong to fall asleep, her mind crammed with thoughts and impressions. When she did drift off, she sank deep into the ocean of the night. Kennach's voice, calling her back, caused physical pain.

But ja, his words did penetrate and instill an immediate sense of dread. She sat up in her nest of blankets and clawed her hair out of her eyes.

"The harbor?"

Kennach held a rush light that lit his face garishly. "The seafarers' boat. It is under attack."

Embra swore bitterly and got to her feet. She slept in nothing more than a thin underdress with her hair loose around her, both now tangled from her restless night.

"Ulrik?" she grunted as she searched for her boots, fruitlessly.

"Aye. Half the settlement is awake and hurrying there."

Embra could hear them yelling and hollering outside, streaming past the wall of her quarters. Ach, by sweet Freya's heart, what next?

"Where is my knife?"

"Mistress, there is no time."

"I will not go unarmed."

Kennach thrust a weapon into her hands. Abandoning the search for shoes, she ran out with Kennach behind her.

The harbor was on fire. Or, nei, those gathered there merely had a large number of torches. Even from a distance, up the slope of the land, Embra could see the dark knots of excited people. She could also see several torches and dark forms moving on what must be the seafarers' boat.

She went breathless and ran—not a good combination.

She'd been fleet in her youth, able to best her brothers at least some of the time, and usually went barefoot then. Now her heart pounded so hard she wondered if she'd make it to the harbor.

Ach, what would she find?

Heedless, she shoved her way through folks who scowled until they recognized her. When she reached the shore, she splashed out into the water as she was.

How had this situation slipped so far out of her control? She had set guards. Perhaps they had given the alarm.

Men—armed warriors—stood in the water all around. It took Embra a moment to realize they were from the settlement and not Magnus Tolljursson's boat.

Where was he?

Suddenly someone seized her arm. She swung round, knife in her hand, but it was only Vanja.

"He has Ulrik!"

"Ulrik? Who has him?"

"The seafarer. Magnus Tolljursson."

"Ach!" By Tyr's balls! What was she to do now?

"Come no closer!" bellowed a voice from the boat, the prow of which towered above Embra's head. Then, "Ach, it is you."

She looked up, and up. Magnus stood balanced at the front of the boat with his arm clasped around her brother's chest and a knife to Ulrik's throat.

She could not see Ulrik's expression clearly, but his posture spoke loudly of outrage and indignation. Her brother fancied himself a fierce warrior, and to be caught out so must be a sore humiliation.

"Mistress Embra," Magnus said. "Come aboard."

A line was tossed over the side. Cursing bitterly, Embra climbed up it, dimly aware Kennach followed her, and arrived dripping wet.

A body lay sprawled nearly at her feet, with another just beyond. Both warriors of the settlement, both dead. Ulrik's friends. He'd made good on his threat of attack, but clearly had not succeeded in the attempt.

She wanted to skin him alive for such temerity. But she'd have to talk him free of Magnus's hands, first.

Straightening herself to face the two of them, she barked, "What is all this?"

Everyone on board swung toward her, all the members of Magnus's crew, many of whom held prisoners of their own.

Magnus had a rakish cut running down one cheek, just above the night-time stubble that covered his jaw. There had been a skirmish previous to the captures.

The seafarers had proved victorious.

Ach, that would put a wrinkle in Ulrik's ass.

Indeed, he looked furious enough to spit flames, eyes wide, chest still heaving.

Magnus, on the other hand, appeared calm. He took a moment to eye Embra up and down from her bare feet, along her sodden underdress and wet hair, to where the damp fabric outlined her breasts.

She had to discipline herself, because it felt as if he touched her with his hands.

He tossed his wild mop of hair. "As you see, we were boarded and attacked in the dark. Violating your own assurance of safety, I might add."

Embra raked Ulrik with her eyes and glanced around the deck before asking, "How many dead?"

Ulrik said nothing but his eyes blazed.

"He cannot answer you," Magnus drawled, and she grasped for the first time that he too was angry—furious. "I have the knife pressed too hard against his throat. If he speaks, he will die."

She should have known something like this would happen. She had known—which was why she'd sent Kennach with the warning. She had not wanted a boatload of murdered seafarers on her watch. She hadn't expected Magnus's men to turn the table quite so completely.

A splashing heralded the arrival of someone else. Please do not let it be Vanja, she thought. When she glanced over her shoulder, she saw Runi climbing aboard.

"Allow him," Magnus called to his men, and Runi took the place at Embra's side.

"Well, little brother, what have you done?"

"Made a cock-up," Embra answered for Ulrik.

Runi laughed.

"Master Magnus," Embra began after drawing a breath, "release my brother, and you and I will sit down again to negotiate."

Once more, he examined her in the soaking underdress, as good as naked. She had no hope of reading what lay in his eyes, but the heat rose and suffused her.

"It does not work that way, Mistress Embra. Your brother boarded us with treachery in mind. Here in your harbor, this boat stands as Sorvagur."

"Ja." Embra understood that.

"It is our right to defend Sorvagur."

"As you have done." Embra grimaced and spread her hands. "Successfully."

"It is my right to cut his throat."

As he had Fadir's? Or Gunnar's? The words were implied. Embra's stomach clenched.

"Perhaps," she returned. "Or perhaps you might provide your hosts with a show of good faith and release him."

Magnus shook his head. The muscles of his arm flexed as he pressed his knife still deeper into Ulrik's throat. Ulrik tried to shrink from the blade and a thin line of blood appeared on his neck.

"It is not going to happen that way. He has attacked us and is now a prisoner of Sorvagur."

Ulrik reacted to that. Flexing his body, despite the pressure of the knife, he twisted in Magnus's grip. A brief scuffle ensued, at the end of which Ulrik lay on his back with Magnus's boot in the middle of his chest.

Ulrik's eyes glared up at Embra as if all of it was her fault.

Impetuous ass.

"You mean to hold him hostage?" Her voice did not sound like her own. "You do realize how many score men are in my settlement, and might attack you."

"You do realize I have only to finish cutting his throat, or pull anchor and sail away with him."

"A fortuitous way to get rid of our troublesome brother," Runi muttered for Embra's ears alone.

So it was. Yet the repercussions just might tumble her from power. What kind of jarl failed to protect his—or her—own?

She shrugged, feigning indifference. "Take him. Much good it will do you."

Magnus laughed with what sounded like real amusement. "Much good will it do you."

Curse it all!

"I may not harm him, Mistress. I may but tie him up and make him our guest for a time, as so many have been guests here in Husavik."

A slave? Was that what he meant? Would he make the son of Friti Gunnarsson a slave?

"Or I may return him to you. In pieces. A finger here, an ear there."

Ulrik howled.

Runi chuckled. "By Odin's eye, I begin to like this man."

"Shut up!" Embra breathed into Runi's ear. "What am I to do?"

"I cannot do both, Sostir—shut up and tell you what to do. Besides, *you* are jarl."

"We will negotiate," Embra called to Magnus. "What do you want?"

Again, his gaze dropped to her breasts. Truly? He wanted that?

Ach, and it might be a clever ploy, to accommodate him. Take him somewhere they could be alone. Her chamber, possibly. Bare her breasts to him. Find out how it felt, being touched by those hands, those lips. Then she could put a knife between his ribs.

He said, "We will sit down come the morning, Mistress Embra, and talk about it. Right now, I want my bed."

Did he!

"Meanwhile, as a show of good faith, we will release these others of your men who accompanied your brother on his misguided raid. Except for the few who did not survive." He tipped his head. "Would you like to take them too? For burial? We are not savages, and have no further use of them."

Bastard! Handsome, clever bastard.

She gave a hard nod. "We will take them."

"Ja, and Mistress, you are aware that if we are attacked again, or if I am ambushed when I come to deal with you on the morn, Master Ulrik will be the first to feel the consequences."

"I am aware of that, ja."

He gestured with his elbow to his men, who released their prisoners.

Eyeing the men with disfavor, Embra told them, "Bring the others," and they moved to collect the dead.

She did not so much as glance at Ulrik as she and Runi turned and followed them off the boat.

But Runi whispered in her ear, "I still say you should let them kill him."

"Tempting," she returned. Very tempting indeed.

Chapter Twelve

"You find yourself in a great deal of trouble," Magnus remarked to the man who sprawled at his feet. "Perhaps you are regretting your recent actions."

Ulrik Fritisson glared back at him. They had tied him to the mast, tightly enough that he felt the bite of the ropes. They had also, at Apsel's suggestion, stripped him naked, just to provide an extra measure of humiliation.

He'd fought back, so he bore numerous wounds, including a superficial cut to the throat. That would not kill him. He was too valuable to kill—yet.

Magnus crouched down next to him, the better to glare into his blue eyes. Mad eyes they were. Or perhaps that was just anger. Magnus had to give him credit—he did not display much fear.

He might, anon.

"I must thank you for the advantage you have given me with your sister."

Ulrik spat. "You err if you think you can use me to bargain with her. She does not care about me."

"No love lost among you, eh?" Magnus thought briefly of his own sister, Gyda, whom he adored. What might he not do for her? "You shock me, truly."

"Go bugger yourself."

"I will assume that is the fear talking."

"It is the hate. You will not survive long, once you

set foot ashore."

"You think not? But if I die, you do also. And the way I see it, Mistress Embra cannot allow that. How, then, to hold her place as jarl?"

Ulrik grunted.

"A place you want for yourself, is it?" Magnus leaned closer. "Would you like me to see if I can remove her from your path? Perhaps strangle her, when I get her alone?"

That was not what he wanted to do with Embra if he got her alone. He had a whole list of other things in his mind. He wanted his lips at her throat, ja. And perhaps his tongue. At her breasts, which he'd as good as glimpsed last night. And lower.

How would she taste? Spicy and vital as the sea?

Interest flared in Ulrik's eyes. He gaped, "Why bother to meet with her? You and I, ja, can negotiate. Here and now."

Ja, and that sounded like the brother of Gunnar Fritisson speaking. Gunnar had come to Sorvagur last summer asking their help in a power struggle with his father, warning them Friti planned to attack their settlement. All charm and guile, he'd held a knife in his hand, one which he planned to plunge into their backs. In Ulrik, he heard the echo of Gunnar's voice.

"You," he told Ulrik, "are a vicious asp. I would as soon spit as trust you."

"Watch your back," Ulrik called after him when he rose and moved away. "And watch out for Runi. He is a thousand times smarter than you."

****

Embra paced the interior of the great hall, just as she had most of the night. She'd had little sleep following the attack at the harbor. First she'd needed to speak to the people of the settlement and send them all home. Then Vanja had assailed her, and she'd needed to try to reason with her also. Even when she and Kennach were alone, Embra having told Runi, when he left, to come back in the morning, her thoughts would not allow her rest. She'd fair worn a path in the floor.

At the first morning light she'd gone home, dressed in some of her finest garb, and returned.

To pace some more.

Would Runi come? One could never tell with Runi, mostly because one could seldom define his motivations. Other members of the family were moved by greed. By hate. By lust. Runi rarely wanted what you might suppose he wanted. Difficult to measure.

She would be glad of his support in this instance. He had seemed to support her last night. And in this, she dared not step wrong.

She had guaranteed the safety of the seafarers—common practice in her world—and Ulrik had defied her in that. Yet if she allowed Magnus Tolljursson to kill him, all of her father's associates, and enemies, would step forward and cry foul.

They would use it as a reason to depose her.

And then what? Orve was still too young to serve as jarl, but some might try to persuade Runi to step up. She did not think he would. Others among the elders of the settlement might support Ulrik's claim, no doubt recognizing something in him, or even believing they could manipulate him.

Embra did not want the place of jarl for the sake of it, but because she foresaw the chaos, the pain and darkness that might ensue if she lost control and it passed to someone else.

Ach, maybe she should just let the seafarer kill Ulrik, and let the ashes fall where they may.

A shadow blocked the sunlight that streamed through the open door as Kennach leaned in and huffed, "He comes."

"Runi?" She spun.

"Nay, Magnus Tolljursson."

He entered the hall swathed in sunlight, his hair lit to the warm color of flame. He'd come alone—walked through the angry and dangerous settlement as if out for a stroll, with his shield and—

Ja, that was an axe.

He favored the axe, did this man from across the water?

"Welcome," she told him.

He nodded and said nothing.

Looking past him, Embra bade Kennach, "Leave us. And make certain we are not disturbed."

"Mistress—" Ja, Kennach recognized that as an impossible order.

"Do your best."

Magnus made his way toward Embra slowly, glancing around the hall as if checking it for hidden enemies.

"It is just the two of us, Magnus Tolljursson."

He turned his attention to her, made a slow inspection as he had last night aboard his boat. Even though she now stood well-clad in at least three layers of finery, her flesh pricked.

"Have you killed my brother yet?"

He smiled and lines bracketed his cheeks. He wagged his head a little. "Not yet."

"No doubt you want to." She turned away and poured out two cups of mead. "He is mightily aggravating."

"You speak the truth. It amazes me no one here has yet silenced him."

She handed him one of the cups. Their fingers brushed.

He quirked a brow. "It is early for mead."

"I suggest we drink a pledge, before we begin."

"Do you, Mistress? What sort of pledge?"

"One of honesty. You and I, it seems, must deal with one another. We are not enemies, despite the fact that our fathers were."

"And our mothers. Did you know your mother once tried to kill my mother?"

"She is a woman of strong passions."

He stepped closer, the cup in his hand. "Like you, Mistress? Are you also a woman of strong passions?"

She gazed into his eyes. Hazel green mixed with gold and brown, wickedly bright. "Nei, I am a woman of reason. Like my father. Whatever else might be said of him—"

"A great many things."

"A great many things," she added deliberately, "some quite evil, he was by and large immensely practical. Eye always upon the ultimate outcome."

Another step closer. "And what outcome do you seek?"

"Peace, of course."

"It is a worthy aim. Whether it is possible here in Husavik—" He wagged his head again, in mock sorrow. "I do not know."

"Nor do I. Will you drink a pledge of honesty with

me?"

"Most certainly."

He laid the axe aside and took his shield from his shoulder. "But like this."

As the old ones did when they made a pledge, he looped his arm, the hand holding the cup, through hers. The move brought him much closer, and she could smell him—warm sunshine and healthy male. "I drink from your cup and you from mine."

"Ah." An avoidance of poison? Very well then. Her voice came in a husky rasp. "To truth."

"Truth."

He did not look away from her as he drank. His lips came away wet from the rim of the cup. She had the mad desire to capture them with her own. To taste and taste, and taste.

Instead she disengaged from his grasp. Her knees wobbled beneath her. "Let us sit. And speak honestly."

"Ja."

They sat more or less where they had met before, beside the hearth. Magnus drained his cup. "That is very good mead. Nearly as good as what we have at home."

"It is kind of you to say."

He flashed a smile. "Truth."

"Let us begin more plainly than we did last time we met. No talk of—of old quarrels, perhaps." That tended to prompt strong feelings.

"All right."

"I need my brother back. Tell me what I must do to get him."

"You walk a fine line here, Mistress Embra. A dangerous one, establishing your power. It would not be easy for anyone, given the word I have brought from Sorvagur. And for a beautiful woman, even less so."

He thought her beautiful, or he just employed the word in flattery. Ah, but he'd sworn to truth.

She regarded him steadily.

"You dare not put a foot wrong."

"It is so. The men of Husavik tend to think their women good for but two things. They do not want to take me seriously. But Runi does not want the place of jarl, and the others of my family . . ."

"Ja."

"So I hope with Runi's backing, I may steer a safe course for the settlement."

"Were I or one of my men to slit Ulrik's throat—"

"It might be convenient, but it would be seen as a mark of weakness on my part, that I allowed it to happen."

He spread his hands. Strong, beautiful hands they were, still flecked with small wounds from the fight aboard the longboat. "So we bargain."

"Why do you not finish what you began before you left in a huff, and tell me what you want?"

Chapter Thirteen

Magnus narrowed his eyes at the woman who sat opposite him, and he struggled to order his thoughts. He might want to argue with her accusation that he'd gone off in a huff the last time they met to bargain, only he had. He did not like being reminded of a slave's supposed worthlessness.

Mistress Embra proved a terrible distraction. Everything about her lured him away from his intentions, even though she now sat properly dressed like the daughter she was of a wealthy Norse jarl. Not like he'd seen her aboard his boat last night—feet bare, hair loose around her as if she'd just come from her bed. Underdress dampened and as good as transparent.

Beautiful, ja, yet he did not quite understand why she affected him so powerfully.

"Last time we spoke," she began, "you said you'd come for three reasons, yet I know of only two—to tell me of my father's death and to see the land of your forefathers."

"Ja. It might be well to establish trade between us also. Given, there is an immense amount of ill will. But establishing a trade route might serve to avoid a repeat of what happened last summer."

"Bringing news of my father's death at your hands tends to prompt more ill will."

"He did not die at my hands."

"At the hands of your folk. Also, holding Ulrik prisoner is not a good way to sue for better relations."

"Mayhap not, but certain points should be understood."

She refilled his cup from the jug of mead. "What points?"

"Husavik may consider Sorvagur weak and vulnerable. Yet if you attack us, you will bleed."

"I see."

"Our fathers may have been enemies." He gave her a tight smile. "And our mothers. But we are related in blood. I hoped to leave here with a treaty of peace. Having met you, Mistress Embra, I hope for more."

Her gaze flew to his. "More?"

"You are a reasonable woman," he echoed her previous words. "And we have sworn to deal honestly."

"You would have us forget all the bad blood between us?"

"If possible."

"Tell me what became of my father's body. And my brother's."

"They were put to the flame with a number of other dead. A large number."

"Did all the men who accompanied them on their voyage perish?"

Magnus wondered at the question. Friti had come with a longboat crammed full of warriors. Had this young woman's lover been among them? Hard to imagine she did not have a lover.

He shook his head. "Not all. A number were wounded in that final battle. We gave them care. Some decided to join the settlement. Two are still prisoner."

"And Lodvar Haraldsson? He decided to join with

you also?"

"He did." Magnus would not tell her Lodvar had wed his sister, nor how deep their bonds reached. "Our shaman, Kaddi, also perished during the battle. Lodvar has taken his place."

"I have heard of Kaddi. He was shaman here, at one time."

"Over a score of years ago." Magnus drank of the excellent mead. "That brings me to my third reason for coming."

"Name it."

"Catrin."

"Eh?" Her brows flew upward.

"A Gael, a slave who became wife to Harald Ericksson. Is she still living here?"

He held his breath waiting for Embra to answer. If Catrin had perished, all this would be for naught and he would have terrible news to take home.

"I—should need to inquire. What do you want with her?"

"She was a dear friend to my mother." Magnus would not emphasize the connection to Lodvar, though Embra would likely arrive there. "You may know that when my parents left Husavik, they took with them not only whatever warriors chose to come, but as many Gaelic slaves as Fadir was able to purchase and thus set free. They were in truth the foundation of the settlement at Sorvagur. Catrin was captured, like Modir, from the island of Lewis. But Harald refused to let her go. I understand he has now died. I wish to take her back to Sorvagur with me."

"Well as I say, I will have to ask about her. After their master dies, slaves may be disposed of in many ways—"

"He married her in the end. Would that not protect her?"

Embra shrugged. "I will find out. What was her name, again?"

"Catrin. Wife to Harald." Magnus tried not to squirm where he sat. At Sorvagur, there were no slaves. And he struggled with the attitude toward them here. Indifferent. Unconcerned. As if they were only possessions.

"About Ulrik."

"You shall have him back, given he has not done something foolish in my absence and forced my men to cut his throat."

"When?"

"Just as soon as you bring Catrin to me."

"So important is she, this woman?"

"My modir has spent many years regretting that she could not bring her friend away with her to freedom. I wish to make that right."

"Very well. I will try and determine what has become of her. There are many slaves and many Haralds."

"Act swiftly, Mistress. It will not be easy to keep from killing Ulrik."

Magnus got to his feet. Embra followed. As he turned away, she spoke again, softly.

"And is there nothing else, Master Magnus, that you want?"

He whirled back to face her. She held him with that pale blue gaze of hers, and suddenly the desire between them sprang to life. It sizzled along his skin and expanded to fill the chamber.

He inspected her once more as he had aboard the boat, allowed his gaze to slide along her cheek, graze her lips, and dance down the length of her hair. He let it hover at her breasts and his blood heated within him.

By Odin's eye, she'd asked for the truth, had she not?

"I want to kiss you."

That should shock and offend her. It should make her step away from him. Instead she moved in closer, and the blue eyes dilated.

"I should like that also. Perhaps a single kiss to—to seal our agreement."

He needed no further invitation. With a growl deep in his throat, he snagged the back of her neck with one hand. Like a man diving for treasure, he captured her lips.

Fire roared through him, a wall of heat so powerful it took an instant to grasp that she felt it also. Desire pounded in cadence with his heart, and the top of his head seemed to fly away, taking all good sense with it. He lost the next few moments. Sensation flooded too bright and seared all else away into a fog of staggering pleasure.

Embra. In his arms. Her body flattened against the muscles of his chest, pressed so close he could feel everything. Her mouth open beneath his, soft lips asking, beseeching, her tongue wooing his and making bone-melting promises.

With a groan, he plunged his fingers into her hair. She tasted of the mead, better than the mead. He wanted her more than he knew a man could want anything.

One kiss, she'd said, and it was only one, but it went on and on while the pleasure of it continued to burn his senses, and reality threatened to abandon him entirely.

A primitive part of his brain argued he must take her—here, now. It warred with an even older part that bade him *breathe.*

Gasping raggedly, he came up for air, his heart thudding.

They still held one another fast, she clinging to him like a limpet on a rock. Even though he hadn't entered her, they felt like one person. The same dazed wonder he felt reflected in her wide eyes. Astounding enough that he felt this. That she felt it also—

He needed to say something, but he had no words. He could barely hear his own thoughts for the blood pounding through his veins.

"I—" she began, and her voice broke. "I—I—"

Mad laughter rose to Magnus's head. He had shaken this nearly unshakable woman.

"Why do you look at me that way?" She managed an entire question.

"Because you are so beautiful. And—" And out of a world of women, he thought he could fall in love with this one. Or at least take her on a night voyage she would not soon forget.

Something inside her called to him. The determination in her eyes, perhaps, or her stubborn strength. Her honesty. That incredible heat.

Why here? Why now?

"I—" she attempted again. "I will inquire about this Catrin." She groped visibly for her composure. "Then you will return my brother to me."

"Ja. If he survives." He bent his head to her but resisted taking her lips again. "Truth. We have sworn to it. Kissed on it."

She still had hold of him, so he felt it when her knees wobbled. Ja, he had the same effect on her that she had on him. Heady knowledge.

"I'd best begin, then." The words gusted from her.

"You had best." He smiled into her eyes.

"And then—then perhaps you had better come back so we can speak again."

"Speak. Ja."

"You will return?"

He had her asking for him. *It was well*.

Chapter Fourteen.

She had asked him to come back to her. Virtually begged. And Embra Fritisdottir never begged for anything.

She paced and pondered it, there in the empty hall after Magnus left. What was it about the man? What, that reduced her to this condition, made her stutter, and turned her into a throbbing morass of need?

She did not know, but she needed to kiss him again. The truth was she never should have kissed him in the first place, pledge or otherwise. She'd had a pretty fair idea what would happen, though she'd never imagined a reaction of such power. Such splendor. Like a tide sweeping through her.

Nei, not like a tide. He made her think of fire, did Magnus Tolljursson, with his wealth of reddish locks and his freckle-burnished skin. Fire burned. It destroyed everything in its path.

He had just destroyed her. With a single kiss.

She wanted—she wanted him to come back so she could look at him. Touch that magnificent chest once again. Gaze into those eyes, filled with light. Watch for his slightly wicked smile that flickered with wry promise. The one that showed he knew what she was thinking.

She wanted to look at him, ja. To touch him. She wanted far more.

She could scarcely make a more disastrous choice

for a lover. On the other hand, the rules governing such choices here in Husavik were so lax, they might not exist.

The truth was, she wanted Magnus in her bed for a night that lasted a fortnight or so.

As jarl, she had a right to tumble whomever she chose. The gods knew, Fadir had. Slaves, maidens, the wives of his friends, with or without their permission. Even Vanja, most probably. Why should Embra not help herself to one solitary seafarer?

She did not want anyone else.

The next time she saw Magnus Tolljursson, she must bid him to her bed. She knew that to her soul, and the very prospect made her shiver from head to toe—shiver with heat, were such a thing possible.

"Sostir, we saw him leave. Has he gone to free Ulrik?"

Embra spun to see not only Vanja but Dagmar entering the hall. Ach, as if one alone was not trouble enough.

"Nei, not yet. We were but bargaining." Heat flooded her cheeks. She need not share the nature of that bargaining. Fortunate, though, her sisters had not arrived a few moments earlier.

Vanja looked like a madwoman. In fact at this moment she looked so much like Modir, beautiful and wild, Embra found it unsettling.

Dagmar looked calmer, but simmered visibly with anger. "He is arrogant, that Magnus Tolljursson. Only see the way he stalks through our settlement, unafraid, as if nothing can touch him."

Balls as big as Odin's head, Embra thought irreverently. Well, she meant to find out.

"He has berserker blood," Vanja pointed out. "He may be berserker as well."

"Is he?" Dagmar asked Embra.

"I do not know."

"He is also half slave," Vanja pointed out. "That may cancel out the endowment of the blessing from our gods."

"Do not say that to him, Sostir, not if you want Ulrik back."

"I am not sure I do. But we cannot allow that outlander to hold him—or kill him. It is a matter of pride."

"I agree," said Dagmar starkly. "This is outrageous, that they should sail into our bay and take our brother captive."

"What would Fadir say?" Vanja rejoined.

Very little, Embra suspected, since he was dead. "We must deal with Magnus Tolljursson, and send him on his way. Then get back to establishing a strong government here."

"You think Fadir's cronies will ever accept you as jarl?"

"If I show them strength enough."

She thought about asking for her sisters' backing, their support. The more members of Friti Gunnarsson's house she could persuade to stand with her, the better.

Vanja leaned toward her and widened her beautiful eyes. "And after all the deals are made and Ulrik freed, we will kill the berserker's son. We will have our revenge for Fadir's death."

****

"We had to gag him," Apsel explained when Magnus returned to the boat. "He would not stop spewing curses, even when we gave him a kicking. And he pissed all over the deck. Just so you know, none of us is willing to clean that up."

Magnus bent his gaze on Ulrik Fritisson—now a pitiful sight. Still naked except for the filthy cloth tied over his mouth, lashed to the mast and surrounded by a pool of piss, he glared back with furious eyes.

"He tried to bite me when I gagged him," Rojd offered.

"Most unwise. His temper gets the better of him, I think." Magnus bent toward the prisoner. "Your sister is considering ransoming you. She will make up her mind."

His sister. Hot and pliable in Magnus's arms. By Tyr's beard, what had she done to him?

"We have had an audience all morning," Apsel said. "They stand on the shore and glower. Probably thinking of ways to sink us."

"If we sink, so does he." Magnus pointed his axe at Ulrik. "And he's in no position to save himself."

"Why do we not send him back to his sister the jarl in pieces?" Knut suggested. "It will give us something to do. I am bored, and it makes me feel edgy."

They all felt that way.

"Not yet. I think we should pull anchor and sail out farther into the bay. Just to make attack more difficult for them. Then we will take it in turns sleeping. Two men at a time."

"Ha!" Knut chortled. "What will they think when they see us preparing to sail off?"

Odin alone knew.

****

"The seafarers are sailing away. And they still have

101

Ulrik with them. Come, look!"

Ulla's cry called Embra and Runi from the hall where they'd been speaking together. Embra had finally tracked her brother down, but he was in one of his difficult, uncooperative moods.

He laughed when he heard Ulla's call. "This Magnus Tolljursson does begin to amuse me."

Embra frowned. Why would Magnus decide to leave when they had an agreement? And ach—her heart skipped a beat—what if she did not have a chance to see him again?

Kiss and run. She could murder him for that.

She hurried outside with Runi behind her. Down at the harbor, figures scrambled. It looked like men prepared a *skuta* to pursue Magnus's longboat, which indeed headed north toward open water, moved by powerful strokes of the oars.

Orve ran up. "He pulled anchor just moments ago!"

"Watch," said Vanja, who also joined them. "He will slit Ulrik's throat and throw him over the side."

"Wait." Embra narrowed her eyes, fixed upon the longboat, and tried to discern the thoughts of the man aboard. He had given her his word. A pledge. A kiss. "He is merely withdrawing a distance to avoid trouble. Orve, run and tell our men not to pursue."

He gave her a doubtful look but ran off.

Runi glanced at Embra. "How do you know he is not just leaving?"

"We have an agreement." Besides, she had to wager Magnus wanted to see her again as much as she wanted to see him.

"Agreements have been given before now, with every intention of breaking them."

"You are thinking of Fadir. And Gunnar. You know very well when they went to the Faroes last summer they intended to lie, cheat, or do whatever else they must, to see Tolljur Magnusson dead. Gunnar—he went smiling. All a plan for betrayal."

Runi shrugged. "Whatever works."

"There is Fadir speaking. But it did not work, did it? Fadir and Gunnar are dead, and the berserker is not. Instead his son has arrived on our doorstep."

"Huh."

Sure enough, the longship paused and began to come about just inside the arms of the harbor, at a good distance. Embra could barely see the figures moving around on deck. They pitched the anchor.

"There now," Embra whispered, "he will wait for me to give him what he wants."

"What is that?"

"That is just what I was trying to tell you. Maybe now you will listen."

****

"I suppose we must remove his gag in order to let him eat."

Magnus and his fellows all looked at Ulrik, who languished naked in the sun.

"Are we planning to feed him?"

"Jorg, what kind of hosts would we be, if we did not?"

"Have we enough food to waste on him?"

"Maybe a crumb or two."

Ulrik's glare declared he did not want their food.

"A shame to waste good fare, if we intend to kill him."

"His sister wants him back. Do not ask me why."

And Magnus desired giving Embra everything she wanted. Preferably while in her bed. Over and over again.

"If it were up to me," Knut drawled, "I would hang him over the side and see how long he can hold his breath under water. It's deep enough out here."

"Interesting." Apsel nodded. "Might alleviate the boredom."

"For a short while."

"If I were his sister," Apsel went on, "I would be hoping we kill him."

Magnus, his gaze still fixed on Ulrik, tipped his head. "I wonder what she would give me if I performed that service for her and brought her his head."

"While you are making up your mind," Knut suggested. "Let us sup and play a game of bones."

"Fair enough."

****

"The woman's name is Catrin, you say?" Runi lounged on a rug beside the hearth, the same place where Magnus had been. Runi rarely drank. He'd once told Embra he'd seen what too much drink did to men of their blood, and did not think once he started, he would be able to stop. But he sipped from a cup of broth Embra had offered him.

Not that Runi did not have other appetites he indulged. Embra once heard a rumor that he'd been with three women at the same time.

"Ja, Catrin. A slave from the Alban isles."

Runi looked at her. "And she belonged to a man called Harald?"

"I think so, ja."

"You do know who that is?"

Dumbly, she shook her head.

"Well, you know Lodvar Haraldsson. Harald used to oversee the old hall, before this was built. In the wild old days. Fadir rewarded him with the gift of a slave. I do not remember her name, but she was taken in raiding. Harald is dead now, but he had a son from her. Lodvar, the shaman."

"She is Lodvar's mother?" Embra stared.

"Lodvar the turncoat, apparently, who has decided to forsake us for a life in Sorvagur."

"Forsake us." Forsake what? Embra wondered. Unending insults? Slurs hurled at him? The status of slave above which he could never quite rise, even though he spoke with the gods?

"Perhaps," she suggested, "he had no choice. Magnus told me Kaddi—you remember Kaddi?"

"I have heard tell of him."

"He left Husavik before we were born. He died there at Sorvagur, and they wanted a new shaman."

Runi shrugged.

"The berserker may have pressed Lodvar into service. Then again, it may not be the same slave or even the same master. There are so many Haralds. But we will have to inquire, find out what happened to her, and get Ulrik back."

"I suppose we must get him back? The settlement has been very peaceful today. It occurs to me he is by and large a disruptive influence. It would serve the berserker's son right if we made him keep the little bastard."

Embra shrugged in turn. "They will not put up with him for long. They will soon put him over the side."

"Mayhap they already have."

"All joking apart, Runi, will you inquire after the woman, Catrin, for me? I think such inquiries will be taken better coming from you. Less—less fuss."

"By Thor's balls, Embra, I do not like to. I will have to go among folks. Speak with them."

"I am saving you from the onerous task of serving as jarl, Runi. You owe me."

"Ja, well. I will ask."

"Tonight?"

"In the morning."

"In the morning, then." She hoped he would not drag his feet. She wanted an excuse, any excuse, to see Magnus Tolljursson again.

Chapter Fifteen

"You are Catrin, wife of Harald?"

The woman who stood before Embra held herself humbly and had a thin, lined face. Her clothing, though not rich, looked clean and decent. She wore her hair tucked up in a cloth like any good matron. Embra could not see its color, but her eyebrows were brown.

"I was his slave."

"Wife," Embra corrected patiently. "It is said Harald wed with you."

The woman flapped her hand, an odd gesture that spoke of both strength and helplessness.

"He wed me. Before he died."

"How did he die?"

"A fall, after drinking. His joints had crippled him. He would go out drinking with his cronies anyway."

"I see."

"Many days, I tended him. He moaned and shat himself like a babe."

Embra lifted her brows. "And where do you live now? With whom?"

"Alone. He left me enough to afford a tiny place."

It must be a bleak existence. Of course, the woman might have friends, but her stark expression argued for loneliness.

Fortunate, perhaps, that Magnus Tolljursson came asking after her. A kindly thing. Embra did not see much of kindliness, and she rarely felt sympathy for others. Doing so seemed too much like offering to share their ill luck. No one wanted to catch Loki's notice or have him turn his eye upon them.

Had this woman ever been beautiful? Hard to tell, now. And it did not matter. The men of the settlement would use any woman, and use her frequently.

"Please, Mistress Catrin, will you sit?"

"If you will forgive me, I do not wish to sit in your presence, Mistress Embra."

"Why not?"

"I would not so dirty myself."

Hostility! The woman must possess some inner strength, to have maintained a capacity for it.

"As you choose. Are you modir to Lodvar Haraldsson?"

That snagged her attention. Her defiance died. "Do you have word of him? The boat that came—it is said they are from the settlement at Sorvagur."

"Ja."

"They brought word of the expedition that went there? The news of Jarl Friti's and Gunnar's deaths?" she sneered over the names, as if unable to prevent it.

"They both died in the fighting there. If Lodvar is your son, you will want to know he still lives. He holds the position of shaman in Sorvagur."

Catrin sagged where she stood. "Bless him. May the gods bless him!"

She did not speak of Norse gods, Embra felt sure of it. She wondered to what other gods this gaunt woman might pray. They must be strong, to have let her survive.

"Magnus Tolljursson has inquired after you. You

were friend to his mother, he says."

"Magnus. Eadha's son? I was friend to Eadha, long ago. Is she well?"

"So far as I know. When I speak to Magnus Tolljursson again, I will tell him you are also well."

"Ja, Mistress."

"Thank you, Mistress Catrin. You may return home."

Without question, the woman went. Embra gestured Runi forward from the shadows where he had stood listening.

"What do you think?"

"I think Magnus Tolljursson wants her for a reason beyond what he has disclosed."

"He is willing to trade Ulrik for her."

"For that scrap of a slave woman."

"She is slave no longer. Free to go if she wants."

"We will not tell her that just yet."

"I need to meet with Magnus Tolljursson again." Embra needed to see him. Touch him. Breathe the same air as him. "What shall I say?"

"That the woman is here. Alive. Is that not what he wanted to know?"

"I will send him a message."

"How?"

"Kennach will row out on a *skuta*."

"Bid Magnus make the trade and leave on the next tide."

Embra's heart thudded within her breast. "He has spoken of setting up trade."

"The best thing he can do is take his slave woman and sail away, Never return."

Ja, and how would Embra bear it?

****

Kennach delivered the message before noon. Embra herself watched from the harbor as two armed men rowed him out to Magnus's longboat. An exchange took place, and she held her breath.

Mayhap he would come back with Kennach, decide to meet with her directly. But nei. She gnawed her lips when she watched Kennach come back alone, save for the guards.

"What did he say?" she asked her servant before his feet hit the pier.

"He said to thank you for locating his mother's friend."

"Will he now return Ulrik to us?"

"Mistress, he did not say."

"Will he come in and meet with me?"

"He did not say that either."

By Freya's heart, she found it frustrating. She wanted to see the man. At the same time, she could scarcely warrant the fact that she could not work up a measure of indifference.

Indifference had always been her means of survival.

He was but a man. He belched and broke wind and probably snored in his sleep.

Only he was *not* just a man.

"He has not yet slain Ulrik?"

Kennach looked startled. "If he has, he did not say so. I did not go aboard."

All the rest of that day, Embra waited. She endured visits from her siblings and sent them away in turn. Only Runi did not pester her.

He will come at nightfall, she told herself over and

over again. But well before nightfall, rain swept in from the sea, a storm on its skirts. Thunder shook the settlement, and the sky grew dark betimes.

He will not come now. She tried to handle her disappointment and, giving up her place in the hall, went home.

Even that brief journey left her soaking. She was half changed out of her wet clothing, damp hair hanging all around her, when Kennach called from outside the door.

"Mistress Embra, a visitor."

"Eh?"

He put his head in the door. "Master Magnus."

Ach, by Freya's heart!

"Give me a moment and show him in."

She had but the one room—a bed and a fire met her needs. A small space for Kennach to prepare most her meals. Kennach slept in a separate nook, out back.

Not luxurious, but hers alone.

Magnus Tolljursson came pushing through the leather door curtain before she was ready. He stood just inside, hair plastered to his head, garments clinging to him, looking so handsome it hurt.

"Ah, Master Magnus." She gasped for breath, and fought for control. "I thought the storm would keep you away."

"You suppose me afraid of a little rain?"

A little rain. The thunder shook the building and the rain threatened to tear the roof down.

Did he disregard all dangers with the same careless aplomb? And, was she dangerous to him?

"Come, sit beside the fire. Let me find you a drying cloth."

He laid down his shield and axe, both within reach. He shook the wet hair down his back and it rippled in sodden waves. Embra passed him the cloth she used for washing.

He rubbed his wet face with it before looking at her with a smile. "It smells of you."

"I apologize. I have naught else to hand."

"I am not complaining." He finished drying his neck, his arms, with his gaze on her all the while.

"I went to the main hall—you were not there. Your man directed me back here. I hope you do not mind."

"I do not mind." She wanted him here. With her. Alone. "How is my brother, Ulrik?"

"Wet, very wet. At least he has no clothing to worry him."

"You stripped him?"

Magnus nodded. "And bound him to our mast."

Suddenly she wanted to laugh. She should not find that amusing, she truly should not. "Why?"

"It is our opinion he needs to learn some humility."

"No doubt you are right. But it will not teach him that. He was ruined years ago."

"You cannot fault us for trying."

"You are right. I cannot." She poured two cups of mead. "Will you sit?"

He did, his sodden boots creaking.

"Take those off, if you like. I do not mind."

He removed the boots and set them near the fire to dry. "Your man says you have found Catrin."

"Ja." She handed him a cup and could not help pausing to study the picture he made there beside her fire. All that hair, dark and sodden, eyes so bright with intelligence. The front of his tunic unlaced.

"She is well?"

Embra shrugged. "Well enough. Not happy."

"Will she be willing to come away with us?"

"I did not raise the matter with her." Embra sat down opposite him. "You failed to tell me she is Lodvar Haraldsson's mother."

Magnus shrugged. "Does it matter?"

"I think it does. We pledged honesty with one another."

"I gave you honesty."

She shook her head. "If Lodvar has turned on his jarl and this settlement and betrayed us, it will be a sore spot with those here. If I make a deal to benefit him, it may cost me support I need to consolidate my position."

He considered that. "Ja." Slanting a look at her, he asked, "Does our pledge of honesty still hold?"

"Of course."

"Lodvar has become my friend. Your father and brother brought deception to Sorvagur. Lodvar did not agree with what they tried to do. Gunnar turned on him and would have killed him." His gaze searched hers. "You must know what Gunnar was like."

"Ja." Pure deception behind a pair of smiling eyes, that had been her brother.

"Lodvar," Magnus said slowly, "found something in Sorvagur he never had here. Who could blame him?"

"Hundreds, here in Husavik."

"I did not lie about Catrin. She was my modir's closest friend."

"As well as Lodvar's mother."

"Mistress Embra, let us make this deal. You will get Ulrik back. I will take Mistress Catrin away with me."

She thought about it, wishing Runi were here, with his clever mind. Only she did not want Runi here. She liked being alone with Magnus Tolljursson. She craved this man's company the way a thirsty man craves mead. She had to be careful—

"To be sure," he said softly, "Lodvar is worried about his mother. Would you not be?"

Embra's mother was a madwoman, and she did not comprehend how others felt.

When she did not speak, Magnus said, "Catrin is a free woman. Surely she can choose to come away with me."

"She can, and she cannot. Popular opinion governs much here in Husavik."

"Embra," he leaned toward her, "Make the deal. Let me take the woman and sail away, removing this problem from your life."

Sail away over the water, out of her life. Never to see him again.

"Surely," he continued to urge, "that is what you want."

How earnest he looked, leaning toward her with his gaze fixed on hers, his hair already drying in the heat of the fire, turning to flame. Should she tell him the truth? Should she admit to him what she really wanted?

"Nei," she said softly.

He looked disappointed. He must care a great deal for Lodvar, if this meant so much to him. It occurred to her that no one here in Husavik cared so much for her. Husavik was a place of scheming. Of trickery. Of power.

Boldly, she met his gaze. "I do not wish for you to

sail away back to Sorvagur. At least not before—"

It took him a moment to grasp what she meant. When he did, his eyes widened and his lips pressed together.

"Mistress Embra—"

"We are free to choose, are we not? No one need know what we do here." Fire raced through her blood at the prospect of having him. Here, alone. Naked. In her bed. "It is storming. Too hard for you to return to the boat that brought you in. Stay here, Magnus Tolljursson.

"Stay with me this night."

Chapter Sixteen

They should be negotiating. That mad thought speared its way through Magnus's mind but failed to make the impression it should. He could scarcely believe the offer Embra Fritisdottir had just made to him. Had she truly said what he thought he heard? Had he misunderstood what she meant?

He wanted her. Tyr's sacred balls, he did. No ordinary desire, this. It rode his blood like fever that would not ease. When apart from the woman, it served as a distraction. When in her company, it flared into a ferocious conflagration. When near enough for him to touch her, he turned short of breath and aflame with desire.

He could touch her now, if he wished. She invited him to do so. She offered—his mind stuttered over it.

Would it be a bad decision for him to stay? Would it complicate the deal he'd come to make? He needed to consider that, to think of more than his own desires.

When she looked at him, he could barely think at all.

He said it aloud. "We should be negotiating."

She answered softly, "It is customary when people negotiate, they each get something they want. I think we both want this. Am I wrong?"

Honesty, he reminded himself even as his throat closed. "You are not wrong."

"Then stay here with me tonight. One night. In the morning we will conclude our deal."

Coercion? Was this coercion? Did she offer herself as a bargaining piece? What kind of woman did such a thing?

He reminded himself, the rules were different here in Husavik. Everything was. He struggled to think about it objectively. "Not a good idea, mayhap."

"Mayhap not," she agreed. "But I want it anyway. I want you, before you sail away."

Truth.

She slid across the rug toward him. "Tell me you have not wondered how it would be between us."

"I've wondered." Constantly. It clouded his head and riled his blood.

"Perhaps if we put the wondering to rest, it will leave us in peace."

Perhaps. Make love to her once. Touch and taste her everywhere, spill his seed. If they both wanted that, why not?

He got no farther in his thoughts because she leaned forward and kissed him, and the desire exploded.

Once more, he could taste the mead she'd taken on her tongue. Never again would he be able to drink mead without thinking of this, thinking of her. She welded her mouth to his and her body followed. They fell together as he went backward onto the rug, with her on top of him.

Need poured through him from his crotch upward. Another sensation, equally strong, accompanied it, curling through his brain the way music might, the first snatches of a beguiling song. *Rightness…*

She broke the kiss and stared down into his eyes,

her tumbled hair all around her.

"Magnus Tolljursson, will you gift yourself to me?"

"Ja," he said hoarsely. "Ja."

What did he see in her eyes then? What, besides blazing desire? A flash of possessiveness? Certainly no doubt, no uncertainty. A thread, perhaps, of helplessness, the same as he felt at being swept away on a wave of something he could not deny.

"Take off your clothes," he rasped. "I want to see you."

She smiled at the request. He followed her movements avidly as she untied her kirtle, slid it down. She wore a fine and well-woven garment beneath, dusty blue in color. She slipped out of it with no shame. She wore nothing beneath.

Ach, she was perfection. A slim body and long legs—she was tall for a woman—with small breasts, firm and high, the rose-colored nipples growing tight in the air. The cluster of curls that hid her most secret place was darker than the hair that flowed over her shoulders. Her gaze burned him.

"Beautiful."

That seemed to please her. She came back down to him and gestured with her hands. "You. I want to see what will be mine, this night."

Hers. He shucked his damp clothing, no easy feat with her half on top of him. She watched closely, her gaze following every movement, sliding over each muscle, every scar he revealed. It caressed his chest and ran down the line of hair that led to the place where he ached for her.

"You are terribly wet," she observed. "Allow me to

remedy that."

She applied her tongue to his skin, licking him the way a cat might, up the quivering muscles of his stomach and across his chest. She worked her way up each shoulder, gathering moisture with her tongue, and a word groaned its way past Magnus's lips.

"Down."

She laughed. "Not. Just. Yet."

She fastened her mouth to his, and his vision went white. He distinctly felt all coherent thought fly out of his head. His impulses, in the absence of the ability to think, took over.

He palmed her breast, and she sucked his tongue into her mouth. A promise. Or so he hoped.

After that, even the ability to hope escaped him.

Nothing existed except sensation and the heat rushing through him—rushing through the both of them. The knowledge that she felt what he did, as strongly as he did, pushed him over an edge he'd never seen coming. They consumed one another luxuriantly until she released his mouth, reared up and straddled him, her beautiful body moving with lithesome grace. Her eyes, glowing like blue ice, met and held his as she lowered herself upon him. An exquisite impalement.

She rode him with abandon, and he lost himself entircly to her. When she came and he, without any hope of control, as swiftly followed, he could have shouted. Or sobbed.

She collapsed on him with her hair spread everywhere, a fragrant blanket, and her lips touching his.

While trickles of sanity slowly returned to Magnus's mind, he tried to identify what he felt.

Wrung out. Shattered. Strangely moved. He flattened his palm across her naked back and drew her closer. Tenderness for her swamped him, all unexpected.

She sighed and slid her lips across his.

"Well, Magnus Tolljursson, was that as you anticipated?"

"Better." He could barely speak the word. "Did you get it out of your system?"

"I do not know. Give me a moment. My heart is still pounding."

"Ja." He felt it.

Her tongue came out and traced his lips. "You taste so good. I have never known aught like it."

"I am happy to please."

"Ach, I forgot to check one thing." She slid down his body, pushed his knees apart, and performed a swift examination. "Ja, just as I thought."

"Eh? Do you doubt I am intact? After that?"

"Nei, and nei." She nestled back upon him, a smile curving her lips. "I but needed to verify. As big as Odin's head."

"What!"

"It is a private joke."

"I hope so. I would not like to think of you going around the settlement—"

"—bragging to one and all about the size of my man's endowment?" She gazed at him, her eyes going suddenly serious. "But you are not my man."

Magnus wanted to be. He surely did. "Nei. Ja. Perhaps."

"Honesty," she reminded.

He gusted a breath. "I would like to be."

"Well, then. I would like that also."

"It is impossible."

"Is it?"

"I will at some point hand your brother over to you. You will release Mistress Catrin to me. I will go home."

The breath caught in her throat. She said nothing.

Overhead, thunder boomed. Magnus could hear the rain crashing down outside.

She tipped her head. "Thor does not approve."

"Nei?"

"He protests the prospect of our parting."

"Or perhaps," Magnus caressed her smooth back, "he merely approves of what we do here together."

"I like the way you touch me."

"Do you?" He slid his hands lower to her butt and fitted her more snugly against him.

"You are not rough. Well, just rough enough."

"A man should never hurt someone he—" Magnus halted.

"Someone he—" she prompted.

"Cares for." That other word should not, could not slip past his lips.

"What should a man do with someone he…cares for?"

"Protect and defend her. Cherish her. Die for her, if necessary."

"Make love to her?"

"As often as possible."

Draped across his chest, she contemplated that. At length, she said almost plaintively, "Magnus, Magnus, I find my craving for you is not eased after all."

"Is it not?"

"Nei, nei, the desire remains just as bright. What is

to be done?"

He licked his lips and drew his fingers through her hair. "I cannot imagine."

"We have the rest of the night. I fear it is storming much too hard for you to return to your longboat."

"Is it?"

"I believe so." She lifted herself up on her elbows to look at him. "I seem to have fostered a belief in so many things I never—never before imagined."

"Ja." Again, his throat grew tight. He'd believed in love all his life. He witnessed the bonds of it—strong, unbreakable—between his parents. He saw what lay between Gyda and Lodvar, infused with magic and tenderness. He'd hoped but perhaps he'd never quite believed it would come for him.

But now, now—

He began to believe in that, too.

Chapter Seventeen

Embra woke with a buzzing in her head and rhythmic music in her ears. She felt like she'd taken too much to drink and now descended from a delightful mead high, one that had fairly numbed her mind.

Last night's storm had passed, but rain still fell outside. Was that the source of the music she heard?

Nei.

Warmth suffused the front of her body, and wrapped around her. She felt sore in unaccustomed places, her flesh tender and swollen. Alone in her room?

Again, nei.

She opened her eyes. Magnus Tolljursson lay just beneath her, still sleeping. His breathing provided the music she heard. They had—

Ach, sweet Freya, what had they done?

She lifted her head and looked at Magnus. Caught deep in slumber, he was. His lashes lay thick and brown upon his cheeks. His hair had finished drying during the night and spread like a cloak of warm, red-brown fire. His skin, burnished beneath the freckles, gave off a heady fragrance.

She liked the way the man smelled. And she could not deny, she had never seen a man to equal him. Never touched one, either.

Her scheme—ja, her scheme of exorcising her

desire had proved a dismal failure. It had not truly been a scheme anyway, merely an excuse to have him. Did that violate their vow of truth? Or had he known all along that when it came to him, her desire overruled her? Had it overruled him also?

But nei, she was not sated by all they had shared, all she'd had of him. Oh, by Freya's heart, what she'd had of him! She now knew how he tasted everywhere. And he, her.

How long before morning light raised the settlement? It grew light early at this time of year though the rain kept it darker than usual. She needed to awaken him. She must send him away while yet the throngs remained at home.

How could she?

She leaned on one elbow, continuing to study him, and contemplating her feelings. So tangled were they, and so foreign to what she usually felt, it proved difficult.

What they'd shared last night had been both wondrous and unsettling. She could not believe how she'd behaved. Not that she felt ashamed of it—no shame in honesty. Yet as a customarily controlled woman, she rarely moved beyond the boundaries she herself set.

Last night, Magnus Tolljursson had destroyed her boundaries as if they'd never existed.

Even now, she longed to touch him. Wanted to run her fingers through the hair on his chest, trace a path lower. Wanted to plunge her hands into that rich brown mane, as she had when she kissed him.

Ach, those kisses! Enough to claim a woman's very soul.

But as she'd told him last night, a relationship between them was impossible. Anything more than what they'd already shared—purely physical pleasure—was impossible.

Even though she thought—she feared—she could come to love this man.

That thought appeared without warning and made her eyes go wide. It terrified her, but not so much as the one that followed: *Mayhap she already did love him*.

Nonsense. She had no room in her life for love. No time for it. She had problems enough without worrying about a man. For they were trouble, each and every one of them.

Anyway, what they'd shared last night hadn't been love. It had been self-indulgence, the satisfying of pure need, hot and wild. The fact that they'd admitted to it honestly, that its power had been shared, merely made it seem like something more.

He'd been tender at the end. The last time he entered her, he'd run his fingers through her hair and whispered her name.

Embra.

The memory nearly brought tears to her eyes.

"Embra?"

Awake, he gazed up at her, slightly puzzled and wondering. "By Odin's eye, did I spend the night here?"

"You did." And spent plenty of himself with it.

"Is it morning? I must away."

So he must. She should present him with his clothing, his axe and his shield, and send him off. Back to his longboat. Back to Sorvagur.

Fiercely, she blinked any tears away.

"What is it?" Gently, he touched her cheek. There was that tenderness again. It had the power to undo her.

"Naught. I am just—"

He sat up, muscles rippling. His hand cradled the back of her head when he rested his forehead against hers.

"Shattering, was it not?"

"Ja."

"Who would have thought we would fit together so well?"

Who, indeed?

She strove mightily to gather her emotions. "In the interest of honesty, I never—never imagined such a joining."

"Nor I." He smiled, the rueful smile that so delighted her. "Did we do all I remember?"

"Truly? Ja."

Thoughts—and remembrance—moved in his eyes. What would he say to her? What could he say? Would he make excuses? Pass it off as holding little importance?

His lips quirked again. "You are beautiful, Embra Fritisdottir." He bent his head and kissed her naked breasts, one after the other. "So beautiful. I hope you do not regret what has passed between us."

"I regret nothing. Nothing."

"Nei, nor I."

She scrambled up from the bed where they'd ended up last night, and searched out her clothing. The garments lay scattered where she'd discarded them.

He arose also.

She could not help but watch him from the corner of her eye.

"Where do we stand?" he asked once he'd climbed into his leathers.

"With—"

That smile again. "Our negotiations."

"Negotiations." She paused in tying up her kirtle, and looked at him. "I think further talks are required."

"Do you?" His eyes brightened with interest, or something more.

"Ach, ja. You must return here so we can continue to discuss the situation."

Emotions worked in his face. Doubt, and desire. "What of your brother? Naked and tied to our mast."

"He is young and strong. He will survive."

"Yet—"

She stepped up and kissed him. "Return to me, Magnus."

"When?"

"Tonight."

He picked up his axe and shield. She followed him outside.

Dawn just showed in the east, a line of light against the thick clouds. She longed to say something to him, something meaningful that would assure his return. She wanted to express the powerful emotions that filled her, but having known so little of softness, she could not tell how.

She wanted to touch him, curl her fingers around his arm—claim him. But out here, eyes would be watching. Already there would be questions about him having spent the night in her quarters.

Instead, she said, "I will see you?"

"Ja."

He walked off, still possessed of that air of

powerful competence. With every step he took away from her, Embra's heart grieved.

But nei, her heart could not be involved. She could not allow it to be.

****

"We thought you were dead, or captured." Apsel directed a speaking look at Magnus when he returned to the longship, his dark eyes performing a swift evaluation. "Do not tell me you were there all night? With her. By Odin's eyes, you tumbled her, didn't you?"

The other men gathered round, their expressions avid.

"Why should you suppose I did that? We were negotiating."

Apsel raised his eyebrows and swept his fellows with a glance.

"You have the look," Jorg stated. "That of a man well tumbled." He raked Magnus with a glare.

"Besides," Knut added, "I have seen the way she looks at you, like a hungry woman eyeing a feast."

Jorg wagged his head. "When a woman begins to look at a man that way, there is but one thing for it."

"In addition," Apsel contributed, "your boots are laced up backward."

"Are they? They were wet when I got there last night. I took them off to dry."

"I do not believe that for a moment. Are you mad?" Knut demanded. "This is a nest of asps, and all of them crazed. Why would you get involved in that?"

"I am not involved." Magnus gave up the lie. "Merely—"

"Negotiating," they all chimed.

"And," Knut pressed, "was the deal made?"

Magnus thought of Embra reaching for him, parting her lips and her thighs. "Not quite yet."

"Oh, ho!" Rojd chortled. "I conjecture he must go back for further negotiating."

"Perhaps. Ja. At the lady's insistence."

They clapped him on the back, though Apsel protested, "I call that unfair. You bid us stay away from all those beautiful women, and then take one for yourself."

"And what about him?" Knut jerked his thumb at Ulrik who lay against the mast, looking like a drowned rat after weathering the storm.

"Leave him where he is."

"Do we have to feed him?"

Magnus gave Ulrik a long stare. Would Embra wish him to? "I suppose we must offer a modicum of hospitality."

As soon as they removed Ulrik's gag so he could eat, he started cursing and hollering again. Not too smart, this one. He did not learn.

"Shut up," Knut bawled at him. "Do you want your breakfast?"

Ulrik scowled and glared at Magnus. "When am I to be released?"

"That is still being decided."

"It is an outrage! I am the son of a jarl. For you to keep me tied up this way, treated like an animal—"

Magnus crouched down beside him. "When you capture slaves, what do you do with them? How do you transport them here to Husavik? Do you not bind them? Do you never take your pleasure or ease your need upon any of the women?"

Ulrik's head jerked up. "I am not a slave. Nor," he added scathingly, "the son of one."

"Let me kick him," Knut begged.

"He is too stupid for it to do any good," Apsel growled.

Magnus told Ulrik, "Your sister is contemplating whether to ransom you. Deciding if it is in her best interest. You want the place of jarl for yourself, do you not?"

"It should be held by a man. One of my father's blood."

"You?"

Ulrik shrugged and gave Magnus a savage look. "If Runi does not want it."

"Because, why?" Magnus challenged. "Women are not worthy to lead?" His own mother had led beside Fadir all Magnus's life. Her advice was valued, and usually sound.

"Men were made to lead, women to follow. They have their other uses."

"One good kicking," Knut beseeched.

"He is not worth soiling your boots. But by Odin's eye, gag him again. I tire of listening to the fool."

Chapter Eighteen

Embra sat amid the chaos of the hall at midday and imagined Magnus Tolljursson running his hand up her leg. His palm, rough from handling ropes and hefting weapons, dragging across her skin with heat-building friction. The caress of it on her calf. Around her knee and still higher. Gently, gently urging her legs apart. By Freya's heart, she liked the way the man touched her.

"Embra? Embra!"

Vanja's demanding voice cut through the fog of desire that possessed Embra's mind. Her siblings had all descended upon her to argue about the seafarers.

The trouble was, Embra could think of little but Magnus. His hands, ja, his lips. That powerful, supple body and the way they'd mated, without restraint.

Her siblings had argued away half the morning and continued now, while she calculated how soon Magnus might return.

She still felt the effects of their joining, her body sore in some places and wanting in others.

"She is not listening," Runi observed dryly. "Perhaps our sister has something else on her mind."

His gaze met Embra's. Did he know?

How could he possibly? Even if someone had seen Magnus leave—early as it had been, someone could have—they would not know what had taken place during their negotiations. Ja, there would have been guards at the harbor who had watched him row back to his ship. Even they would not guess she had done more than reason with her guest.

But Runi—Runi was spooky sometimes. He knew things.

Ovre said, "We must get Ulrik freed from the incomers. It is unthinkable he should remain in their hands."

"We shall get him back. My negotiations with the seafarer continue."

Dagmar spread her hands. "Why is that taking so long?"

"Ulrik is a valuable hostage. Magnus does not wish to surrender him without getting a fair return."

"Sostir, you should have murdered the man while you had him here. Runi says you and the seafarer remained in discussion all night."

They all stared at her, even as she bent a glare on Runi.

Spite flared in his eyes. "I think Embra concentrated on other things last night."

"Rutting?" Vanja fairly screeched. "You rutted with him?" She looked like a madwoman, hair in disarray and eyes wild. In fact, she'd never looked more like a madwoman.

Embra glared at Runi, even as her heart sank. "I did not say that."

"Nei," Vanja waved at Runi. "He did. It is not fair."

"I understand it may not seem—"

"If you can have one of the seafarers, I want one. The one with the black hair and the wicked eyes."

"Nei," Dagmar promptly faced off with her. "I

have my eye on that one."

They began bickering over it. Embra assumed they meant the man Magnus called Apsel. Ja, he was handsome. But naught to Magnus.

Ovre rolled his eyes, and Ulla looked troubled.

"Enough!" Embra roared at last. "Never mind all that. No one is to tumble the seafarers."

"Why not?"

"It is unwise. Dangerous." And Embra could scarcely wait to do it again. "It is best I continue negotiations."

"Tonight, I suppose," Runi posed.

"Whenever Magnus chooses to return."

"Not fair," Vanja muttered again.

Dagmar eyed her. "Tell you what, Sostir. Since I am in a generous mood, I will share the black-haired seafarer with you."

"In turns?"

"Or, ja, we might please him together."

Runi started to laugh. In an aside to Embra, he said, "This is what you must deal with, Sostir, if you want the place of jarl. Frankly, I do not know why you want it."

"Frankly, nor do I."

****

No sooncr had Embra's siblings cleared the hall than Embra got another taste of what she must deal with as jarl. A contingent of the settlement's elders descended in turn, voices raised and militant aggression in their eyes.

When Embra saw them coming, she snagged the arm of Runi, who prepared to follow their other siblings out. "You—stay."

He crooked a brow. "You speak to me like a hound?"

"I refuse to face that lot alone."

Embra knew all these men. Cohorts of her father, most of them aging warriors. One of them, called Asger, was a man of considerable means who'd made noises in the past year about trying for leadership of the settlement.

Embra and Runi had always put him off with the probability that Fadir and Gunnar would return. That would not work this time.

The elders marched into the hall, a band six strong of big impressive men, Asger and his likely backers.

"Master Runi," Asger began. "Mistress Embra. We must discuss this outrage."

"Outrage, ja," the others muttered, their eyes flashing. Trouble, indeed.

Embra stepped up to Asger. "You refer to Ulrik's capture."

"Of course we do. You must retaliate. The fact that you have not already done so proves you unworthy of this place you have assumed."

Another of the men spoke up. "To permit Friti Gunnarsson's boy to be held by an offlander, what is more the son of that truant berserker—"

These men would have known Tolljur Magnusson. Most would have sailed and fought with him at their head. A berserker—a true berserker—was a highly valuable battle weapon.

She'd heard it said they believed that Tolljur had betrayed them by leaving Husavik. Him and that slave wife of his. Growing up, she'd never thought much about it. But last summer, Fadir had gone to take his revenge.

Steadily she said, "I am negotiating for Ulrik's release."

"Negotiating." Asger spat. "You should send a band out there to burn his boat and kill the seafarers as they jump off into the water, like rats."

She looked him in the eye. "And by the time we attack the boat, Ulrik's throat will be cut. Is that what you want?"

"At least our honor will be intact!"

"What does a woman know of honor?"

"I say," declared another of the men, one of Fadir's old drinking companions, "we take this berserker's son captive in turn, next time he comes to negotiate. He walks through our settlement as if he owns it."

"Ja. See if his men will trade him for Ulrik."

"Magnus Tolljursson lies under my protection!" Embra reminded them. "I have given my oath on it."

Asger stepped up to her in turn. "And what oath may not be bent for good cause?"

There, Embra acknowledged, lay the philosophy at the heart of Husavik. But what else might she expect? Her grandsire, Gunnar, had been a criminal when he founded the settlement, an outcast from Norway who had lied and cheated his way to power. And Fadir—Fadir had raided, pillaged, and shared his women, quite likely with these very men. Even Modir, it was said—with Modir's enthusiastic approval.

"That promise will not be bent. The seafarer's safety is assured. I will get Ulrik back. Believe it."

"And what of revenge?" Asger's eyes gleamed with spite. "This last year you have been telling us your father would return from his voyage. Now we find he and Gunnar, who should have become our next jarl, who thought and acted as we approve, were murdered in the Faroes."

"Not murdered. They died in battle, a battle they began."

"Why," Asger glared at his fellows, "this bitch believes the stories the seafarer tells."

Anger licked through Embra. She strove not to reveal it.

"Any leader worth his or her salt would pay back those who killed their jarl, even if he was not her father."

"Revenge," others of the men cried, and repeated. "Revenge!"

Embra glanced at Runi who stood silent. Why did he not back her up? As Friti Gunnarsson's eldest surviving son, his words might carry some weight.

"Revenge," she said succinctly, "is beneath us."

Asger howled at her. "Husavik was built on revenge, or the desire for it. Ah, bah—what do you know?"

He turned to Runi. "Tell her, Runi Fritisson. Tell this sister of yours who would be jarl!"

Only then did Runi look at Embra, before he said, "Revenge is good, ja, as is deceit in its place. The seafarers expect such from us. Do you forget, this man's father knew mine—and my grandfather? If we mount an attack, he will sail out of the bay with Ulrik aboard. We will either lose him to a long capture in a foreign land, or they will slit his throat and toss him over the side."

"That is why we must capture this Magnus berserker's son the next time he sets foot ashore."

"He wants something," Asger glared at Embra. "Over what do you negotiate with him? Gold? Silver?"

Embra shook her head. "I cannot say. I must continue to bargain."

"Why, you are as poor at that as everything else. Runi, you should accept the place of jarl. Either you, or one of us!"

Everyone looked to Runi.

Many a time had Embra heard him say he did not want the place of jarl, especially since Gunnar's failure to return from the Faroes. True, Fadir had trained Gunnar to step up after him, and they were spun from the same wool.

Runi—Runi was different.

But now he stared into the faces of his father's cohorts and said slowly, "I will consider it."

That seemed to satisfy them, at least for the time being. Still grumbling and with many a glare for Embra, they filed out of the hall.

Embra looked at her brother. "You will consider it?"

He met her stare. "What did you expect me to say?"

"Perhaps that you back me. You could have thrown your support behind my claim. It would have meant much."

"Would it? If they want another Fadir—or another Gunnar, for that matter—they must look to Ulrik. He has the fierce spirit."

"The foolish heedlessness."

"Call it what you will, Embra."

"Do you want the place of jarl?"

"Nei. But saying I will consider gives you some

time, ja? To finish your *negotiations*."

As for that, Embra was not at all sure she could finish them, or that she dared allow Magnus Tolljursson to come ashore again.

Chapter Nineteen

"Someone is coming. In a *skupa*. One man on his own." Apsel made the call while shading his eyes with his hand. Last night's rain had all cleared, making way for the sort of day Magnus liked best. Far-reaching, fresh-washed skies and seas that danced with a light breeze.

Far out here in the bay, the light sparkled on the water all around them, making shards of brightness that dazzled the eyes.

He stepped up next to Apsel as the others gathered behind him.

One man, ja, rowing hard—a challenging pull out into these choppy waters at the edge of the wide sea.

"It is that wee man," someone said, "the one that belongs to Mistress Embra. Her slave."

So it was. The Erin man came with his back to them, peering over his shoulder.

"Toss him a line," he urged when the *skupa* drew near enough.

But Kennach—ja, that was the fellow's name—refused to come aboard. Instead he gazed up into the dragon boat and called, "Master Magnus?"

"I am here."

Kennach peered at him. His plain face gave away little beyond mild anxiety. Magnus wondered at what went on behind his eyes.

"My mistress sends you a message."

"What is it?"

"Do not come to Husavik this evening. Negotiations are halted for the time being."

The men behind Magnus swore. They were bored with hanging out here in the bay and wanted to go home. This did not prove the grand adventure they'd anticipated.

Magnus strove to master his own disappointment. He'd been living for evening, dying for the taste of Embra. Eager to touch her and discover just how many ways they might pleasure one another.

"Why is that?" he called.

"Eh?" the fellow hollered back.

"Why have negotiations been halted and how long before they resume?" Before he could touch her, inhale her scent.

"I am sorry, Master, I do not know. She sent me only with a message: Do not come."

Magnus growled. Someone behind him snickered.

"What are we to do with her brother?" Apsel called. "Does she not want him back?"

"We are sick of him!" Knut added. "And may put him over the side tonight."

Kennach looked startled. "Och, do not do that."

"Come on board," Apsel invited the man.

"Nay, thank ye, sir."

"Abandon your little boat and come along with us. We told you, you need be a slave no longer," Apsel persuaded.

"Och, master, I could not do that. Whatever would Mistress Embra do without me?"

"Why do you care?" Knut bellowed. "You can

return to Sorvagur with us. We keep no slaves there."

"Nay, sir." Quickly, Kennach fumbled his oars. "That is my message. I must return."

They all watched him turn his boat about and row off slowly.

Magnus slanted a look at Apsel. "Why did you do that?"

"What?"

"Try again to persuade him to run away with us."

"If the lady jarl values him, he would make a good hostage." Apsel turned and aimed a kick at Ulrik who, still naked and bound, listened to all. "Clearly she does not value the one we've already got."

"Ach, and I thought you acted from a desire to spite the lady jarl."

"Perhaps some."

"You have been here too long," Magnus observed, "and begin to take on the ways of Husavik."

"We have all been here too long," one of the others protested. "Magnus, this is not viking. Where are the women? The riches? Where is the gold?"

"Ja, where?" Jorg aimed a resentful glare at the shore. "You know they have it all."

****

"What did he say?" Embra demanded when Kennach returned and put his head through the doorway of her dwelling.

The man stepped in. "He asked why he should not come."

He should. He should be with her, touching her. Kissing her. Spending his passion on her like some sort of magical blessing.

She'd never believed much in suing the gods for

favors. She knew folk who did. They held rituals and made sacrifices. They branded and tattooed themselves to honor their deities.

She also knew such acts were often mere lip service. Men sued the gods' favor before a voyage, before a battle. She'd seen her father and brother do so. But there'd been nothing behind it, save empty custom.

She herself prayed to Freya, when she did pray. Usually the vow or oath just came from her without thought. But she'd spoken to Freya, sending imprecations the whole time Kennach was gone. *Bring him to me. I want him. I need him.* How send a man a message he should keep away, and then expect him to defy it?

"How did he look?" she asked Kennach in defiance of her better judgement.

"Master Ulrik, Mistress? I did not see him."

"Nei, Master Magnus." Kennach, despite his carefully bland expression, was not stupid. Embra did not doubt he knew exactly what had taken place between her and Magnus last night. "Did he look…disappointed?"

A flash of something did appear then in Kennach's eyes. Sympathy? He said only, "Mistress, I could not tell."

"To be sure." Ach, what was she to do with these feelings? She craved the man. not just the taste of him, or his touch, but his slow smile and the light in his eyes.

"I am sorry," Kennach whispered.

"Naught to you of blame," she returned. "Thank you for your long row out and back again."

"Mistress, if I might ask—"

"You know you may."

"How will this end?"

"Kennach, the gods alone know."

"Mistress, you will be careful?"

She did see emotions in his mild gray eyes, then. Fear? Ah, and he probably worried what would happen to him, should something happen to her. Few men acted from aught but self-interest. He led a protected life, so long as Embra did not fall from grace.

She touched his arm. "Do not worry yourself over it. I am a sensible woman, am I not?" Yet all sense flew from her head when Magnus touched her. *By Freya's heart, she had to see him.*

Kennach nodded. "I am thinking only if you anger the wrong people, Mistress, they may well take it out on him."

Embra should have heeded those words, she truly should. But in Husavik it was very hard to keep from angering the wrong people.

****

Her sisters, all three of them, descended upon her the next morning, crowding her quarters. Embra, not having slept well, found herself in a less than forbearing state of mind. Certainly she had not the patience required to deal with Vanja, Dagmar, and Ulla before breakfast.

"What do you want?" Still braiding her hair, she tossed the words at them.

Dagmar spoke up. "I heard you have halted further negotiations with the seafarer."

"I have."

"What about Ulrik? You cannot leave him in their hands. You are supposed to be making a deal to get him back."

"Ulrik chose his path."

"You have never favored him," Vanja accused. Once more this morning, she looked like she'd just crawled from someone's bed after a hard tumble, hair in disarray and eyes wild. Whose bed?

"It is not my place to favor him."

"Nor is it your place to abandon him to the same men who killed our father and brother. Their ship, hanging out there in the bay like a hawk waiting to pounce, is an insult."

So it was, in a way.

"Why did you refuse to meet with the berserker's son?"

"I did not think it safe for him to come to Husavik. If someone attacks him here, all hope of getting Ulrik back dies." Only half a lie.

Her sisters exchanged glances.

"What?" Embra demanded.

"There are rumblings from some of Fadir's companions that the place of jarl should be secured. Folk grow dissatisfied with you."

Embra flushed. "Where did you hear this?"

"Never mind where." Vanja smirked. "One man in particular prepares to step up."

"Whom?"

"Asger."

Ja, the man, who had been on many voyages with Fadir in days gone by, had made his disapproval known when he visited her yesterday.

Would the settlement as a whole support Asger? Did he have a claim? Could he depose her?

If Runi and Ulrik both backed her—but nei. Once Ulrik was freed, he would make a claim of his own. As for Runi, would he stir himself to back anyone?

She eyed Vanja. "How do you know this?"

Dagmar smiled again. "How do you suppose? She slept with him last night."

"With Asger?" Embra could not help but stare. "But he is—"

"Older men," Vanja told her smugly, "have the most experience. And, Sostir, a man will say near anything while teetering on the knife's edge of pleasure. There is a great deal of power there."

Power.

"You should try it some time."

Try it. What she'd shared with Magnus—well, it had been *shared*. And it had less to do with power than connection.

She could feel that connection, still.

She glanced at Ulla who, at thirteen, should not be hearing all this.

"I am certain you are mistaken. Our house still stands strong. A man like Asger would not dare try to depose us."

"A man like Asger would, with Fadir gone," Dagmar snarled at her.

"He merely awaits the right moment," Vanja said. "And Sostir, you would do well to remember there are more ways than one to legitimize a man's claim."

Chapter Twenty

"I think he is dead." Apsel kicked at Ulrik's foot, which sprawled, as naked as the rest of him, on the deck. The men had removed Ulrik's gag and untied one of his hands so he could eat, and growing weary of his ensuing complains had plied him with mead in an effort to shut him up.

He was quiet now, most certainly.

Magnus peered at his prisoner. "How much did you give him to drink?"

"Enough. First, he wanted something besides water to wash down his bread. Said he might die from drinking water." Apsel blinked. "I did not think you would want him dead before you made your deal."

"This is so. But he appears to have died anyway."

Apsel scowled. "Perhaps he is merely passed out. You see, he complained about the quality of the mead."

That took some cheek, though the mead they drank in Husavik did rival that made by Magnus's mother and the other women back home.

"So to make him stop complaining, Knut held him down while I poured a flask of mead down his throat."

Waste of the drink, in Magnus's estimation. They might need that before they got home.

"It was Apsel's idea," Knut declared. "I told him it would just make the lout piss himself more. He already stinks."

Apsel narrowed his eyes at Knut. "I thought that was you."

Knut gave him a shove.

"Listen to me." Magnus nudged Ulrik again. "He is no good to us dead."

"He is little good to us now, since you are not even bargaining over him. What is the hold up? Let us make the exchange for Lodvar's mother and go home."

"I am working on it."

"You are not. You are standing here on this boat, staring at what may or may not be a dead man."

Was Ulrik dead? Magnus stared hard and determined the man was breathing very low. "Do not give him any more mead," he instructed, "at least for the time being."

Knut stepped up to Magnus. "When are we leaving this place, Magnus?"

"You wanted an adventure."

"Sitting here in the bay is no adventure. We have stolen nothing, and all the women are on shore."

"Patience, Knut. Let us play a game of bones."

"I am tired of bones. I am tired of this. I say let us drop him over the side and go home."

"I made a promise. I cannot leave without Lodvar's mother."

Or, indeed, without seeing Embra again.

****

Embra walked the settlement, and everywhere she went folk seemed to stare and whisper. It made her wonder what they knew and what they suspected. If word was out that she'd spent the night with Magnus, it would be on everybody's tongue. Not that morals were so high here in Husavik, but it would call her loyalties

147

into question, and along with that, her fitness for her position.

She hung onto the place of jarl by only her fingernails.

But perhaps talk was all about her failure to get her brother back—not much better, truly.

With Asger on the prowl, waiting for a chance to seize power, she needed Runi to show his support for her. But no matter where she went about the settlement, she could not find Runi.

By afternoon she felt desperate, her emotions frayed. She climbed higher and higher away from the harbor, searching, and always the longboat hanging in the bay made her turn her eyes out to sea. With each glance, her longing grew.

What was the matter with her? Magnus Tolljursson was just a man, was he not? And while she might take pleasure in looking at a well-made man, admiring the strength of his back, the muscles bulging in his arms, the confidence in the way he moved, there were men enough in Husavik at whom she might gawk if she chose. Magnus was not so special.

Only he was.

More than just a man, to her he represented delight, humor, and a curious sense of ease. Belonging. When she'd been in his arms, she'd wanted nothing more, and that made her feel helpless now. Because she still wanted nothing more than to be with him.

Ah, by Freya's heart, she had fallen into a trap, one as old as time itself. She needed to get free of him, break the spell he had woven with his hands and his lips that night. Make the deal to get Ulrik free, and send Magnus Tolljursson on his way.

It would make a show of strength, proving to Asger and the others that she could hold this place that had been thrust upon her, and keep matters in line. If that meant she had to watch Magnus sail out of the harbor, knowing she would never see him again, so be it.

Runi materialized quietly, approaching her with his step light on the stone, and she stared. He wore his light-colored hair tied back, and his pale eyes were narrowed against the afternoon light.

Embra started. "Brodir? From where did you come?"

He gestured vaguely to the wild country behind him. "You are not the only one, Sostir, who needs a tumble."

Embra widened her eyes and took another glance behind him. She had reached the edge of the settlement, and she saw only rocks and undulating green. "There is nothing—no one—out there."

"Is there not?"

"And—" So, Runi thought he knew what she and Magnus had got up to, did he? "What makes you suppose I've had a tumble?"

"Do you think me stupid? The seafarer comes to negotiate in the evening and does it with you—alone— in your private quarters. He does not leave till dawn. And you look—" He flicked a glance at her.

Embra swore under her breath. "Is it all over Husavik?"

"No doubt. I have not been all over Husavik."

Then where had he been?

As if in answer to her unspoken question, he held out his arm. "I went to think. And get a new tattoo."

Indeed, the flesh inside his forearm showed newly

pricked and raw. The outline of a serpent showed there, twining and sibilant.

"That looks sore."

He shrugged.

"You had better hope you do not take poisoning from it."

"I never have before."

"Good. Because this is no time for you to sicken and die. I need your help."

"You want to keep me alive because you need my help?"

"Is it not a good enough reason? Asger has me worried. I think once you announce to him you do not want the place of jarl, he will attempt to seize control."

Runi shrugged once more. "Asger is of the generation that believes women good for but one thing. He may never take you seriously."

"I know that. But your backing will help. Runi, I need you to stand and speak up for me to men like Asger."

"While you indulge in further negotiations with the seafarer?"

"Nei. I mean to make the trade for Ulrik and see Magnus Tolljursson on his way."

"Then you will have one more problem—Ulrik—on your hands."

"I need the old guard to see that I can forge an agreement, and I need them to see that you back me. Runi, do you?"

He appeared to contemplate it, his gaze, like hers, on the bay. When he spoke, it seemed to be off topic. "Did you know, Sostir, that the land holds magic? There are others besides us dwelling here. Some older than time itself."

Why, Embra thought, he is as mad as Modir. She glanced at the raw tattoo on his arm. "Magic?"

"Ach, ja."

"Is that where you were? With some magical beings?" she half scoffed.

He flicked her another look. "Ach, Sostir, you think you know so much, but you understand so little."

"Oh?"

"Look out there at the bay. What do you see?"

"Water. Boats." Perhaps her heart.

"But what is beneath the surface? What lies beneath this green turf and rock upon which we stand?" He leaned his head toward her. "Fire, that is what. The flowing blood of the world."

"Ja, so." Hot springs abounded here. And all her life she'd known about the spirits of the ancients, that might explode. It did not happen often, only when—

"The gods of the land are angry," Runi said. "They do not like the discord here in Husavik. You remember what used to happen when Fadir grew angry?"

Embra shuddered. She still had a few scars, as did they all. "Ja."

"It is the same with the land, here. You must have your pleasure, conclude your dealings with the seafarer, and send him on his way."

"I have just said I intend to. But, Runi, can I count on you to stand with me?"

"Of course not, Sostir. I stand alone. This you know."

Impatience washed over Embra. Bad enough coping with Vanja and Dagmar, with Ulrik and Orve. Must Runi also prove difficult?

She sighed. "Look, I just need for the men of the settlement to see that you approve of me. You are the eldest surviving son of Friti Gunnarsson. It will make a difference."

"Will it?"

"Ja. I care little what you do, in truth. You may speak to what gods and obtain what tattoos you like."

"Just so you know, I will go where I choose—where the wind leads me. Or, where the fire drives me."

"Understood. Are we agreed upon it?"

The ground rumbled beneath their feet. Runi began to laugh.

As near as she would get, or so Embra guessed, to an agreement.

Chapter Twenty-One

"The gods are angry!" Asger shouted the words in an accusatory tone. He pointed a finger at Embra. "They do not like her being in charge."

Murmurs greeted his words. Embra could not tell if they were all sounds of agreement. Just before nightfall, nearly all the settlement had descended upon the great hall. She, with Runi at her side, had met them outside the door.

Asger appeared to be in an ugly mood, and he had a crowd of other aged warriors at his back. He would, ja, use anything to discredit Embra, even the rumblings of the land.

She shouted back, "We all know this happens from time to time. The spirits will settle down. We are in no danger."

"We need the seafarers gone from our bay." Now he pointed out to sea. "That boat is bad luck. It brought ill news of our jarl, and darkness hangs around it in a cloud. Embra Fritisdottir, if you will not deal with those interlopers, I will."

Ach, Embra thought, here he makes his play. With tempers strained and fears high, he thinks he can seize control.

"You shall not, Asger. Friti Gunnarsson's house still stands. Has he not left three sons and four daughters?"

"His sons are not the ones seeking the place of jarl."

Embra glanced at Runi, wishing he would speak up. "The children of Friti Gunnarsson stand united."

"I do not think so. One of them remains captive on that longboat. Not all of them are happy with your seizure of power." He sneered. "You, a woman."

Embra tossed her head. "I will send for the seafarer and conclude our dealing tonight. But I need the word of everyone here that he shall meet no harm when coming or going. Should he be captured or slain, we lose all hope of regaining Ulrik."

She glared around at the crowd, now gone silent. "Do you agree?"

She heard a few mutters of agreement. No one disagreed.

Asger railed at her, "Have your negotiations, Mistress. But calm the spirits of the land, or step aside for someone who can."

The crowd began filing away.

Embra turned to Runi. "Why did you not speak up for me?"

He shrugged.

"I need you to go and fetch Magnus Tolljursson. Take a number of guards with you, if you must. But make sure he arrives safely at my quarters."

"Your quarters? And would not your negotiations go better here at the hall?"

Perhaps they would. Perhaps it would better allow her to resist the temptation Magnus represented.

"Too many eyes and ears."

Runi quirked a brow. "Do you mean to tumble him? Again?"

"Nei, I do not."

"Then what matter how many eyes or ears?"

"It is a mere matter of preference."

Runi smiled. "Mayhap you would like me to sit in on these negotiations with you."

"That will not be necessary."

"I merely thought since you require my backing, and all—"

"So I do." Outwardly.

"Sostir, you have got yourself in quite the tangle."

So she had.

"Very well." She tossed her head. "I will meet with Magnus Tolljursson, get Ulrik back, and send the seafarers away. You may sit in, if you like."

"Ah, Sostir, would I be so cruel?"

****

"Someone coming," called Rojd, who was on watch, and Magnus's heart leaped painfully in his chest. Swiftly, he walked forward to the prow. "Is it Mistress Embra's man again?"

"Nei—a *skupa* with several men."

Evening was just falling—the dark as complete as it ever became at this time of year. Radiance hung to the north in a steady afterglow, and not a breath stirred the water. So quiet was it as the *skupa* neared, Magnus could easily hear the creaking of the oars.

He counted heads. Two men rowing and a third at the front of the boat.

"Who is that?" he asked Apsel who, along with the others, had come forward to look.

"It appears to be—ja, Runi Fritisson."

Ach, and so it was, as Magnus saw once the *skupa* came alongside and the man got to his feet.

"Magnus Tolljursson, may I come aboard and see my brother?"

Magnus thought swiftly. "Ja. But you may not take him." He drew his dagger, and his men did likewise.

Runi nodded and sprang aboard easily. Magnus measured him with caution.

A tall man was Runi Fritisson, taller even than Magnus, who overtopped his own father, and of a lithe, narrow build. He wore his fair hair braided, and his pale eyes revealed little about the thoughts in his mind.

Ulrik, who had sobered and acquired a sour mood along with it, called out as soon as he saw Runi. "Brodir! Brodir, get me away out of this."

With a flick of a glance for Magnus, Runi shouldered the men aside and crouched down beside Ulrik. For several moments he eyed his brother thoughtfully.

Desperate, Ulrik ordered, "Well? Untie me! You have come to rescue me, have you not?"

"Rescue you? You are the great warrior, following in Fadir's footsteps. What need have you of rescue?"

Ulrik swore bitterly. "You see how they treat me, the son of a jarl!"

"Son of a dead jarl now. Embra fights for the place."

"Curse Embra. Do a deal and get me out of here. Or tell our bitch of a sister to do so."

"Ach," Runi tipped his head, "there is Fadir I hear speaking from your lips, ja. Embra says you never should have attacked our guests, given she had assured their safety, and that you have got what you earned. I do not know if she will bargain for you."

"Then by Tyr's balls, stick a knife in her back and

take over the negotiations!"

Runi put on a sorrowful look and straightened back up to his full height. "You bid me murder our sister?"

"Not murder. Remove. She is in the way, is she not?"

Runi made a curious gesture with his hands. "And then, if I did as you asked and freed you, would I not be in your way, little Brodir?"

"Nei. Not like that."

"I think I'd best leave you where you are." Swiftly, Runi turned to Magnus. "My sister sends me to escort you in for negotiation. Once again."

Magnus's heart leaped painfully.

"Will you, Magnus Tolljursson, accompany me?"

"Ja. Shall I bring one of my men?"

"No need. I will myself assure your safety."

Apsel clapped Magnus on the shoulder. "Come back with a deal so we may rid ourselves of that sack of shit."

As he climbed into the *skupa*, Magnus thought he heard Runi laugh.

****

Embra paced like a woman demented. If she kept this up, she would wear a path right into the floor of her quarters.

This was not like her. The steady one she'd always been among her siblings. The sane one. Not prey to her emotions like Vanja, or to spite like Gunnar.

But, ja, she'd fallen prey to her emotions now, so she could barely think straight. Waiting for Runi and Magnus Tolljursson to arrive, her control slipped steadily from her grasp. Her hands shook and her heart pounded in her ears.

She must—must—keep her eyes on her goal. Make the deal for Ulrik's release and send the seafarer back to Sorvagur where he belonged. End all this madness.

Send him away.

Truly, it was her only option. Yet it felt like a dagger to her heart.

She heard a noise at the door and whirled, nerves tightening impossibly. It was only Kennach, putting his head inside.

"Mistress, do you have all you need for your negotiations?"

"Ja, Kennach. Go to bed."

His mild gray eyes regarded her with doubt. "Are you certain?"

"Go."

Ach, she was going to perish before Magnus arrived.

Could she trust Runi to bring him safely? One never knew about Runi. He was like the wind above a maelstrom, blowing one way and then the other. She had no one else to trust. But if he allowed any harm to come to Magnus before they arrived, she would gut him herself.

A short span of time—one night—for negotiating. That was all they would have together. Time for her to look at Magnus, watch the smile flicker in his eyes, see how he used his hands.

Not enough.

"Sostir?"

They came.

She whirled with her hair flying around her. Runi entered the chamber with Magnus just behind him, and guards at their backs.

Her gaze met Magnus's, and a fierce wave of joy arose inside her, so powerful it seemed to ignite her where she stood.

"Welcome," she told him, and it meant so much more. *Be with me. Take what you will of me. You are welcome to my body. My heart.*

Magnus nodded. "Mistress."

Those lips of his had been all over her body. Just watching them part to utter one single word set her to tingling.

Runi glanced from one to the other of them. "Embra, did you say you wish for me to sit in?"

She strove for a negligent tone and failed miserably. "That will not be necessary."

"Very well. As we discussed, I will station the guards outside. They will not leave until your— business—is ended."

"*Tak.*"

Very quietly, Runi went out. Embra heard him speaking to the men. She could only hope those he'd chosen were trustworthy.

She nodded at the shield and axe Magnus once more carried. "Keep your weapons close. I would not be surprised if we come under attack."

He lifted a brow.

She explained, "There are factions who do not believe me fit for the place of jarl, men who would move to seize power. It is why we must conclude our negotiations as quickly as possible."

"I see."

Did he appear disappointed? Had he thought he came here so she might bed him again? If so, he gave little sign. Instead, he stepped to the hearth and laid his weapons there.

"I will confess, my men will be happy to rid themselves of Ulrik. They will be happy also to sail for home."

"And you, Master Magnus? Will you be happy to sail?"

He gave her a long, steady look. It started at the crown of her head and moved downward, and she swore she could feel it like the touch of his hand.

"I will be honest with you, Mistress Embra." He cocked his head. "I assume our vow of honesty still stands?"

"It does."

"I am no longer certain how I feel."

Breath gusted in Embra's lungs. "Nor I."

"This is a treacherous place, one filled with pitfalls and dangers. Naught is what it seems." Again he crooked a brow at her. "Even the ground shakes beneath my feet. On the way in, I overheard one of the guards say the gods here are angry. I scarce imagine how you endure it."

"I am as devious as the rest of them." Against her better judgment, she stepped up to him. "Except when I am with you. I am honest when I am with you."

"A quite remarkable thing. As my modir would say, there must be some magic in it." Almost delicately, he raised a finger and touched her cheek. He barely brushed her skin, yet the intensity of the sensation had her closing her eyes.

In bliss.

She whispered, "I am not certain I believe in magic."

"You must. It is everywhere. In the light on the

water. In the flight of a bird. In *this*."

He brushed his lips across hers and she felt every vestige of her hard-won willpower drain away. Just like that, she stood helpless as if he'd stripped her naked. Trembling.

She knew then he would not leave this place without making love to her again. But first, but first—

She hauled on the tattered shreds of her control and whispered, "We are in grave danger. You are. Those who would depose me take the restlessness of the land as a sign that the gods disapprove of my tenure as jarl. We must conclude our dealing. You must return Ulrik to me."

"And then?"

"And then we will see one another never more."

Chapter Twenty-Two

The woman spoke sense. Whatever else Embra Fritisdottir might be—charmer like her brother Gunnar, deceiver like her accursed father—Magnus did believe she offered him the truth now. That might well make him a fool. But when she looked him in the eyes, he believed she wished him no harm.

They must, ja, conclude their dealing, and have it done. That meant he should not, as every particle of him wished, plunge his fingers into the wealth of her hair. Haul her up against him and kiss her as if only the two of them existed in all the world.

They did not, and he had no call to spend himself on Friti Gunnarsson's daughter. No matter what he saw in her eyes.

They would conclude their bargaining tonight. He could have Mistress Catrin in his hands as soon as tomorrow, and sail away.

Thus he stepped away from Embra, though it took every bit of his strength. He sat down beside his shield. She sank to her knees also, as if her legs lacked the strength to keep her upright.

"So we are agreed, Mistress Embra? I will bring your brother to the harbor at first light. You will have Mistress Catrin waiting to depart with us."

"If she wishes to go. She is no longer a slave, after all, but a free woman."

"One whom someone may prevent from leaving."

"Nei." She shook her head.

"If not prevented, then why would she not wish to leave?"

Embra shrugged. "Believe what you will, she has lived here a long time. This is her home."

"She will want to go to her son, so you will bring her to me. I feel it safest the exchange be made at the harbor. Send a *skupa* with Mistress Catrin in it. I will put your brother ashore."

Embra gave him a long stare. "I have your word, you will send Ulrik back?"

"Ja. We speak only truth with one another, do we not? Besides," Magnus gave her a tight smile, "my men want rid of him."

She drew a breath. "Very well."

He quirked a brow at her. "That was easily done. It seems there is naught else for me to do but leave." Disappointing. Once he walked out of here under guard, he would not see her again save from a distance. Never touch her nor experience the intense rush of feelings that accompanied that touch.

But leaving was the sensible thing to do. And surely he was every bit as sensible as she.

"Wait. Do not go yet." She jerked her head at the door. "We cannot make it seem we have failed to hash the matter over until each of us has the better bargain."

"Each of us having the best, is it?"

"Ja. Have a cup of mead."

Ah, her excellent mead, connected somehow in his mind with the still-more-heady taste of her. Did he dare?

When he hesitated, she added, "To seal the

bargain."

She filled the cups and handed one to him. Suddenly he had a vision—a wedding out in the open on the cliffs above the sea, back home. Embra dressed in finery, her hair well-plaited. A cup of mead, shared. Truth shining in her eyes, just for him.

He had seen many a wedding. Never his own. If he imagining wedding anyone, it would be Astrid.

Not this woman.

His sister, Gyda, was the one who experienced visions. He might well believe in the gods' magic, but he remained a practical man.

Except, perhaps, when he gazed into Embra's eyes.

She leaned forward, close to him. "Magnus Tolljursson, I have enjoyed knowing you."

"And I, you."

"I value our vow of truth. Perhaps if we drink now, we may make another such vow—to see one another again sometime in the future."

Was such a thing possible? Sorvagur was not so far away, and he could well plow the seas. But this was a place of treachery to which he might well prefer never to return.

Except—she was here.

Slowly and regretfully, he shook his head. "I have a life to live. So do you. You will wed—"

"Me? Wed with any man here?" Scorn filled her eyes. "I want none of them."

"But surely—"

She leaned still closer. So close her lips nearly brushed his. "I want none of them."

Ah.

"Magnus Tolljursson, I will be honest with you, as

I must. I did not call you here merely to bargain. I called you here because I want you one last time before you sail away. I am not certain I can live without it."

His pulse leaped. Not wise. The guards stood just outside the door, and would surely hear anything that passed between them, beyond conversation.

"Unwise." He said it in a whisper. "It will only make me want you more."

"You think so?"

"I know it." Already the ties that had formed between them last time they were together pulled at him. Best to pick up his weapons, to walk away.

Yet he had only to reach a hand to touch her hair, her cheek, her breast. Had he the strength to resist?

"Kiss me," she begged.

He shouldn't. He dare not. *He must.*

Their lips met and the floor trembled beneath Magnus's feet. His world exploded.

****

There was fire, a roaring wall of it, and sweetness, and the smooth slide of skin on naked skin. The softness of Embra's breast at Magnus's lips. Not a soft woman, or an easy one, she nevertheless relented when she came to him. They melded in the heat and became one. Stronger together. Magically invincible.

"Shh," she whispered against his lips, a breath that addled his senses. "We must remain silent." Then those same lips traveled over him, making him want to shout. Her mouth wooed him, stole from him, gave back in equal measure.

More than just pleasure, it became a holy exchange. The fire beside them burned down and the light failed.

The ground moved.

Ja, Magnus had heard that said before, when men spoke of mating with a woman, but this time it truly happened. Flat on his back on the rug, beneath Embra's hands and mouth, he distinctly felt the earth shift under him and decided the gods truly did try to make their wishes known. Did they approve of what he and Embra did? Or otherwise?

He heard voices exclaim outside in the dark and considered arising, going out to see what terrible thing had happened. The world might well be ending. But then Embra slid her lips once more down his body, and the quivering of the earth became no more than a part of his mind-numbing pleasure.

"There now, Magnus Tolljursson, I am part of you, and you part of me." She glided up his body and gazed into his eyes. Twining her fingers through his hair, she kissed him.

And he felt it, he felt the bonds curl deep inside him like the roots of the tree of the world. Not just pleasure, this, though the fever possessed his blood. As he'd been inside her, she now dwelt inside him.

"You may sail away from me," she half-sobbed, "but you will remain. Always mine."

"Always mine," he echoed.

"Ja. From this moment, whatever happens, I am yours." Tears fell from her eyes. This woman who he imagined wept but rarely. She wept for him.

She lived and breathed for him.

How he knew that, he could not say. Yet the truth of it shone from her eyes.

"Mine."

"Magnus—Magnus, I know you must sail, but vow

you will return for me."

"Embra—"

"If you make the promise, I will believe it. Until you return, you will live here, in my heart."

"Embra, nei. You can sail with me. Come away with me now."

He got no farther. Voices once more rose outside and someone called, "Mistress Embra!"

They dressed hastily and went outside, Magnus careful to take his weapons with him. There, the guards and what looked like half the settlement stood out in the open watching the sky.

And nei, he had not imagined it while in the throes of passion. The earth not only trembled as from the footsteps of trolls deep beneath the surface, but orange light filled the sky.

"Mistress Embra!" The guard who had called to her spoke as soon as she stepped outside. "The gods unleash their anger upon us!"

Embra stared, her pale eyes wide and reflecting that distant orange light. "Perhaps."

"What must we do?" The man eyed Magnus without liking. "The gods do not like this bargain you make. A sacrifice, perhaps?"

"Ja!" Other voices joined in and folk moved in closer, hemming Embra and Magnus together.

"Nei," Embra shouted. "The powers stirred before our bargain was made."

"But only since the seafarers came!" one man declared.

Embra turned on him. "That is not so. For years we have felt this, from time to time."

"Times of chaos and darkness! The gods are

displeased. We must mollify them by killing the intruders."

Magnus shifted his axe in his hand. Surrounded, he might not fight his way free, but he could do much damage before he went down.

Embra called out, "Our bargain is concluded. The seafarers will leave come morning. Ulrik will be returned. If you wish to displease the gods, act in defiance of the promise I have given."

A tall figure stepped up beside Magnus. "Come," Runi said smoothly. "I will escort you back to the harbor."

"Ja." Embra turned to her brother in relief. "Do that."

Yet her gaze clung to Magnus as he turned from her, and he felt her emotions pull at him.

Would he ever see her again?

The ground rumbled beneath his feet as Runi led him away, a number of guards falling in behind. Folk parted reluctantly before Runi, though Magnus could feel the ill will on every side. Embra did not follow, and he could hear her voice addressing her folk.

The *skupa* awaited them in the harbor. Suddenly Magnus could not wait to shake the soil of this place from his feet, to conclude his task, pull up anchor and sail away.

Yet when he did, he feared he would leave a vital part of him behind, in Embra's keeping.

Chapter Twenty-Three

"Mistress Embra, the woman is nowhere to be found."

"What?" Embra whirled and faced Kennach, all her raw senses leaping. He looked distraught, which was nothing to how she felt.

She'd sent him at first light to bring Mistress Catrin, that she might put the opportunity to leave before the woman. The events of last night, everything from her moving experience at Magnus's hands to the near-uprising, argued for urgency. Even if they did carry a tinge of unreality.

Nei, being in Magnus's arms was real, and the promise she'd sought from him. Before that, everything else faded.

Now her heart fell, and she narrowed her eyes at her servant. "You must be mistaken."

"Nay, Mistress." Kennach spread his hands. "She is not there."

"Impossible. Where would she go? You have merely sought her at the wrong house."

"I asked the neighbors. She was there yesterday. Her dwelling is now empty. No one saw her go."

Embra swore bitterly. "Were there any signs that harm has come to her? Disorder in the house, or—or blood?"

"Nothing."

Embra's mind raced. She was set to complete the exchange for Ulrik this morning. Already, light wound its way through the settlement. The ground had quieted, as if the gods were satisfied with their agreement. A calm morning, now suddenly gone awry.

By Freya's heart, she should have sent for Catrin last night, made sure of her bargain. But she'd been profoundly shaken last night. Watching Magnus walk away had been like receiving a livid wound.

She would see him again this morning at the harbor. But not if she had no former slave woman for the exchange.

Frustration warred with a thrill of gladness inside her.

She told her man, "Go find Master Runi. Bring him to me if you can."

"Aye, Mistress."

Kennach hurried off, and Embra surveyed her quarters. She'd taken time to straighten up following their lovemaking, after Magnus's departure last night. It no longer looked like the scene of desperate longing and passion as it had. The memory of it all, though, circled through her, not so easy to banish.

She pictured Magnus lying on the rug beneath her hands, his hazel eyes filled with light. She felt the way his muscles quivered under her fingers when she touched him. A powerful man, one who possessed humor and intelligence. A beautiful man who—

"When do we leave for the harbor?" Vanja spoke from the doorway, banishing thoughts far better gone. Embra's ragged nerves leaped, and she turned with a groan. Just what she did not need, her troublesome sister. Nei, as she soon saw. Both of them.

"Soon."

Dagmar pushed past Vanja and stepped in. "The earth has quieted. The gods must be happy with the bargain you have made. As am I. It is high time we freed our brother from the hands of those savages."

"I am not happy." Once again, Vanja looked like she'd just come from someone's bed, clothing in disorder and golden hair in a tangle.

"You are never happy," Embra said dismissively.

"Ah, you never cared. Why, if it hadn't been for Fadir comforting me—"

"Comforting? Is that what you call it?" Embra faced her sister.

Vanja pouted. "I do. I could go to him when I might go to no one else." Her blue eyes gleamed. "He taught me things. How to make a man do whatever you want."

Sickness rose into the back of Embra's throat. She choked it down. "You will end up like Modir if you are not careful."

"I will not. I am much too clever."

Dagmar interrupted impatiently. "Let us go to the harbor. I am tired of waiting."

"Let us stay until Runi comes."

It took a while. Folk had begun drifting up, and some even made their way toward the harbor before Runi arrived.

Embra gave him a searching look. "Where have you been?"

He shrugged. She snagged his arm and dragged him away from her sisters. "There is a problem."

"There usually is."

"The woman, Catrin, has gone."

"So?"

"So I bargained to exchange her for Ulrik."

"Ach." Runi's teeth showed in a brief smile. "So, Lodvar Haraldsson will get what he wants."

"Nei, he will not. Are you not listening? Do you know where Catrin is?"

"How should I know?"

"That is not an answer. Runi, answer me."

"Have you asked Vanja? Or Dagmar?"

"I am asking you."

"Has it occurred to you it might be better if we do not get Ulrik back, if Magnus drops him over the side or somehow otherwise murders him?"

"Of course I have considered it. But it would not be better. It would break this family, such as it is, apart."

"With Fadir gone, and Gunnar, a new center of power must be found. Curious, how Fadir managed to keep control even when he was dead for a year. You wish to be the next center of power—"

"I do not, Runi. You refuse to take the place. And I am merely the most sensible one left."

"The riches do not concern you? This is a place of great wealth. Everything from silver to slaves."

"I do not care about that."

"I am certain Asger does. Why else do you suppose he puts up with Vanja?"

"Because she is pleasing in his bed."

"Mayhap."

"Runi, do you think Asger has found out the details of my bargain with Magnus, and seized Catrin?"

"It is surely possible. The guards may have overheard what you said, and talked of it. Ah, look." Runi gazed toward the harbor. "Your hero makes his way in."

So he did. In the bay, Magnus's longboat was on the move.

Embra tightened her grip on her brother's arm. "You must help me."

"How?"

"Stand with me against Asger."

"That, Sostir, might be tricky. You think you may seize power because you are daughter to Friti Gunnarsson. But so is Vanja."

"What do you mean?"

"Use your head, Embra. Think about it. And meanwhile, you'd better go to the harbor and make your excuses."

****

The men had unlashed Ulrik from the mast, forced him back into his clothing, and trussed him up like a prize boar. Initially they'd taken the gag from his face, but he spewed so much venom and complained so vociferously they put it back on.

Magnus had given the order to ship anchor and make their way inshore. Already, he could see people gathering in the harbor. Was Embra there among them? He narrowed his eyes, feeling again the persuasive wooing of her lips against his, and the silken rush prompted by her tongue sliding over his skin.

Such a woman! He had grown up surrounded by strong women—former slaves who had endured being dragged away from their homes, subjected to captivity and to forcible rape, and had survived.

The gods knew his mother had a dangerous strength. As for his sister, well she was, in truth, the daughter of a berserker. He should be used to women who spoke for themselves and were not easily cowed.

Embra—ja, she had a sense of entitlement that the women in his life did not share. Being raised in this place of power and betrayal, how could it be otherwise?

But having tasted her, having held her in his arms and become one flesh with her, he would swear that, despite her parentage, there was something more—or other—than a cruel desire to dominate.

She knew what she wanted, did Mistress Embra. And she wanted him. He had no objection to that, save that she tugged at his emotions as well as his flesh. And there was no future in it. Absolutely none.

Despite that, when they neared the shore and he saw her making her way down to the water, his pulse leaped. A rush of memories flooded his mind. How she'd shed her clothing for him, so eager she'd fumbled the ties. The way she'd looked at him, with sensual demand. The way she'd run her hands across the muscles of his arms and shoulders, with a hesitant reverence that should be foreign to her.

Yet wasn't.

When alone with him, Embra Fritisdottir was a different woman than she was here among her people.

He stood beside the prow of his boat and had Ulrik hauled up next to him so she could see he was alive and whole. The trouble was, the people of the settlement saw him also and immediately began clamoring for his release.

Magnus narrowed his eyes. There were Embra's two mad sisters and her younger brother and sister. Her brother Ovre, barely out of his youth, yet looking dangerous. There, Embra's Erin-man slave. A hundred other faces. Nowhere could he spy anyone who could be Lodvar's mother.

"Halt!" he called to the men at the oars. "Prepare to come about. Something is wrong."

Ulrik stiffened at his side. Tied as he was, it was difficult for him to keep his head upright, but he fought to do so. Ach, he must be tasting his freedom.

"Here, take him." He thrust Ulrik at Apsel and drew his sword. He preferred the axe but not in such tight circumstances.

"There is going to be trouble," he told his men. "Be ready. Apsel, if he moves, slit his throat."

With a glint in his eye, Apsel nodded. Magnus leaned out over the front of the boat and engaged Embra.

"Mistress! Where is Mistress Catrin?"

She strode forward into the water. As she had the night she'd come aboard, she heeded not the waves soaking her clothing. Her hair hung partially loose down her back, and she looked as composed as ever. But Magnus felt her uncertainty and saw it in her eyes.

Embra waded still closer, tipped up her head and said, "She is not here."

"What?" Dismay nearly clogged Magnus's throat. A trap, was this? Had all her kisses been meant to lure him, lull him? Had the vow of truth been a lie? Ach, ja, she was Friti Gunnarsson's daughter, after all.

He bellowed, "We had an agreement!"

She nodded evenly. "We do, still."

"This is meant to be an exchange."

"We have searched for her. I suggest—"

The crowd behind her swelled, like an angry sea. Magnus bellowed over his shoulder, "Pull away. Pull away!"

Too late. The warriors of Husavik rushed the longboat, surging into the water and splashing past Embra even as she hollered at them, "Stop. Stop!"

Like a tide, they refused to pull back, and the morning swiftly moved beyond Embra's control.

Chapter Twenty-Four

One thought possessed Magnus's mind as enemy warriors poured over the sides of his boat and swarmed aboard. *I am going to die*. Here on a cold, foreign shore. He had no time for anything more, save regret. Not with an unholy battle on his hands.

Half a score men he had on board, only, to face this throng. The intruders intended to take Ulrik back, but he'd given Apsel an order and could hear his friend bellowing even as the invaders engaged others of his men.

"Back! Back, or I will slay him."

Close beside the prow where Magnus was, he engaged his first opponent, a brawny man with narrowed, feral eyes. Magnus could, ja, fight with the sword though at this moment he longed for his axe.

No time for choices now. No chance to do anything but fight.

He took out the man with the feral eyes, who fell away back into the water, only to face another, and another after him. He heard screaming, hollering and— he thought—Embra's voice. He would not make it out of this alive. Nor would his men.

And then, abruptly, the battle madness arose.

It came with a rushing in his ears like the wind, and made the air dance all around him. The deck of the boat shook beneath his feet—or perhaps his feet trampled the deck—and his vision went red.

The berserker's rage. He'd experienced it only once before, during a battle at Sorvagur. But as the son of a berserker, it rode his blood.

And with a roar, it now burst from him. The air glowed bright, too bright for his eyes. The muscles of his body turned to fire. After that, he remembered no more.

****

Voices murmured nearby, mere threads of sound. They teased Magnus's ear and called to him through the pain. By Odin's eye, he hurt. Pain possessed every muscle, and weakness that bordered on paralysis kept him flat on his back where he lay.

Wherever that might be.

By all that was holy, what had happened, and why did he feel so ill? Thoughts came to him but dimly, sifting through the pain. His boat. His men.

The berserker's rage.

He groaned. The place where he lay was dark, or nearly so. He could still hear someone speaking, whispering, near at hand.

He knew this place, the feel and scent of it. He knew the voice—

The shadows in the room shifted. Someone moved beside him. As soon as she touched him, he knew her. A wave of emotion pounded through him and he groaned again.

"Magnus? Are you still with me?"

Ah, ja. With her, but barely.

She gusted a breath above him. "I thought I had lost you. I thought you were dead." Something warm and wet touched his face. Weeping? Could Embra

Fritisdottir be weeping? Nei, not this strong woman.

He growled in response, all he could manage. When the berserker's rage lifted, it took much. He remembered last time, the weakness and pain.

Fighting against it, he tried to speak. "What happened? My men—"

Had she betrayed him? Had she bedded him only to lure him into the trap that had sprung there on the shore?

Had her vow of truth been naught but a lie?

"You did not tell me you were a berserker like your father."

"Nei."

It did not come to him often, or easily, this power. Only when he sought to defend his own.

"My men—" he repeated.

"Prisoner. Those who survived."

Ah, Odin! Nei, nei. Into what had he led his friends?

"How many dead?"

"I do not know. They were being pulled from the boat when we left. I dared not linger and feared only for you. *For you.*"

She pressed her face against his. Ja, she wept.

"Ulrik?"

"Dead. Your man slit his throat."

Apsel had. Just as Magnus had instructed.

"Apsel?"

"Is that the black-haired man? Prisoner. Not here. It is all beyond my control."

She had betrayed him. She must have. But he would think about that later, when he was able to reach beyond the pain.

"I hurt."

"You are wounded, beyond what—what the fit did to you. The healer has seen you and bound your wounds. He did not know if—when—you would recover from the fit."

How had Fadir endured this over and over again? Tolljur Magnusson had served as berserker in battle many times, both here at Husavik and abroad. He never spoke of it. Magnus knew the old shaman, Kaddi, had helped by feeding Fadir draughts both before and after he came out of the trance, to ease the transition.

Magnus had naught but this woman at his side.

"Where are we?"

"My quarters. I have taken charge of you. But, Magnus, as I say, everything else has slipped from my grasp. The outrage over Ulrik's death reaches far. Those who supported my father and do not support me will use it as a cause. Already, Asger seizes control. They prepare a grand funeral for the son of Friti Gunnarsson."

Magnus gasped. He had to get out of here, find a way to gather his men. What was left of them.

He still did not know if this woman had betrayed him.

"Help me up."

She tried. Winding both arms around his body she hauled at him, but he could do little to aid himself, and his weight was too much for her. When she turned her face he got a glimpse of it, twisted in agony and wet with tears.

"Hush," he breathed, unable to keep from minding how she felt. Because he cared about her still, even as he might doubt her. He could not prevent that either.

"Where are my men being held?"

She sat back on her heels, her breasts heaving. "Here and there about the settlement."

In the limited light, he tried to see her expression. "Am I a prisoner also? Are you holding me here?"

"Ja, but just for show—"

He swore bitterly.

"Magnus. Magnus, listen to me. The truth still stands between us."

"Did you betray me?" In that instant, it was all that mattered, or nearly all. His men, prisoners. His mission, failed. Yet it meant almost more to him, whether this woman had broken faith with him.

She stopped breathing. "Is that what you think? Nei. Nei! I did not. I would not."

"What happened on the shore—that looked and smelled like a trap."

"I did not!" Fiercely she kissed him, a touch of fire on his lips. "By all the gods, Magnus. I swear it."

He shook his head. The fog in his mind cleared slowly. The pain remained. "I know not what allegiance you pay your gods, or what a promise means to you." It had meant nothing to her brother, or her father. How had he thought she might differ from them? "I know you scarcely at all."

"You do. You know me."

"Nei." Gently he pushed her away from him. His brain still moved sluggishly. "My men, my boat—"

"Your boat lies safe below, in the harbor. They wanted to fire it, but I said you were under my protection yet, and prevented it."

If they fired his boat, they might just as well murder him. He would never reach home again.

He struggled to breathe through his pain, not all of it caused by the berserker's fit. "You made love to me." Blinding, almost holy love. "Just to deceive me."

"I did not. Magnus, Magnus look at me."

She trapped his face between her hands. "It is truth. It is truth, what happened between us."

"Nei."

"Do not speak that word! Do not let me hear it pass your lips. I will get you out of this, I swear it. You need only give me the chance."

"How? How will you get us out of this?"

"I do not know that yet. Listen to me. I meant to make the trade, the woman, Catrin, for Ulrik. I could not find her. I can no longer find my brother, Runi, either. It is possible he has made off with her."

"Where?"

"I do not know."

"Why would he take her?"

"Why does Runi do anything? I will find out. I will sort it. Meanwhile, I can hold here, keep you safe."

"I am your prisoner," he accused.

"Under my protection."

He grunted, and she laid hold of him again. "Listen to me. Even if Asger gains the upper hand, and right now the whole settlement is divided on that, I do not think they will kill you. Everyone saw that you are berserker—a rare and valuable man. We have not had a berserker here since your father left Husavik."

Magnus struggled to comprehend what she said. Did she imagine he would ever offer his services here, as his father had once done? Witnessing his agony, would she allow such a thing? Did she care so little for him?

Fadir spoke so rarely of his past, but had once told Magnus that Modir had saved him. Her love, her music, and her magic had.

He narrowed his gaze on the woman who knelt in front of him. He could no more guess what she might do—or why—than she could gainsay the actions of her brother, Runi. But he very much doubted she acted out of love. The kind of love Modir and Fadir shared. How had he imagined differently?

"Rest," she urged. "Recover your strength. My man, Kennach, is still out looking for Catrin. If he finds her, or hears word of her, we may put the question to her, whether she wishes to leave with you."

"And Ulrik's death? Will we be permitted to leave?"

"Ulrik perished because of his own foolishness. Whatever else, we are a pragmatic folk and I hope, once the anger clears, will recognize that."

And did she care nothing for her brother? Ja, the relationships among the members of this family were complicated. They did not feel for each other the way he felt for his sister. He would die for Gyda, and she for him.

He could not fairly say whether Embra was capable of such emotion.

"Here." She put a cup of mead in his hands. "Drink. Rest. And, Magnus, believe in me."

Chapter Twenty-Five

Embra stood on the rise of land just outside her dwelling and gazed at the harbor below. The weather had turned, all the blue skies giving way before a wall of fitful cloud. The wind buffeted her where she stood, and beneath her feet the ground once more rumbled.

Did the gods disapprove of what happened in Husavik?

The tremors were not as violent as before, but whatever forces tore at the fabric of the world had not quieted.

Embra could feel discord throughout the settlement. The attack in the harbor had been a product of that discord. Though she could see Magnus's boat riding in the harbor, under guard, the trouble was not done.

Behind her, inside her quarters, Magnus slept watched by Kennach, who had returned exhausted by his fruitless search. Embra had no idea how to care for a berserker, what he might require. She knew, though, how the minds of those who inhabited this settlement worked. To many here, such a man was no more than a weapon, a valuable one. That might well overshadow the loss of Ulrik who was, after all, but Friti Gunnarsson's third son.

Were there not two others left, and one of them the eldest?

To say nothing of her, Embra, who stood between Magnus and all harm.

Her fingers hovered above the hilt of the knife she wore, and her mind darted back to the battle at the harbor. She'd been raised among warriors. Never had she seen anyone fight as Magnus had under the power of the berserker's rage. He'd become someone else, his face a mask of fury. Impervious to pain, he'd inflicted much harm before being swarmed and hauled off the boat into the water, borne down and half drowned.

Everyone there had seen what he was. The value of what he was may have kept him alive more so than her commands, as she sought to reassert her tattered power.

Now she had to get him out of this. Him, and his surviving men, for he would not agree to leave without them. For his own good, she must send the man she loved away from her forever.

The man she loved.

Ja, she might as well admit it, if only to herself. Love had come to her late, so late she'd nearly lost any belief in it. She'd understood attraction, which she also felt for Magnus, powerful in its own right. She'd acknowledged the existence of foolish infatuation, though it had never befallen her.

But, love?

She hadn't known what that meant till she watched Magnus, snarling and bloody, near drowning in the water, and feared she would lose him.

Anything, anything would be better than that. Even sending him away.

They had taken a vow of truth, she and Magnus, and she owed him the truth now. She should tell him she loved him. But he did not trust her. She could see that in his eyes. He was not sure but that she'd lain with him only for an opportunity to betray him.

She did not know how to convince him otherwise. Not when he could see for himself that Husavik was built on deceit. Even its foundations trembled.

Magnus would recover from the wounds he had taken. The healer she had brought in—the best Husavik had to offer—said he was strong. Three of his men, though, lay dead, and the others languished in captivity. She did not know how to solve this.

She must find a way.

The wind buffeted her more strongly, and she narrowed her eyes, watching a group of figures move up the slope toward her. Here came trouble, and no mistake.

Asger it was, looking for his opportunity to seize control of the settlement. He had directed the attack at the harbor and would have killed Magnus, but for what he was.

It took a bold man to murder a berserker. Her own father had tried it, and failed.

Now Asger came to face her, and he did not come alone. He had a stout group of other warriors at his back, and Vanja walked at his side.

He had Vanja's backing. And Embra needed Runi's if she were to succeed against this upstart.

Where was Runi?

At that moment, she wanted to strangle him. She asked very little from the members of her family and expected less. She had hoped Runi, as Friti's eldest surviving son, would weigh in on her side.

"Mistress Embra!" Asger hailed her when the group drew near enough. He looked confident to the point of arrogance, his eyes bright. "We request a meeting. Come to the hall with us. We have important news to share."

We. Embra shifted her gaze to her sister, who looked as disheveled as usual. She also appeared dissatisfied—though, to be sure, Embra could not guess why. But Embra recognized the restless expression in Vanja's wide, blue eyes.

Was there something here, a weakness that Embra might exploit?

She said, "I have no desire to meet with you, Master Asger."

"Do not be hasty. We must discuss your brother Ulrik's funeral. He has been taken to the hall. Surely you wish to honor him as is his due?"

Honor? Was that Ulrik's due? Perhaps as a son of the former jarl. If she wished to draw upon the power of her house, she supposed she must try to keep the demands for respect intact.

Not awaiting an answer, Asger nodded at the door of her quarters. "How fares the berserker?"

The berserker. Had Magnus, then, ceased to be the man he was, one full of intelligence and passion, and in the eyes of the settlement become naught more than a commodity?

"He will recover."

"To be sure he will. Great strength and endurance, such men have. I knew his father, fought many times at his back."

Ja, for in battle a berserker was sent in first, to cow the enemy.

"I want you to know we wish him no harm." Asger flicked a gesture between him and Vanja.

187

We, again.

"If you can persuade him to stay and fight for us, we might be convinced then to forgive him Ulrik's death."

Vanja twitched her shoulders as still another rumble passed through the ground beneath their feet. "So you say, Asger. I am determined to take my revenge upon Magnus Tolljursson."

"Or his men."

"Or his men."

Embra puffed out a breath. Could she believe Asger had any influence over her sister? If so, she must handle things very carefully indeed.

Asger fixed Embra with an assessing glance, up and down. "If you can get a son off him, better still. Such men often breed true. But know this." Asger's gaze became intent. "I will be taking the place of jarl. It is what we go to the great hall to announce."

He would, would he?

"You and I, Embra Fritisdottir, we can bargain, ja? For the good of the settlement. And for the good of your berserker."

"He is not mine."

Asger's brows flew upward. Vanja leaned forward and began to speak. He forestalled her. "Save it, my love. For our announcement."

Ja, so that was the way the wind blew.

"The gods," Asger stated, "are not happy with a woman for jarl. Everyone can feel their disfavor. They shake the very ground in frustration. They pour fire into the sky. You will step aside, ja?"

Embra stared at him stonily.

"Because," as Vanja had, he leaned closer, "I am

being very forbearing. Sentiment towards your berserker could turn. You want to be careful, if you wish to defend him."

"What makes you think I do?"

"Your sister says it."

Vanja swept her ragged, streaming hair back from her face. "Sostir, I saw your face at the harbor, when you thought the berserker would drown. And I know he spent at least one night here with you."

"So?" Embra glared her sister in the eye. "Not every woman jumps every man with whom she finds herself alone."

Vanja shrugged. "I know only what I can see in you."

Curse Vanja anyway! And Dagmar. Curse Runi also—all the members of her blighted family.

She glanced behind at the door of her quarters, firmly shut. Was Magnus safe there? She could keep him so only if she played this game well enough.

"Very well, I will come and hear your announcement." As if she did not know already what it would be. "But may all the gods help you, Asger, if you betray me."

"He knows better," Vanja laughed, "than to betray either of us. Are we not the daughters of Friti Gunnarsson?"

Chapter Twenty-Six

Magnus woke from a sleep dark as death, wondering where he was. By the gods, he usually slept well. Back home, following a day spent drilling, or worse yet, working the stony fields, he enjoyed a sound rest.

He was no longer at home.

The pieces of his reality fell into place one by one. He could feel them slotting into their assigned spots. Husavik. The battle aboard his longboat. Ulrik's death. The berserker's fit.

His pain had eased, the agony possessing all his muscles faded in intensity. It still simmered beneath the surface of his awareness, the way a pot simmered over a fire. If he moved too quickly, if his emotions stirred too violently, it would return with teeth.

And his wounds—ja, there had been a healer who tended those. Half a score of wounds great and small, the worst a cut to his left arm. The healer had been here, and Embra. She—she had wept over him.

Here—here was her quarters, back beside the hearth where the two of them had made love. Flat on his back and wondering if he had the strength to rise.

Dared he try?

Renewed respect for his father flooded through him. He wondered again how Fadir had withstood a life of this for so long? Strength. Fortitude.

Modir's love.

He, Magnus, surely could claim a measure of that strength and fortitude also. As for love—

He heaved himself to a sitting position, a groan tearing from him. Where was Embra? Was he here alone?

Nei. Barely visible in the dusky room, a figure sat beside the door. With effort, Magnus recognized him.

Embra's man, called Kennach.

He sat the way a guard might, with a long knife in his hands. Had he been stationed there to keep intruders out or Magnus in? A curious thing, to afford a slave such a weapon. Would he not be expected to escape? Kennach had told them he did not want to escape, and where would he run? They were trapped on an island.

When Magnus sat up, Kennach eyed him with alarm.

"Where is Mistress Embra?" Magnus's voice came in an ugly croak.

The Erin man jerked his head to the door. "With her sisters. And that cur, Asger."

What a way for a slave to speak of one of his masters! Kennach's accent reminded him of his mother's—strong in cadence, like a song.

"Do they decide my fate?"

Kennach shrugged. "Most likely. She's given her word ye will not be killed. Ye can trust that."

Magnus lifted his brows. He reached stiffly for the mead jug and cup, left nearby.

Beneath him, the ground rumbled.

"The gods be upset," Kennach said, as mead sloshed into the cup. "No one seems to know why. Is it because ye be here on this land? Because Friti

Gunnarsson is dead? Because my mistress holds the place of jarl? Who can tell?"

Who, indeed. "Is it this Embra has gone to discuss?"

"Aye, so I expect."

Kennach sounded at ease about it. He sounded curiously comfortable, withal.

Magnus drank and asked, "What did you think of Friti Gunnarsson?"

Kennach made an odd sound, as if he spat though no spittle appeared. "A bully and a braggart. I hated him."

Well, that summed it up nicely.

"Tell me, master, who killed him?"

Magnus tossed back the rest of the mead and poured more. "My father beheaded him in a fair fight."

"Ah." Kennach apparently reflected upon that. "I do not remember your father. The berserker. Though people speak of him, I did not come here till after he had left."

"How long have you been here?"

"Nearly twenty years. I was a young man when I was seized in a raid. Little more than a boy, really. Friti Gunnarsson claimed me and gave me to his eldest daughter as servant, and her naught but a bairn then."

"You have been with Embra a long time."

"Aye."

"You must know her well." Magnus ached to ask—was she like the others, like the rest of her family? Half mad, deceptive and cruel? Did Kennach hate her, and hate his place with her? He did not seem to.

Before he could phrase the question, Kennach said, "I did search for Mistress Catrin, you know. Mistress

Embra sent me. The woman is nowhere to be found."

"What do you suppose happened to her?"

"I do not know. Perhaps Master Runi took her away. He had been seen in the vicinity of her dwelling."

"Why would he do that?" Magnus drank again. The mead made a poor breakfast, but it helped steady him.

"No one can tell why Master Runi does anything." Kennach shrugged.

"Is he—mad?" Like his sister, Vanja.

Kennach shook his head. "Clever. Very clever. But unpredictable."

"Is he as cruel as the rest of them?"

"Cruel?" Kennach looked started, as if he'd never considered the word. "Mistress Embra is not cruel."

"Nei?"

Kennach shook his head violently. "Many times has she protected me."

Magnus did not say, but most Norse protected their possessions.

"She is like—like a daughter to me. I would die for her."

A brave avowal. "You trust her."

"Aye."

Magnus wondered if he could.

"If she wants ye, Master Magnus, I will fight to defend ye. It might hclp if you'll fight to protect me—and her—also."

Magnus spread his hands. "I have lost my axe. And they have taken my other weapons."

Kennach grinned and shuffled forward. He extended the long knife he held to Magnus. "Take it. I have another." He drew a dagger from his boot.

A slave who possessed not only one weapon but

two. Now, Magnus had seen everything.

Was anything here in Husavik what it seemed?

****

Morning light bled through the sky and poured in through the open doors of the great hall. Folk streamed in also, mostly men, and swiftly filled the space.

Embra shifted uneasily where she stood. Events, so she suspected, were about to get ugly. She must keep her priorities in mind. Protect herself and Magnus. Find Mistress Catrin. Keep things from spinning off into madness.

She did not know if she could achieve that last one.

Things here in Husavik had always been mad. Her father had kept them balanced, somehow, between greed and cruelty. His followers—and his children— vied for his favor, though Gunnar always possessed it. The rest of them were but afterthoughts, got on a madwoman.

It made for unnatural loyalties. With Gunnar gone, with Ulrik gone, it left limited options. She needed Runi to come walking in through that door, preferably with Mistress Catrin in tow. She needed him to stand with her so she could complete the deal with Magnus, and send him home.

Never to see him again. Because, nei, she did not believe even a berserker mad enough to return here for any reason.

Save love?

Yet Magnus did not love her. She loved him—ach, ja she did, with a kind of wild, complete devotion of which she'd not imagined herself capable. He enjoyed their matings—who would not?—but she had no knowledge whether his feelings for her stretched to

194

more than lust.

She still felt the effects of her terror when she thought she'd lost him. Even if it meant she must send him away from her, she never wanted to experience that again.

She looked at Asger, who stood on the dais in front of Fadir's grand chair, Vanja beside him. Without hesitation, she hopped up and joined them.

"My fellow warriors!" Asger shouted, and those there quieted to listen. "A time of great change is at hand. Long has the house of Gunnar Thorsson, who came over the water from Norway to settle this land, led us."

Gunnar Thorsson, Embra's grandfather, who had been banished from his home and ordered never to return. He'd founded this settlement, and controlled what happened here, who succeeded, who held power.

"Now the seafarers have brought word that Friti Gunnarsson is dead, and his son—Gunnar—with him." Asgar gestured dramatically to the doorway. "A new day dawns for us!"

Murmurs ensued. Embra took advantage and spoke up. "My father's death does not mark the demise of his house. Certain of his children remain."

Asgar turned to her. "I am glad you mentioned that, Mistress Embra. It is important. Following Ulrik's death, Friti Gunnarsson still has two sons and four daughters. But the gods are not happy. We can feel that by the stirring of the very ground, and the fire they toss into the sky. Shall we sit and wait for them to destroy us? Or shall we choose another path?"

Louder murmurs this time. Curse Runi anyway. Why could he not walk in here now? He alone had some authority, some hope of keeping the settlement from chaos.

She raised her voice. "Our established ways, my father's ways, have served us well. I say this is the worst possible time to rock the boat. We must hold strong. Let me continue to lead with Runi at my side—"

"Where is Runi, then? Where is your brother?" someone called.

Embra lifted her head. "Communing with the gods, seeking to calm their anger and make the upheaval cease."

That went over better than she expected. Men exchanged appraising glances. Some nodded. One called, "If anyone can, it is Runi Fritisson."

Asger did not like that sentiment. He stepped to the edge of the dais, dragging Vanja with him.

"We must put all that behind us and begin a new age. One of increased raiding, prosperity, and fruitfulness."

Embra turned on him. "Would you dismiss my father so readily, Asger Tarbensson?"

"Nei, not at all. I would instead blend the old with the new, moving forward with leadership. I have the experience. I have the knowledge." He raised Vanja's hand in his. "I have Friti Gunnarsson's dottir. Tell them, my love."

Vanja's eyes looked wild. With her hair streaming down and her lips unnaturally red, with her overripe body well displayed by the thin gown she wore, she appeared to have climbed straight from some man's bed.

"I have agreed to wed with Asger Tarbensson. So the blood of my father's house will still hold sway, in

Husavik."

Even though she'd half expected the news, it struck Embra in the gut like a hard blow. "Nei," she whispered. That Husavik should be led by a merciless raider and a madwoman. Again.

"And," Asger went on, not giving Embra a chance to address the crowd, "I have further news about the succession. Vanja Fritisdottir already carries my child."

That would convince these men who listened, those who may have believed Asger too old, and not still vigorous enough to lead.

She glared at Vanja. "Is this true?"

Vanja's half-mad eyes met hers for the first time. "I carry a child, ja."

That did not mean it was Asger's child. Vanja had spent time in enough other men's beds.

But did it matter? If Vanja produced a child, especially a healthy son, and Asger claimed it, his success might well be assured.

She turned to the crowd. "This is not right! You followed my father and my grandfather all your lives. This is not what they would have wanted."

"And what do the gods want, eh?" Asger asked. "Vanja Fritisdottir and I will wed as soon as it may be arranged. And a sacrifice will be made to quiet the gods' ire." Asger stepped to Embra's side and spoke for her ears alone. "Think how pleased the gods will be with the sacrifice of a berserker."

Chapter Twenty-Seven

"Stop with your pacing, Embra, or you will wear a trench in the floor." Magnus's head still ached, and whenever he moved, pain licked through his limbs, like fire. Despite that, he could feel his strength returning. Vitality once more flowed through him, combatting the injuries.

He could also feel how distraught Embra's mood had turned. She'd come back from her father's hall tense and edgy, and that pulled at him almost as if their emotions were connected. As if her welfare affected his own.

"I pace when I am worried. And I am worried now. I do not know where Runi is. I do not know where Mistress Catrin is. Has Runi snatched her?"

"Why would he do that?"

"He could have a reason. Or—" she stopped pacing to look at Magnus, "Asger could have her. He spoke of making a sacrifice."

Magnus's head pounded harder. He could not let that fate befall Lodvar's mother. Or any of his men.

Or did the strained way Embra gazed at him denote he himself might be marked for that particular end?

"Asger seeks to assert his power," Embra said. "He has announced he will wed Vanja." Her face crinkled in distress. "He even claims she carries his child."

"Ah. That will lend weight to his claim."

"It certainly will, if it is true."

Magnus grunted. "Have you discovered where my men are being held?"

"Three were killed in the battle aboard the longboat. I am trying to discover where the others are and how they fare. I have sent Kennach to find out."

"I need to free them and assure their safety."

"I will do my best to help with that. But, Magnus, if Asger seizes power, anything could happen. He might make examples of them." She fixed him with a hard look. "Or of you."

"I see." And so, would his life end here in this land where his father's began? "I thought berserkers were considered valuable."

"Ach, ja. And thus you would make a magnificent sacrifice. I need Runi to return and back me so Asger cannot gain control."

"If Runi does return, will he back you?"

"I hope so." She got no farther before Kennach entered the dwelling. "Have you found Master Magnus's men?" Embra asked him.

"Aye, Mistress. Most of them are being held where the slaves are taken, after a boat comes in. Suffering from their wounds, to be sure. Few have been tended."

Magnus swore softly.

"A couple o' them—" Kennach hesitated.

Magnus's heart fell. Had his men been singled out for sacrifice? "My friend, Apsel," he began.

Kennach's gaze moved to him. "Separated from the others."

"For sacrifice?" He got to his feet.

"In a way. Mistress Dagmar has him."

This time Embra swore.

Magnus looked at her. "Has him?" he repeated.

"In her quarters, no doubt. She will eat him alive." Embra added concisely, "He may enjoy it."

"Ah. But—"

"Her interest may keep him alive. Kennach, is there no sign of Master Runi?"

"Nay, Mistress, or of Mistress Catrin."

"Keep searching. And bring me word at once if you hear further talk of a sacrifice being scheduled."

As soon as Kennach left, she began pacing again. "You see how things stand," she said bitterly. "It has very nearly slipped from my hands."

"Come and sit down."

She ignored him. "For the time being, I believe my word can still protect you. If Asger seizes full control—"

"Embra—" He held out his hand. "Come and sit."

With a sigh, she obliged. They sank to the rug together.

"Magnus, I have been thinking and thinking. What is my best course of action? Some of the younger men admire Runi. If he were here, he might persuade them to release your boat and your men. You might slip away home. On the other hand, many of them were loyal to Ulrik. With him dead—"

"A tangle."

"I fear the older warriors may move to back Asger. I felt the mood shift in that room when Vanja announced she will marry him. They probably know she's been in his bed. And most of them would not mind a chance with her."

"Surely he would never allow that."

"Who knows?" She looked at him. "I will do my

best to protect you, in whatever way I can."

"And my men?"

"Their lives hang in the balance. I will do what I can for them also."

She leaned forward and gave him a fierce kiss. What started off desperate soon gentled as her lips softened and molded to his, drawing first one of his lips and then the other between her teeth. Hazy pleasure curled through him, and he felt it possess her also.

"Magnus—Magnus, are you recovered enough to make love to me?"

Strength seemed to come with the pleasure. "Embra, I am."

"We may not have many more opportunities, and I—" She broke off abruptly and looked at him. Deliberately, holding his gaze with hers, she unfastened her tunic.

Her high breasts came to peaks when the air hit them. She straddled him and plunged her hands into his hair as he took a nipple into his mouth. His pleasure spiked.

As did hers. He felt it in the bow of her body, in the way she cradled his head and urged him closer.

"Ach, by Freya's heart—"

He feasted on first one breast and then the other. Before he finished, he stood rigid for her.

"I need you, Magnus. I need you inside me."

"I need that too."

She unfasted his leggings before raising her skirts around her waist. She rode him where he sat, face to face, and it felt like she claimed him, took his heart and his spirit along with his seed.

Even then, she was not done. She pushed him back

onto the rug before removing her mouth from his lips, moving downward and tasting his throat and chest. Continuing still lower, ever lower. When she reached her target, she licked him slowly and with intent, employing long strokes of her tongue until she had him upright again.

"Embra." A man could well lose his mind under such treatment. A man might lose his heart.

"Hmm?" She answered her name while her hair trailed over his skin, setting up an intense heat. "Do you wish for me to talk to you, Magnus? Because my mouth is otherwise occupied."

"I would not interrupt you."

"You taste—so—good." Her mouth encircled him. "Let me have you. All of you."

He'd already given her all, but her mouth persuaded winsomely, and all too soon she had him on the verge of unbearable pleasure. Helpless, his body convulsed, and she accepted all he offered. If he died now, he might have no regrets.

"Embra—"

"Eh?" She cuddled close, naked breasts pressed to his chest. The warmth of her seeped into him. He tangled his fingers in her hair and kissed her long and slow.

"You are so beautiful."

"You think so?"

"I know it. Beautiful and strong and—and like no one I have ever known."

She caught her breath. "You could ask anything of me, do you know that? Anything. And I would grant it you."

"Nei."

"Nei? You do not believe me?"

"I believe you." He drew her still closer. "But I believe it is the pleasure talking."

"There is pleasure, ja. It is not just that." She lifted onto her elbows and gazed into his eyes. Rarely had she looked more serious, her blue eyes intent.

"You must understand, I have no time for men, for—for pleasure. I have no patience with it. With you, it is different. That is because I love you."

Emotions rose within Magnus, even as the passion had. Regret, because anything between the two of them—beyond what they'd just shared—was impossible. Sorrow because he did not want to hurt her. Wonder, that such a woman as this might choose him, of all men, to love.

The corners of her mouth tightened. "I can see, by the look in your eyes, you do not feel the same for me."

"Embra, I do not know how I feel. I have been tossed up here on this shore, caught in a tangle." He stroked her hair. "If you have these feelings for me, I am honored."

"If? You do not believe me. Do you suppose I would share myself so, with just anyone?"

"I think we may both be caught up in the moment."

Grief flooded her eyes. She got to her feet, dropped her skirts and gathered her clothing around her.

Magnus sat up hastily and stared at her in dismay.

"What I feel for you, Magnus Tolljursson, is not fancy. And I am not a woman to be overcome by mere pleasure. If you cannot see that—"

"Embra, I care for you. I do." But love—love was a serious matter, a thing of bonds deeply forged, ties of both the spirit and the heart.

Did he feel that for her? Could he, ever?

"Embra," he said again. "I wish to be honest with you. As—as honest as you have been with me."

Her smile, this time, looked bitter. "The vow of honesty that lies between us still stands?"

"It does. I might say anything to you, claim to feel what I do not. You are a remarkable woman, strong and beautiful, as I say—"

"And the daughter of Friti Gunnarsson. Does that make a difference? Our fathers were enemies."

"More than that." His gaze held hers. "My father slew yours."

"In battle."

"In battle, on the shore back home. Embra, think carefully. Our emotions are stirred, as I say. And I—well, I never knew lovemaking could be like what we've shared."

"You are trying to say I'm deceived, that I do not in truth love you."

"It is a possibility."

"But, Magnus, the gods—the gods love to present such ironies to us. It is precisely what they would do, bring to me the one man I can love in all the world, and he my father's enemy."

She had not met all the men in the world. She did not know if he was the only one to stir her this way. But Magnus did not tell her so.

Desire could be persuasive. And he'd never experienced such desire as he felt for her.

"Do not worry," she told him. "This changes naught. I will still do all I can to protect you. And I will still work to get you out of this tangle, whatever it requires."

Chapter Twenty-Eight

Embra stood outside the hall in the dark, with the wind from the sea streaming through her hair and clothing. A storm brewed off shore, she could feel it. Just what they needed in addition to the other rumblings. Fire and water to match what she felt inside.

She stamped her foot in an effort to control her emotions and blinked her eyes furiously. She rarely wept and certainly not over a man. She did not intend to begin now.

Strong, he had said she was. It was true. She'd needed to grow up strong in the face of her mother's emotional absence and her father's latent cruelty. She'd needed to expect whatever might come.

She had never expected this.

She'd needed to provide her own support and deal with the absence of love.

Had it mattered that no one in her family loved her? That Fadir took Vanja to his bed, that Gunnar cared only for the chance of success or to make someone else suffer. That Runi held himself apart, living a reality she couldn't quite understand. That the members of her family cared always for themselves but never, never for her.

It mattered now, that Magnus did not love her. By the gods! So twisted, so warped was she, she could not even convince him that her feelings for him were genuine.

She swiped angrily at the tears slipping down her face. She would not weep over him. She would not!

"Sostir?"

She whirled to find Runi just behind her. He'd appeared as from the thin air, and she gasped.

"Where have you been?"

He shrugged. "Here and there."

"You have not been in the settlement. We searched everywhere for you."

"If you had, you would have found me." He eyed her. "What has angered you?"

"How do you know I am angry?"

"It is the only time I have seen you weep."

"What has not angered me? Asger has decided he will take the place of jarl, and Vanja has decided to marry him and so back his claim. Ulrik is dead. The woman, Catrin, whom I might have bargained for Magnus's life, has disappeared. Magnus's men are all captive."

"I would not worry for them."

"Why not?" She worried about anything that concerned Magnus.

"They are being entertained, most of them. Dagmar has got her hands on the one called Apsel, and is providing him ample pleasure. I was just there—a more satisfied captive I have never seen."

"By Freya's heart!"

"Where is Magnus?" Runi jerked his head toward the back of the hall, beyond which lay her quarters. "Inside? Have you also been entertaining him?"

"What if I have?"

Runi shrugged. "That, too, is unlike you, as

unlikely as those tears."

"My life has come apart, Runi. And it was never all of a piece to begin with."

"Ja."

"Magnus and I swore a vow of truth."

Runi's brow quirked.

"But when I told him how I feel for him, he did not believe me."

"How do you feel for him?"

Embra eyed her brother with caution. Did she want to admit it again? Runi was capable of making light of anything, and at the moment she could withstand little ridicule.

Weightily she said, "I suppose you would scoff at claims of…of love."

"I should, should I not? As should any member of this family. We have seen little evidence of it, or of any genuine feeling beyond grasping cruelty. Do not blame your Magnus too much if he fails to believe you. He has seen what we are. We should not be capable of love."

"True." She tossed head. "But I find—I find I am capable of it."

"Ah. Then I suppose you shall need to convince him."

"I don't know how."

"Ja, we are severely limited, are we not? Crippled, I might even say. But if you can learn to love in the face of your history, you can surely learn to convince him."

"I tried physical persuasion."

"Did you? Truly, a remarkable occurrence. Nei, physical persuasion, while enjoyable, does not work. Any man will accept such attentions, just witness Master Apsel."

"Ja."

"If you want to capture his emotions, you must meet him where they lie."

"How can I tell that?"

"I do not know. I can speak only for myself.

"You talk of touching Magnus's spirit." She eyed him again. As warped as she by their upbringing, she could barely imagine the state of Runi's spirit.

"Sostir, I care about you—in my way."

She snorted. "If you cared about me, Runi, you would have been here to back my claim."

"You think so?"

"I do."

He smiled. That smile, Embra decided, was one of the things that made him so maddening. "Well, I am here now."

"And will you stand with me against Asger? Will you help me find Catrin so that if I succeed in getting Magnus away, I can send her with him?"

"Do not worry about Catrin. She is—safe. Hidden."

Embra rounded on him. "Hidden? Where?"

"With a friend of mine. Where no one will find her."

"What friend?"

"That you need not know. I will produce Catrin when the time is right."

Embra gusted out a breath.

"Sostir, just because you cannot see me, it does not mean I am not elsewhere working on your behalf." Runi tossed his head. "Think of me as Freya—whom you cannot see either."

"A goddess?"

"A god."

No conceit there, then. Embra resisted the desire to snort again. "If you have the power, pray quiet these rumblings. Asger puts forth they are proof the land itself is dissatisfied with us."

"The land is dissatisfied. But it is nothing a sacrifice can mend."

"Tell Asger and his followers that. Sentiment is divided. If you stand with me—"

"Am I not here, Sostir? Am I not standing? But—if I may offer a word of advice—"

"Go ahead."

"Fadir is dead. Gunnar is dead. Ulrik is dead. Do you truly wish to place yourself in the line of such a progression? Better perhaps to kick the soil of this place from your boots and leave with your Magnus."

A lump formed in Embra's throat. "And if he does not want me?"

Runi shook his head, his expression inscrutable. "You may have to bend your pride. I understand it is not easy. I sometimes think pride is all Fadir ever gave to us."

"Ach, Brodir—you may consider my pride well and truly bent."

****

"Magnus, I am going to accompany Runi to the great hall, to speak with Asger. He—Runi that is—returned last night."

Magnus eyed Embra doubtfully. Morning had come, a gray and fitful morning, and the rumblings beneath the earth had subsided. That did not deceive him into thinking the trouble had died with it.

"I heard the two of you talking." He jerked his

head at the door. "Outside."

She did not look at him as she replied, only continued dressing. "You need not worry about the woman, Catrin. She is safe for now."

"Where?"

"I think Runi has her hidden. He is not revealing where, even to me."

Magnus got to his feet. His wounds had stiffened overnight and pulled maddeningly, but the weakness prompted by the berserker's fit had faded. He felt his vitality returning in full.

"I cannot leave without her."

"I know that." She flicked him a glance. "You shall have to trust me, me and Runi, despite how difficult that may be."

"Ja, I understand."

She faced him fully. "I have sworn an oath of truth to you and I—I have confessed my feelings. I cannot make you believe them."

Emotions stirred within Magnus's breast. He'd slept little last night, even after Embra came in and lay down beside him, not touching. Thoughts had pillaged his mind.

He might doubt she truly loved him, that a member of her accursed family could be capable of love. But he believed that *she* believed it.

He must be gentle with her. Surely she deserved that.

Before he could speak, she went on, "Runi says I should let Asger have the place of jarl. That would mean stepping aside from all Fadir and his father built here."

"Would that be so terrible?"

"It would mean opening the door to chaos. All rules would break asunder—the only things holding the darkness at bay. Property, including slaves, would no longer be safe. The few protections we have would fall away." She gave him a level stare. "Perhaps this is why the land stirs."

"Mayhap."

"If I step aside and relinquish my power, I may not be able to defend you, should they come for you. Some want revenge for Ulrik's death, and for Fadir's and Gunnar's deaths. Others would use you in battle. They have not had a berserker to employ for some time."

Magnus tensed. He could wind up precisely where his father had been. "Let me come with you to this meeting. Allow me to speak for myself, and for my men."

She eyed him. "Do not worry too much for your men. Dagmar has taken the one called Apsel in hand."

"In hand?" Magnus tumbled to her meaning. "Ach—" If ever anyone could handle such a situation, it was Apsel. But by Odin's eye, they needed to leave this deranged place.

And this woman who stood before him with her chin tipped up and hard emotions in her eyes? The one who gave herself to him so fiercely and completely, and confessed she loved him after?

Could he handle never seeing her again?

He could take her with him.

That thought crept in the back door of his mind, the way a wolf might enter a hut, unbidden. He tried to imagine her at Sorvagur, crashing in upon the peaceful life there.

He'd never realized how he valued that peace, till

he saw Husavik.

What would Lodvar say? And ach, by Odin's eye, his mother! What, for that matter, would Astrid say? They did not have an understanding, as such. He never said he would return from his voyage and marry her. But maybe, ja, maybe it was what she believed, or hoped.

He would need to be mad to consider taking Embra Fritisdottir away with him. As mad as everyone else in this place.

She seemed to read the emotions in his eyes.

"Come along with me if you wish. For I would not be accused of keeping you from speaking for yourself. And you are no prisoner to me."

Chapter Twenty-Nine

It had been a bad decision, allowing Magnus to accompany her to this meeting, as Embra soon acknowledged. So far everything, everything had gone wrong.

Despite her hopes, the ground had once more commenced shaking and rumbling even as she and Magnus entered the hall. Runi had not arrived ahead of them, but Asger and Vanja had, along with a strong number of Asger's supporters. Ovre and Ella also showed up. Ulla looked like she'd been crying.

Asger, clearly in an aggressive mood, began right away asking angry questions. "Why have you brought him?" He gestured wildly at Magnus. "Is our business his?"

"It is, if we mean to form an alliance with his people."

"And why should we do that?

"Because in the long run, alliance is always more advantageous than attack. The people at Sorvagur have the same roots as us."

"Slaves?" Vanja sniffed. "We are not the descendants of slaves."

"Norse warriors."

"The people at Sorvagur," Asger pointed a finger at Magnus, "killed your fadir and brodir. Would you ally with them?" He stared around at the listening crowd.

213

"There speaks the weakness of a woman."

"I speak good sense." Embra declared.

But Asger shook his head. "He should be put to the death," he roared, "if only in return for Ulrik's death."

Embra's heart trembled within her. Nei, nei, she should never have brought Magnus here. If by doing so she had endangered him—

Only then did Runi step through the crowd, appearing as if by magic.

"Would you," he challenged, also eyeing the listeners, "be so foolish as to poke the bear?" When they fell silent, he went on. "You have seen the berserker fight. What a waste to put such a man to death—even if you could."

They exchanged glances. "It is possible to kill a berserker."

"Possible, ja, but very, very hard to do. Was his father, Tolljur Magnusson, ever felled in any fight— even against my own father? Does he not live still, over the water?"

Magnus shifted uneasily, perhaps wondering if his own abilities would now be put to the test. Nei, she had been mad to bring him here.

"We meet not to decide all this," she declared, "but to determine who shall lead this settlement as jarl."

Asger stepped forward in turn. "Mistress, one matter hinges on the other. Your suitability to lead depends upon how you respond to your brother Ulrik's death." He eyed those gathered as if measuring their response. "Do you punish his death as you should? Or do you reward it by taking the seafarer to your bed?"

Heat rose to Embra's face. How did he know? Vanja's smirk gave her the answer—her sister had furthered the speculation.

And how dared Vanja hurl blame for sharing any man's bed?

"I suppose," Vanja said, "she looks upon that as forming an alliance."

"As you do?" Embra gazed pointedly from Vanja to Asger.

Asger reached out and seized Vanja's hand, so they presented a united front. "Mistress Vanja has agreed to be my wife. So you see, there is no need to worry about Jarl Gunnar's house continuing. His blood will carry on into the future."

The listening warriors, both young and old, murmured over that. One of the younger, perhaps a friend of Ulrik's, called out, "I say Ulrik Fritisson's death must be avenged."

"Take the berserker prisoner!" another ranted. "Beat him down."

Magnus drew a long knife from his boot. How had he come by that? Following his berserker's fit, the men had disarmed him.

No matter. He shifted his weight, looking dangerous. Embra could lose him, if this broke up into battle. Here, now.

Somehow, somehow she had to regain control.

She exchanged a look with Runi and drew herself up. "Listen to me, all of you! If I remain jarl here in Husavik, I shall wed with Magnus Tolljursson. Then, not only shall the succession carry the blood of my father, Friti, but we may beget a line of berserkers here in Husavik."

Everyone there stared at her, including Magnus Tolljursson.

****

"You had no right to tell them that," Magnus declared furiously. "It is not agreed."

Embra had never before seen him so angry— caught in the berserker's fit, ja, but that was quite different. In her experience, a man's anger was a dangerous thing. Gunnar's had come accompanied by sly cruelty. Fadir's with a hard blow. Ulrik had whined and struck out for revenge.

Magnus, a calm man for the most part, went icy and quiet, a terrifying light in his hazel eyes. Embra did not know how to deal with such a reaction.

Following the meeting in the great hall, where nothing had been decided, they had returned to her quarters accompanied by Runi who, along with Kennach, now listened. It did not help having Runi standing with his arms crossed on his chest.

Embra turned to Magnus, and felt his cold fury wash over her. "I had to say something, to protect you. Do you realize how near you were to being overtaken?"

He took a step closer to her. "You think I need you to protect me?"

"In this instance, ja."

He spat, "Not through marriage. Never that."

Embra flushed in mingled distress and humiliation. "Would it be so terrible, marrying me?" Not giving him time to answer, she rushed on, "Marriage with me would give you immunity to being bludgeoned to death or—or sacrificed." Her true fear. "Even if I am no longer jarl, my family is important enough to prevent that."

Magnus went very still. "So you would legitimize me? The way your kind might a slave? As my fadir did my modir?"

"I did not say—"

"I am a free man in my own right."

"You are. It may not be enough to save you." Did he not comprehend his peril or sense how she feared for him?

Desperate, she turned to Runi. "Runi, tell him."

Runi, who leaned against the inner doorway, arms still crossed, shook his head. "He does not trust my words any more than yours, so it seems."

Magnus spun to face him. "Trust?" He gave a hiss. "What is there here to trust? Nothing but treachery abides in this place."

"And scheming." Runi held up a finger. "Do not forget the scheming."

"You mock me?" Magnus's eyes narrowed and he took a step toward Runi, his long knife once more in his hand.

Embra's stomach did a somersault. If he slipped into the berserker's fit again—

"Do not," she barked with far more force than she felt. "Not under my roof." She appealed directly to Magnus. "That is but Runi's way. He has a strange sense of humor."

"I do not feel like laughing."

Nor did Embra. In truth, she wanted to throw herself down upon her bed and weep a river of frustrated tears. She could not see a way forward. Nothing she had endured, surviving in this place, had prepared her for what she felt now. The first time, the very first, she offered anyone her heart, and he could not trust her enough to accept it.

"If you want my advice," Runi began.

"I do not," Magnus snapped.

"Marry her. You can still leave Husavik with your men, once Mistress Catrin returns."

They both turned on him.

"In fact, it will assure that you might."

Embra's throat went dry. Her heart thumped in big, desperate beats.

Magnus eyed Runi. "Do you know where Mistress Catrin is?"

"Ja. Safe. I will bring her to you at the right time."

"Now. Bring her now. I will collect my men—"

"By what authority?"

"Eh?"

"By what authority will you gather your men? Certainly not as husband to the jarl."

Magnus returned the knife to his boot and forced his fingers through his hair, fighting visibly for control. He swore under his breath.

Runi spoke calmly. "You hesitate to wed with her because you believe she seeks to use you." He gestured at Embra. "Do you not see you may use her also? It is the way things in Husavik are done."

"By Odin's eye, I hate this place."

And her? Did he hate her, Embra, also? Her very spirit shrank from the thought.

Runi shrugged. "What does it matter? Once you leave, you will leave the marriage behind you."

Again they both stared at him. Magnus said nothing.

"After you are wed," Runi went on, as if he discussed the minor details of a gathering, perhaps, "I will bring Mistress Catrin to you. You may then prepare your boat to sail—once you have, as you say, regained your men." He looked at Embra. "If they all survive."

Magnus twitched, a whole body flex, as if struck by a flail. "It is coercion."

"It is bargaining, what we here at Husavik do best." Runi turned to the door. "Give it some thought and let me know your decision."

He stepped out. Embra followed and caught his sleeve.

"Runi—"

He smiled at her. "You can thank me later."

"Thank you? For what?"

"He will take the deal, mark my words."

"Do you truly suppose I want him to accept me— wed with me—only because he's forced to?"

He flicked her with a look, up and down. "I suppose you will take him any way you can get him."

Embra flushed, and tears stung her eyes. "And what good is it, if he does naught but leave?"

"Ach, Sostir, it is your task to persuade him he needs to stay."

Chapter Thirty

Magnus's fury died slowly. Never a hasty man, or one who easily lost control of his temper, he did not like falling victim to his anger now. That, he reflected bitterly as he waited for Embra to return, was why succumbing to the berserker's fit went so hard with him. Therein lay loss of all control.

Embra Fritisdottir prompted emotions in him, however, such as he'd never experienced. Rage, indignation—and ja, if he were honest, lust. He did not like being equated with a slave, nor treated like one.

Was that how she'd always seen him? Surely so, for they were arrogant, these people of Husavik, and Friti's offspring most of all.

He glared at the door and narrowed his eyes. He could hear Embra and Runi talking—whispering—but could not catch their words. He wondered what Runi was about. With such a man, who could tell?

Embra let herself back in softly, and her man, Kennach, who'd been there listening quietly throughout, moved to slip by her.

She prevented it with a touch on his arm. "Where did Master Magnus get the long knife he carries?"

Kennach looked blank. He shrugged.

"You might as well admit it. That is the one I gave to you."

Kennach met her gaze then, his expression

unreadable. Magnus took a half step toward them. Would Embra retaliate against the man? Magnus would not allow her to punish Kennach on his account.

The slave spoke quietly. "No man should go unarmed. Is that not what you said, Mistress, when you gave the weapon to me? He is not like me, a slave, but a man in his own right."

Embra scowled and said nothing. With a jerk of her head, she dismissed the man.

To Magnus's astonishment, as Kennach slipped out, he gave Magnus a wink, one Embra did not catch.

"Will you punish him?" he asked once the man had gone.

She gave him a sharp look. "You suppose I could ever hurt Kennach? He has been with me since—"

"Since you were a child, ja. Yet he remains a slave."

"I protect him even as he seeks to protect me."

"You might best protect him by giving him his freedom."

"And what then? What would happen to him?"

"He might go home, where his heart lies."

She retorted, "You know nothing about his heart."

"Embra, look at me."

She did, her chin lifting with unconscious pride, light flaring in her eyes.

He challenged, "Is that how you think of me? No better than a slave to be used and manipulated?"

"By Freya's heart, nei. I have told you how I feel for you. You refuse to believe me."

He stared at her stonily.

"Or perhaps," her chin jerked higher still, "you merely do not want what I offer you."

221

He wanted but three things—to recover Mistress Catrin, gather his men, and sail away from this place, never to return.

With defiance in her eyes, Embra went on, "You are angry because you believe I seek to use you. Could I not accuse you of the same? I am fit for coupling, but the prospect of marrying me horrifies you, so it seems."

When again he said nothing, she spoke further. "Why will you not believe I have proposed this marriage in an effort to protect you?"

"As you protect Kennach."

"Ja. Ja! Magnus, you perceive not the danger in which you stand."

His anger rose again. He waved an arm at her. "You play at some game. With Asger, with your brother. Who can be smart enough, and sly enough to hold the place of jarl? You care for little beyond that."

She closed her eyes an instant, a woman in pain. "I cannot convince you."

"This place is a bed of deceit, inhabited by madmen and women."

"Perhaps. Perhaps so."

"Why has Runi seized Catrin and hidden her?"

"He might tell you he did it to protect her."

"I am asking you."

She shook her head. "I do not know."

Disgust and dismay filled Magnus in equal measures. "I will return to my boat and there await the outcome of this tangle."

But at the door, she barred his way. "I cannot allow it."

"Eh?"

"If you go to your boat alone, Ulrik's supporters

will attack you again. They will fire the boat. You are already sore wounded."

Ja, and if he slipped into the berserker's fit again, depleted as he was, he might pay a hefty price.

By Odin's eye! He was trapped. And it seemed he needed Embra, needed to use her, even as she did him.

What was this place, and this woman, making of him?

****

Magnus slept. He lay in Embra's bed opposite the fire, even while she sat beside the hearth alone, afraid to join him.

She, who admitted to fearing so little.

He needed his rest. She told herself that over and over again. His body must heal and so, she suspected, must his spirit. As for his anger, that had left him but slowly. She'd listened while he moved restlessly in the bed, fighting it until weariness claimed him.

Leaving Embra prey to her thoughts.

He hated her. That thought, among the many, had the power to hurt her most. The only man in the world she would ever love, and he detested everything about her.

Well, not everything. He'd enjoyed her body and the sharing of it. The passion. That, she saw quite clearly, was not love.

She wanted him, and she loved him—two very different things. When they lay together, when he was inside her, those two things came together and she found perfection, bliss. A kind of wholeness she'd never imagined.

Yet—yet perhaps those things did not come together for him. Perhaps when he spent himself upon her and gave her his seed, it was only an act of release, nothing more.

The thought hurt far more than any blow. She would do whatever she could, whatever she must to protect him. It would not matter what she did, for when the moment came he would sail away from her without a backward look.

Even marriage would not prevent that. It was what Runi had tried to tell her.

Runi—her sole ally, and she wanted to strangle him. Magnus was right, everyone around her played at games.

Everyone except Magnus.

An honest man. Was that why she had fallen for him? But nei, there were a thousand other reasons. The light that filled his eyes. His grave demeanor broken by a rueful smile. His quick intelligence and the humor that lurked beneath the surface.

The truth was—the truth was she admired everything about the man.

To stand above the harbor and watch him sail away—it would break her in two.

At least the ground had stilled, and fire no longer spat into the sky. Were the gods satisfied? Were they appeased by her humiliation?

It did not matter. She had but one aim, to protect Magnus. Changed forever, she arose and joined him in the bed.

****

The dream began with deceptive calm. Magnus stood on the clifftop back in Sorvagur, high above the bay. He could see his father's boats riding below, including the one in which he'd sailed to Husavik.

Home. He had come home.

The relief of it nearly staggered him. He drew a deep breath, expanding his chest, and felt all the lies, all the deception fall away from him like chains.

Far, far across the water—well out of his reach—lay Husavik. He could see it no more. And his heart rejoiced.

He turned his head when someone called his name. His family approached along the green clifftop—all those dear to him. Here came Fadir and Modir arm in arm, his father giving one of his rare smiles at seeing him. And Gyda with a bundle in either arm, side by side with Lodvar, who wore his deep blue robes, and the sigils woven through his brown hair.

No one else? Surely someone was missing.

His heart protested the truth of it even as he watched his family come to meet him.

Modir embraced him. "Welcome home, son!"

And Fadir. "Magnus, you have done well."

Had he? Then why did he feel this terrible sense of loss?

He smiled despite it and stepped to Gyda's side, peering at each of the children in her arms. "Nieces? Or nephews, Sostir?"

She turned back the edges of the swaddling cloths. "Two nephews for you, two sons for me."

He embraced her, careful of the new life she cradled.

Lastly he turned to Lodvar, who clasped his arm as a brother might. Lodvar regarded him with troubled eyes.

"Are you not happy to see me, my friend?" Magnus asked.

"Very happy."

"I did well. I brought your mother."

"And I will be forever grateful to you. Yet you forgot."

"Forgot?" In the dream, Magnus frowned.

"You forgot your own happiness." Lodvar turned and pointed over the water. "You have left her behind."

Lodvar's tawny golden eyes returned to Magnus's face. "You must go back. For you neglected to bring your heart."

Chapter Thirty-One

Magnus awoke when Embra slid into the bed with him. He lay with his eyes wide, contemplating the dream while she pressed her body to his, throwing one arm over him in a gesture of possession—or protection. The feel and the scent of her enfolded him.

Unexpectedly and unpreventably, his heart rose.

He lay with his eyes wide while she planted her cheek against his shoulder, wondering at the dream, and the emotions that filled him. Something more than lust, though his body tightened at her nearness.

He could not possibly be falling in love with this woman. It would be the single most foolish act of his life. He needed someone steady and gentle and, well, like Astrid, when he thought about it. Someone who did not have a mind sharper than his axe and the capacity to deceive.

Yet—Astrid did not make him feel like this, she never had. She didn't accelerate his heartbeat with a single look, a single touch.

If he left Embra here, if he sailed away home just like in the dream, would he leave part of himself behind?

Nei, nei. He did not love her. He might love the way her hair smelled. The weight of her breasts in his hands. Perhaps even the way she looked at him. But there could be no love without trust. Could there?

That question transfixed him. Had Modir trusted Fadir when they met? Nay, for he'd been her conqueror and she a slave. He'd claimed her as a spoil of battle.

Now they could not live without one another.

And Gyda—Lodvar had first come to her as the right-hand of her enemy, Gunnar Fritisson, a man twice as deceptive as this woman who lay beside him.

Her brother.

Gyda and Lodvar had bonded on a spiritual level. They spoke into one another's minds, and hearts.

Would loving Embra truly be a step so far?

He lay while her warmth seeped into him and tried to imagine the future. He'd never been good at that. The women of his family were the ones blessed with clairvoyance.

He was but an ordinary man, willing to work hard, to battle for what he loved. If he could choose, though, he would choose peace.

He could not imagine Embra Fritisdottir bringing him that.

Restless, he turned in the bed and she tipped her face up to his, pressing closer. Their lips met.

Ach, by Odin's eye. No one had ever told him about the fire. His friends, ja, they talked of the pleasures to be found with a woman. He'd never suspected it could fair unhinge a man's mind.

Embra murmured in approval as the flames licked through them both, and parted her lips beneath his. Helpless to resist, he dove in. Capturing his hand, she brought it to her breast.

That was not love. He would need to be a fool indeed to love a woman such as this.

Yet she invited him in, his body and his spirit. Just

like the berserker's fit when it came, she made him something he'd never expected to be.

Mouths joined, they undressed each other, a difficult feat nevertheless accomplished in little time. Skin to skin, things got so much better, especially when Embra slipped beneath him and parted her legs.

Still not love. Merely coupling.

He captured her hands, one in either of his, and pinned them against the bed. Rearing up, he gazed into her face by the light of the dying fire.

Eyes wide, she gazed back at him.

"Embra? Embra, how would you have me?"

"Any way." She licked her lips. "Any way you will take me."

Flagrantly hard, he already hovered at the entrance to her heat, and could readily plunge inside. He could take what he wanted, as she said, and sail away. Or could he?

With a hint of defiance she said, "I have never offered myself so to any man. Only you."

He believed her. Had he forgotten that amid all the deception, they had vowed truth?

"I want you, Magnus." She whispered it. "I want you forever."

Forever. The word possessed his mind as she recaptured his mouth and he slid into her welcoming heat. They moved together with ease and passion, like one person, until it turned wild, and the fire rose to consume them.

Forever, as the waves of pleasure engulfed her first, and milked him dry. The word sang through his blood, pumped through him in time with his heartbeats.

When it was done, he lifted himself over her again,

one hand at each of her wrists, and looked at the picture she made. Hair wild, breasts dampened with sweat, eyes two darkened caverns in which he glimpsed … well, that just might be eternity.

Might he claim this—claim her—for himself? By all that was holy, dared he?

"Wed with me, Magnus." She did not beg, nor did she cajole. She met him stare to stare, equal to equal, and his heart opened in response.

"Wed with me. Make me your bride."

He kissed her, taking his time with it, sounding the depths of the emotions that filled him. still holding her beneath him, he lifted his head to regard her again.

"Ja, Embra. Ja, I will."

****

The wedding was brief, with none of the trappings customary back home—the food, the music, and the fancy clothing. It had to be public, as Embra informed Magnus, in order to secure its purpose. All the elders must be there to witness their joining, along with the remaining members of her family.

She informed him of all this while they dressed the next morning, when the doubts crowded his mind. He'd agreed to wed with Friti Gunnarsson's daughter. Was he mad?

Ja, possibly the madness inherent in this place now infected him. When he looked at Embra as she dressed, though, with her hair spilling down her back and her expression intent, he felt certain.

He did not know why, but wedding with her felt like the right thing to do. Sometimes a man had to act on—well, on faith.

Could he pin his faith to Embra Fritisdottir?

"I want my men there." He looked her in the eye. "All of them."

And so they were. The gathering occurred at the great hall, and everyone came, including Vanja and Asger, the latter looking sour, perhaps because they beat him to marriage. Apsel arrived in company with Dagmar. He did not look like a prisoner, and stood with his arm draped over his captor's shoulders. Neither did he look ill-used, save possibly in Dagmar's bed.

Runi attended, though he remained silent throughout. Bright sunlight blessed the union, and even the ground remained docile and quiet.

A shaman, perhaps Lodvar's replacement, spoke the words that joined them, and asked for their declarations. The doubt that hovered in Magnus's mind remained until the end, when he looked into Embra's eyes and averred, "I am hereforth your husband."

Then he felt—certain. Sure. Triumphant, even. Everything else about his mission, about this place might be wrong. Not this.

After, there was not much celebrating. Asger and his supporters grumbled until Embra spoke up.

"With our marriage, the settlements at Sorvagur and here at Husavik are joined. This, as jarl, I have accomplished for you. You will respect and honor my husband as you do me."

And so she granted him a measure of power. Testing the extent of it, he called out, "I want my men released and allowed access to my boat. We are no longer enemies here."

Louder grumbling, but Embra nodded. "So will it be."

The shaman spoke a final blessing. The crowd

began to break up and drift away, all except for Runi and Vanja, who stepped up with Asger still in tow.

She glared into Embra's face. "I suppose, Sostir, you believe you have got one over on me, performing your marriage ahead of mine."

"That is not why I have wed with him."

Vanja snarled, "Why, then?"

Embra eyed her sister. "I doubt you would understand."

Vanja gave a throaty laugh. "Never tell me you think you love him? Him? I will admit, the fact that he's a berserker is seductive. And the possibility he could father another such berserker upon you. But not enough to make you bond with a half-slave."

Embra breathed, "Better than a grasping, avaricious old man." She flicked a glance at Asger. "I will be surprised if your betrothed can fulfil his duties."

Asger growled and Vanja threw her head back. "He has already given me a child. And he satisfies me right well in our bed."

Runi, standing by and listening, grinned. "I was not aware anything could satisfy you in that regard, Sostir."

Vanja spat at him, "You! Traitor. You should be supporting my claim."

"Why? Embra is the elder of the two of you. She is certainly more fair-minded. If I do not want the place of jarl, she should have it."

"We shall see about that." Vanja glared at him through narrowed eyes before turning back to Embra. "Remember, Sostir, she who is a bride can soon be a widow."

Embra stepped up. "Harm one hair of him, Sostir, and I shall carve out your eyes with a dull knife. Then see what man will want you in his bed."

Vanja looked startled and Runi laughed. Ach, into what had Magnus got himself? Before he could let himself contemplate that fully, he turned to Apsel and Dagmar, who had lingered.

"Are you well?" he asked his man, and good friend.

"I am."

"You are free now to do as you wish. Gather the other men and return to the boat."

"Ja?" Apsel's gaze questioned him. "What are your plans?"

"We will discuss that later."

Apsel nodded, glanced at the woman beside him, and said, "I will gather the men. But if I am free to do as I wish—"

"You are."

"Then I believe I will continue to stay with Mistress Dagmar a while yet."

Magnus's heart sank. He shot a look at Dagmar, who appeared both smug and defiant.

Magnus towed his friend away from her. "Are you mad?"

Apsel failed to look abashed. "The rutting is like nothing I've ever had. She even called in a second woman for a time, so we could   "

"I do not want to know."

"If we are leaving—" Apsel looked inquiring. "Are we leaving?"

"When the time is right."

"Well then, Magnus, I would enjoy myself until that time."

In horror, at that moment Magnus realized that

Husavik had seduced them.
It had seduced them all.

Chapter Thirty-Two

"Now that you have tightened your control," Runi told Embra, "it should be safe to bring Mistress Catrin back." He gave Embra a searching look. "You are in control here, are you not?"

Embra hoped so, although things kept threatening to slip away from her. She'd done what she could to protect Magnus. All it would take, though, to upset the balance was a further scheme on Asger's part, or a rumble from the ground.

Vanja's wedding was set for the morrow. Would that change anything?

She eyed Runi thoughtfully. "Where is Mistress Catrin?"

"Safe with a friend." He jerked his head to the south. "Inland."

"A friend? What friend?" There were, ja, other settlements in Iceland. None within walking distance.

Uncharacteristically, Runi hesitated. The two of them stood outside the hall, following her wedding, while inside, Magnus met with a number of his men. Embra tried not to worry about what he planned.

To leave her? So soon?

Staring away toward the harbor, Runi said, "The identity of my friend cannot be revealed, Sostir. Not even to you." He switched his gaze to her face. "To do so would endanger her. I am certain you, above all others, understand the desire to protect where one—cares deeply."

Embra's brows flew up. An extraordinary statement coming from Runi who, to her knowledge, never admitted caring for anyone.

"Ah. Is your friend a former slave?" Occasionally slaves here in Husavik did try to run. Most were caught and punished so severely—as a lesson to others—many died as a result. She supposed the few who escaped recapture might have joined together and formed a community somewhere, though she'd never heard of it.

Runi gave her a hard stare. "You need not know."

Embra shrugged. She could ask Mistress Catrin, when she returned.

As if he heard her thoughts, Runi said, "And Mistress Catrin will not remember."

"Why not? Have you kept her sedated?"

"Sostir, you ask far too many questions. I will go and retrieve her today. That is all you need to know. But you had better hope the land remains quiet, else the folk of Husavik may decide a sacrifice is required after all."

Her chin jerked up. "If so, you may be sure it will not be my husband."

****

"What is the mood among your men?" Embra asked when she reentered the hall, all Magnus's men having filed past her as they left.

Magnus shrugged. A good question. "Most are happy to be freed and will return to my longboat. Some—" He hesitated. "Some have requested permission to stay where they are."

She perched beside him on the step of the dais,

where he sat. "Ah. This troubles you."

Deeply, though Magnus could scarcely say so. If he admitted Apsel had been seduced by Dagmar, would he not have to acknowledge he had been, by Embra? This woman with her clear eyes and strong mind. Ach, ja, he had been seduced. How could he blame Apsel?

"Many things trouble me," he admitted.

"Runi will go today and retrieve Mistress Catrin. So long as I keep my grasp on things here, she should be safe—as should you. I hoped we might discuss—well, what comes next."

Magnus nodded soberly. He would have to leave her. Shake the dust of this mad place from his heels and sail. The question was, when?

"My reason for coming here was to bring Mistress Catrin back to Sorvagur."

"For Lodvar."

"For Lodvar."

"You lied to me. You said you'd come to bring us word about my father's and brother's deaths."

"That too. It was not a lie."

"And to form an alliance with Husavik."

"That, surely our marriage has accomplished."

Unable to help himself, he cupped her cheek in one hand. "Embra, I have kept my vow. I have not lied to you."

Her eyes flooded with emotions he could not name. "Say you will not leave me."

Magnus kept silent.

"Please—"

"I cannot make that promise. You know I must return to Sorvagur. You have always known that."

"Magnus—" She caught his hand in both of hers.

"I know you hate it here. You think us a pit of poisonous vipers. But you and I—we have found a place of truth among all the deception and lies. Does that count for nothing?"

"It does. But—"

"Does our marriage count for nothing?"

He found he could not claim that. She mattered to him. Far more, in truth, than made him comfortable.

Did he love this woman? Or did what he felt belong under the name of lust? He thought again of the love between his father and mother, deep and sustaining, enough to save one another in times of strife. Of Gyda and Lodvar, who were joined at the roots of their very souls.

Maybe, he thought with a touch of despair, such glory was not for the likes of him, a simple man and little more. Perhaps he, like Apsel, might be satisfied by the physical, bone-deep pleasures of coupling. Embra certainly provided him that.

"I think you are an extraordinary woman, one with a remarkable mind. I admire your strength and the truth you offer me."

"Then," she clasped his hand still tighter, "stay here with me. Send your men back to Sorvagur with the woman, and remain here to help me lead Husavik."

Magnus narrowed his eyes. Was that what she wanted? Had it been her aim all the while?

"Magnus, I promise we will lead together, equally. We can change things here, make a difference in Husavik. With Runi's help, we can make it better for the slaves who live here, hand out fair decisions, and choose members for the council who are less corrupt."

"Or you could come away with me." Magnus's

own words surprised him. He'd not expected to say them. From whence had they come? Up till now, he'd merely contemplated the idea.

Did he want her with him, this daughter of madness, in the peace of Sorvagur? Could he even conceive of it?

Her eyes flooded with anguish. "If I leave here, Magnus, if I cede the place of jarl—especially to a man such as Asger—it will descend into chaos. No rules. No morals. Vanja will act as Asger's means of seizing total corrupt power. Life will be tolerable for no one left here."

"Cannot Runi take that burden from you?"

"Runi plays at his own game. I am not sure where his heart lies. Magnus, send Mistress Catrin home and stay here with me—just for a time. Let us see if we can establish a fair set of rules and find someone to lead in my stead. Then—then I will consider sailing to Sorvagur with you."

"How long? How long will that take?" Magnus shook his head. He could not imagine Husavik being, ever, a place of fairness or sanity.

"I cannot say. But with you, a berserker, at my side we can outface Asger and assure it."

Ah, so was it just politics that mattered to her after all? Even as Magnus gazed into Embra's eyes, he wondered. Hc believed she spoke the truth to him, as she saw it. Perhaps, however, she lacked the capacity for selfless love.

"Should I stay," he said heavily, trying hard to see the future, "it will only become more difficult to leave. You will be loath to release power."

"I will not."

"There may be children, some locked into the succession. Some may be born berserkers. I have seen how the folk here react to such."

She blinked. "Children."

"Surely you have considered that? Given what has already passed between us—"

She released his hand and turned away. He watched her struggle visibly with the notion.

"I intended never to bear children. I did not have a good example of motherhood, with Modir being mad and confined. You are right, carrying the child of a berserker would give me great status." She turned back to look at him. "You cannot believe that is why I chose to wed with you."

"I am not sure what I believe, Embra."

"Our truth—"

"Our truth is strong, ja. But you can only give me, as truth, what you are convinced you believe."

She stared at him. "You think I do not know my own mind."

"I think there are powerful forces at work here, including what we feel toward one another. Embra, listen to this. Let me take Catrin home. You consolidate your power here and I will sail back for you. We can make a decision then. Perhaps the time spent apart will allow us, our minds and spirits, to gain some clarity."

"Sail back for me," she repeated, aghast.

"Ja, so I do vow."

"When?"

"Perhaps next year."

"Next year?" She sprang to her feet.

Magnus followed and they faced one another.

"Magnus Tolljursson, if you can suggest such a

lengthy separation, then you do not love me as I wish. You do not love me at all."

"Embra," Magnus began before the words died on his lips.

Perhaps he did not.

Chapter Thirty-Three

Mistress Catrin appeared unharmed, if mildly confused, when at last Embra saw her. Runi brought the woman to Embra's quarters, and she sent immediately for Magnus, who'd returned to his boat. To speak with his men and see to things, so he'd told her.

She suspected he had other motives.

Following their discussion in the hall—for it could not be called a quarrel—he'd been unable to look her in the eye and had made an excuse to leave.

Was her marriage over before it had begun?

Now she looked at Mistress Catrin and tried to decide what to do. Runi stood silent near the door, preventing Embra from asking the woman such questions as she would.

Embra shot a look at him before she inquired, "Mistress, are you well?"

Catrin inclined her head. She wore her brown hair scraped back from her face and confined in a braid. Today she did not wear a head covering, and her clothing was plain in the extreme. Even though her former master, Harald, had eventually married her, she appeared still the slave.

"No one has harmed you?"

Mistress Catrin's eyes swiveled to Runi. Did she fear him? But she said, "Nay, Mistress."

She did not seem afraid. Her voice, like her

demeanor, remained almost too calm. Perhaps Runi—or those with whom he'd left the woman—had dosed her with some draught.

Greatly daring, Embra asked, "Can you tell me where you have been these many days past?"

Runi stirred but did not object.

Catrin leaned toward Embra, a tick of animation touching her features for the first time. "Mistress, do you believe in magic?"

Embra was not sure she did. The gods, like the spirits of the land, possessed power, ja. Power, she understood. As for anything more—

She shook her head.

"You should," Catrin spoke earnestly. "You truly should."

Embra shot another look at Runi before focusing on Catrin again. Was the woman half mad, like everyone else in Husavik?

Magnus came in through the door, his presence affecting Embra like a sudden blow. Indeed, how could she control her reaction to him?

He moved quietly for such a big man, and exchanged glances with Embra and Runi before hunkering down at Catrin's side.

"Mistress?" He peered into her face. "Do you know who I am?"

She turned a searching stare on him. For a moment her expression remained blank. Then a hint of interest sparked in her eyes. "You—you have the look of someone I once held dear."

"I am Magnus Tolljursson."

"Och, son of the berserker?"

"Ja."

"And son of my friend, Eadha."

"I am." Very gently he took her hands in his. "Lodvar sent me. He wishes for me to take you to him, in Sorvagur."

"Lodvar!"

"He has wed with my sister, Gyda, there. He could not come himself because she is great with child." He smiled. "You may well be a grand modir by now."

Tears filled her eyes. "He is well, my son?"

"Ja, very well, save for worry on your behalf. He holds the place of shaman in Sorvagur, as did Kaddi once."

"This is good."

"Very good, ja. Will you sail back to Sorvagur with me?"

With me. Embra's whole body tensed. He did not say, will you let me send you to Sorvagur?

For an instant she had to turn her face away, so great was the pain. Despite their truth, Magnus did not love her.

What a cruel trick for the gods to play, that the first and only man to whom she could give her heart did not want it.

And could she bear this? Surely so. What was she, a weakling? She'd been raised up on lack of love. Why should she expect anything else now?

"Leave here?" Catrin pondered it, her foggy wits seeming to move more ably. "I have lived in this place more than a score of years—if it can be called living."

"Then come to Sorvagur where you will be welcome. My mother is there. And others you knew here years ago. Your grandchildren—"

"Children? More than one?"

Magnus smiled. "When I left, Gyda was expecting twins."

"A wonder!" She searched his face again. "You have the look of your mother, and her father before her. I knew him because we came from the same settlement. You knew that? Captured in the raids. I was taken first, taken away from all I knew. She came after. I tried to help her, tried to warn her. Do not go to the berserker, I said. None of us wanted to be at his bidding. But she could not choose. And he was good to her, in the end."

"My father loves her very much."

"Aye, she was more fortunate than she knew. Your grandfather—he was a great man in Lewis. He was chief of our settlement."

"Ja, so my modir told me. She says he died in the fighting the night she was captured."

"Death is a release. I believed it the only release available to me. Now, you come."

"Will you sail with me, Mistress Catrin? Sorvagur may not be Lewis, but for us it is home."

"Aye, bonnie lad. Aye, I will go."

****

The figure slipped through the shadows ahead of Embra, more than half hidden by the ground mist that mirrored the clouds overhead. The moon sailed like a longboat in and out of those clouds, flickering. A fine night to follow and not be seen.

She'd come out to gaze at the harbor below the settlement, and in particular at one boat there. Magnus had helped Mistress Catrin pack up her meager belongings before taking her to wait aboard with his men.

Wait to sail.

The very thought made it hard for Embra to breathe. He planned to leave her, and soon—so soon, he felt it necessary to take Mistress Catrin aboard now. And naught Embra said could turn his mind.

Her predicament made it impossible to sleep. And slipping out in the depths of the night, she'd caught sight of Runi.

His tall, slender figure seemed to flicker like the moonlight, silver into darkness. He walked with purpose up the rise that led away from the harbor, and south from the settlement.

With very little hesitation, Embra trailed him.

Curiosity made her do so. Runi kept far too many secrets and shared too little of himself with her.

So she moved lightly, ducking into the shadows, the sound of the wind covering her footfalls. Not difficult to remain unseen while in the settlement, but beyond lay open country, green turf studded with rock and scrub, with little cover.

Runi moved swiftly, as if he knew his path. His long stride ate up the distance. Embra had to scramble at times, and once or twice when he turned his head, she ducked down to blend into the turf.

Where could he be going, this brodir of hers? And why?

When they had walked far from the settlement, and she'd lost sight of the harbor over her shoulder, he veered east. Soon, a sound reached her ears over the rush of the wind—one that sent a shiver down her spine.

By Freya's heart, what was that?

She paused, even though Runi, well ahead of her, kept walking. Her ears pricked, and the chill that possessed her spine seeped into her blood.

Someone was singing.

She scanned the open country ahead of her and could spot no one. Certainly, that was not Runi's voice. Rather, it sounded like a woman, high-pitched and crooning, a song unlike any that had ever before met Embra's ears. More a wail than a song, it drilled its way into her mind.

Runi, now well ahead of her, paused. The land all around him moved with moon shadows, tricking Embra's eyes. When she saw the figure dart forward to meet her brother, she blinked against the flickering light. Who was that? What?

The figure reached Runi and they joined hands. For an instant they stood so, gladness transfiguring them, before they moved into an embrace and became one.

Embra gasped. Impossible for them to hear her at such a distance. But both figures turned in a single movement and fixed their gazes upon her.

Ach, what to do? She would not run from her brother. She did not fear Runi. And if he'd met with a woman—what danger could she pose?

Before the thought crystalized in her mind, the female figure moved. Like one of the shadows, it swooped toward Embra, as if it flew rather than ran.

She wanted to flee then. A prickle of superstitious horror founded the impulse. Nothing human could move that way. This must be some deity.

Runi came behind, running as fast as he could, but Embra spared him barely a glance.

The figure gathered its own light as it came. By the time it reached Embra, it glowed softly, an astounding sight.

She—for the being was definitely female—was small in stature but emanated power along with that light. She wore leggings and a tunic like a boy, though no other hint of the masculine touched her. In the moonlight, her hair, which she wore in a myriad of braids, looked white—the very color of the moonlight—her features sharp, yet beautiful. Her eyes—Embra who feared little, directed one look there before she hastily tore her gaze away.

Not human.

Runi reached them. "Sostir! You should not have followed me."

In his gaze, Embra saw regret and fear that set her back on her heels. Runi feared very little.

"Brodir, who is this?"

The female turned her head to him. "This is your sister?" She sang the words, in a way that argued they were not her native tongue.

"Ja." Runi puffed out a breath. "She trailed me. I did not know."

The small being—for she barely reached Runi's shoulder—looked Embra up and down carefully before she said, "Well, if she is your kin, then I do not suppose I can kill her."

Chapter Thirty-Four

"Who are you?" Embra's voice trembled. Like Runi, she did not fear much. Growing up, she'd faced her father and all his drunken cohorts. She'd weathered Gunnar at his most cruel. She'd endured wild emotions from the madwoman she knew to be her mother. She was strong.

Indeed, the only thing that truly frightened her, up to this point, had been the prospect of harm befalling Magnus. Now fear rose raw in her chest and gripped her by the throat. The fear she felt was for herself.

Ach, with what had Runi entangled himself?

She glanced at her brother, hoping he might answer her question. He looked pale but steady, his gaze fixed on she who had come to meet him.

Then he did answer. "Sostir, this is Borlika." When he spoke, the woman who was not a woman stiffened and turned to him. He grasped her small hands. "She is an elf."

Embra gasped. To be sure, she'd heard stories of the elves in childhood. A part of the land they were, elementals. They could be friendly or malicious. They could be dangerous, if they took a dislike to you. Children who were out when they should not be might well run afoul of them. No one wise ever crossed or angered them.

A near-forgotten memory came into her head. If

one angered them, they might shake the very earth.

Ja, but surely they weren't real?

Only, the creature standing in front of Embra was as real as the ground beneath their feet, the green turf and the gray rocks. Embra could feel that, just as she could feel Borlika's power. Elemental, ja, as fire.

And Runi stood with his hands joined to the creature's like—like a lover.

Nei. Impossible.

All the times Runi had been missing from the settlement, when he'd slipped away—had he been with the elves? A hysterical laugh rose to Embra's throat. An old adage, that—*he is away with the elves.*

"Is this where you brought Catrin? To—to her?"

Borlika said something in a foreign tongue. It flowed like water clattering over stones, even more musical than what the Gaelic slaves spoke.

Runi cautioned Embra, "Show some respect." He hurried on before she could speak. "You should not have come. Now it is too late."

Borlika said in Norse, "What is seen cannot be unseen, not even if I put out her eyes."

To Runi, she said, "You did not know she followed? You grow careless."

He made a face but did not differ with her opinion.

Embra confronted the possibility that she might be about to die. It tasted unpalatable on her tongue. Her life up till now had not been what she might call an easy journey. She did not, however, want it to end—not now, when she'd found Magnus.

She looked to her brother. Could he help her?

He said something to the elven woman, surprisingly in the elvish tongue. They stepped away together and stood with their heads close together, speaking—well, like lovers.

Runi had taken an elven lover.

She should not be shocked. He had always been different. Other. Driven by his own impulses and answering to voices no one else heard. But this—it stole Embra's breath away.

On edge, she waited while they conversed together, Runi persuading earnestly—no doubt arguing for Embra's life—while the wind grew stronger, making the clouds race more swiftly overhead. The whole world flickered in black and silver.

At last Borlika turned and looked at her, looked hard, and Embra felt the power of it just like the wind, springing up from the ground and flowing through her, a physical pain.

Magnus, she thought—only his name—before the silver light exploded around her, and then everything went dark.

****

A fire burned low and steady, a red eye in the darkness. The eye did not blink, but flickered. Alive. The fire was alive.

So was Embra.

The realization brought her little comfort. She hurt all over as if she'd received a sound thrashing, and a bitter taste filled her mouth.

She stirred and nearly cried out when, beside her, one of the shadows that filled the room shifted.

Someone was here with her.

"Magnus?"

"Nei, it is me, Runi."

"Runi. Where are we?" Prisoners of that beautiful,

terrifying creature they had met?

"Home. You are home."

To be sure, she was. She lay in a nest of blankets beside her own hearth. The very place where she and Magnus had made love.

He was not here, though, and her heart ached for want of him.

"How did we get here?"

"I carried you, after Borlika struck you down."

"She struck me down? Did I fall?" Embra did not remember that.

"Ja. Let me tell you, you do not make an easy burden all that distance. But," Runi sounded longsuffering, "my choices were few."

"You brought me home?"

"Did I not just say so?"

"Ach, by Freya's heart, thank you." Embra felt weak with relief. "I thought she would kill me on the spot, or put out my eyes."

"So did I. You have only my persuasive tongue to thank."

Embra struggled to sit up. Runi assisted her.

"You never should have followed me, Sostir. It was a foolish thing to do."

"Well, if you had shared with me that you ventured into the realm of the elves, I would have kept well clear. Runi, I thought their existence a mere tale."

"Clearly not."

"Clearly." She thought about it, struggling for acceptance. "How did you come to form an association with such a—a being?"

Runi sat back slightly. "I have known Borlika since I was a small boy. I used to run away from here when things became, well, unbearable. Much of our childhood was."

"Ja." Embra could only agree.

"I do not know if you remember," his voice became distant, as if he recited an Edda, "for a time I used to visit Modir. From when I was five or so, till I was perhaps eleven or twelve, I stopped in to see her most every day."

"Nei, I do not remember that."

"Gunnar belittled me for it. You know how he was. In front of his friends, he would sneer and call me a mama's boy."

"I know how he was."

"Do not mistake me. I knew Modir was mad. Sometimes when I went to see her, though, she seemed well. She would call me her fine boy. I would watch her comb her hair. It was—ach, comforting, I suppose."

They had all suffered from the lack of mothering and from a father who treated them like mere possessions.

"Then, when I was, as I say, eleven or so, I found her one day in a different mood. Ach, I had seen her raving, angry, impatient, pacing her chamber and demanding release. This day, her mood was like nothing I'd ever encountered." Runi paused, cleared his throat, and went on, nearly without emotion, "She tried to seduce me. I did not understand what she was about, at first. I had seen Fadir with enough women, though, and his men with the slaves at the bath house, to have an inkling. She—she touched me. No modir should touch her son that way."

"Runi, by the gods!"

"No different from Fadir and Vanja, is it? I ran. I

ran hard and I ran far. Into the countryside. I wanted never to come back."

"So I imagine."

"Borlika found me hunkered down in a fold of the land, weeping."

Hard to imagine this brother of hers weeping for any reason. Runi, these days, was all about composure.

"She looked as she does now. Elves age very slowly. I was a child. She took pity on me."

Also difficult to imagine. The being Embra had met did not appear to possess any pity.

"She cradled me. Comforted me. I knew what she was—a part of the land. I considered her a living representation of this place, the rocks, the waters.

"She told me I could come to her any time. So I have done."

"All these years?"

"All these years."

"And no one ever knew?"

Runi shook his head. "There is an advantage, so it emerges, in having no one who cares where you are or what you are doing. Nobody noticed when I slipped away, sometimes for days."

"I noticed. I knew you took off sometimes on your own. Who would not want to escape from our lives? I never thought you went anywhere in particular. Just— just roving."

"Usually, Borlika and I were on our own. Sometimes she took me back to the elven settlement."

"Settlement!"

"It is the closest name I have for it, though it is nothing like our settlement, Husavik. It is mostly underground. Do not bother, Sostir, to search. You will not find it."

Embra shivered. "I will not try."

"Her folk disapproved of her bringing me there, but they never harmed me. It would not be so, for others of our kind."

"I see."

"There are others of our kind there. Some escaped slaves. A few snatched as infants. You would not want to live as they do. But Borlika has status. I am protected."

"What is it like, their kingdom?"

Runi shook his head. "Like nothing you have ever imagined. Full of light, and darkness. Connected—connected as I say to the land itself. It is they cause the rumblings in the ground, the fire in the sky. It is their anger, unleashed."

"Why are they angry?"

"They do not like our settlement, and abhor the growth of it. More interlopers, Borlika often complains to me, and more."

"I am surprised she does not hate you."

Runi's eyes met Embra's. "I am surprised you do not hate Magnus. His kind killed your father."

"Ah. Ja."

They sat in silence for several moments, thinking of possibilities, and impossibilities.

"If Borlika was a comfort to you"—a replacement mother, perhaps—"how then did you become lovers?"

He laughed. A typical Runi laugh it was, wry and self-deprecating. "I grew. I became a man. She and I were already connected in ways I cannot express. We found our bodies fit together. Well enough, anyway."

Embra tried not to feel shocked.

Runi gave her a pained smile. "Anyway, would Modir not have had me as her lover?"

"That is Modir. She is barely sane."

"And Borlika and her kind do not reason as we do. The act does not mean to them what it means to us."

What did it mean, precisely, here in Husavik? Dominance over a slave, self-pleasure, whenever one could get it.

Perhaps not so different, then.

"Do you love her?"

Again, Runi laughed. "Do I understand the meaning of that word? Was I ever taught? I care for you, Sostir, above the other members of our parents' unholy brood. And I care for Borlika on a level so deep I have no words for it. If love is need, then ja. I love her."

If love is need. Perhaps it was. Embra needed Magnus both physically and spiritually. She would be willing to sacrifice anything for him.

She caught Runi's hand in hers. Seldom enough did they touch, and only rarely in affection. His head jerked up, and he looked at her in surprise.

"Brodir," she said, "love is a rare and precious thing. We must take it where found, and hold to it most ferociously."

Chapter Thirty-Five

"Please, tell me about my son."

The request came softly from Mistress Catrin and floated out over the darkened water. Evening had fallen, and Magnus along with Catrin and most of his men had returned to the longboat. The men busied themselves about the craft, checking the equipment, while Magnus and Catrin sat together.

Clouds raced overhead, playing chase with the moon.

She looked worn and tired, her face lined, her brown hair liberally streaked with gray. About her thoughts she revealed little—a skill she must have perfected over the years in order to protect herself. She showed little relief at being away at last from the settlement where she'd served so long as a slave, or gladness at the prospect of being reunited with Lodvar.

"He is well. Happy."

"Good. That is—good."

What did more than a score years of slavery do to a person? This. *This.*

"He is, as I say, wed with my sister. They have a quite extraordinary relationship."

"Imagine—my son wed with Eadha's daughter. We were such close friends, once."

"So she did always tell me. She remembers you fondly, and told me she tried to take you with her when

257

she and my father left Husavik. Your master, Lodvar's father, refused to let you go no matter the price my father offered."

"Harald." She spoke her former master's name with neither liking nor loathing. "Dead now."

"Ja. He married you, so Lodvar said."

"After his wife died, he did."

"Were things better for you after that?"

She gazed at him from hollow eyes. "Better? Who can say? He did it because he did not want anyone to snatch me away. He was old and poorly by then, and wanted someone to look after him."

"I see."

"His children—his legitimate ones, that is—all hated me. As so they should. I was a slave, worth nothing."

The pronouncement shocked Magnus. His mother, too, had been a slave, yet she'd managed always to keep a high opinion of herself, had known her worth.

"You will be comfortable in Sorvagur, Mistress, and very, very welcome. Lodvar is a man of high stature there, and as I say holds the honored place of shaman. He cannot wait to see you, nor can my mother."

Catrin said nothing.

"And I am certain," Magnus continued, hoping to lift her spirits, "you will be very glad to see your grandchildren." He remembered his dream and Gyda with a babe on each arm. Had that been true?

"Part Norse. Part Gael," she said.

"Indeed, like myself."

Suddenly and without warning, Catrin began to weep. The men on the deck looked askance, but

Magnus sat quietly, letting her sob into her hands. Modir had once told him, *Son, when a woman needs to weep, let her do so.*

At length, she dried her eyes on her skirt and lifted her face to the sky. "I wonder if those bairns—blessed bairns—be wee girls, wee boys or one o' each?"

"I know not." Boys, if he could credit the dream. "When I left Sorvagur, they were near to being born. The midwife insisted that there were two of them."

"My son, a father! He suffered so much in the growing. Our status was not easy for him to bear. When the gods began speaking to him, when he found his gift for casting the future, I hoped it might help him find a place in the world."

"So it has."

"Shaman to the berserker. 'Tis an honor. Who would have thought? When your mother was first brought to Husavik, I tried to help her."

"So you said, Mistress."

"I had been taken ahead of her, you see, and already knew a few things. I knew of the dangers. Things worked out well for her in the end, far better than ever for me."

"Take heart, Mistress. You will soon be safe in Sorvagur with your friend, your son, and your grandchildren." An end to her long nightmare, so he hoped.

If such long and evil dreams ever truly came to an end.

****

"What does your elven lover want from you?" Embra asked Runi as she recovered from her meeting with Borlika. In her experience, everyone wanted something.

Runi pursed his lips, not looking at her. "She would like fine to kill everyone in Husavik and wipe the settlement and all traces of it from the land."

Embra glanced at him, startled. "Could she do such a thing?"

"Ach, ja. She might break the ground open with a wave of her hand or send molten fire spilling over us all."

"She does not, because—"

"Because I am here." He said it flatly, without boasting—a fact and no more.

"So, you alone stand between the rest of us and destruction?"

He grinned at her, the kind of smile she but rarely saw from him. "So it seems."

"Ah. Is this why you want no part of being jarl?"

"Nei, I want no part of being jarl because I yet retain a few shreds of sanity. Borlika asks me to surrender my ties and go to stay with her for good."

"You would not do such a thing, would you?"

"Sostir, never say you would miss me."

"I would miss you, Runi." She felt the truth of that to her toes.

He sighed. "Do not turn sentimental on me, Embra. It suits neither of us."

"And can only be interpreted as weakness."

He nodded. "Is that why you love your Magnus? Because he can love and yet remain strong?"

"Magnus does not love me."

That jerked Runi's head around.

"He but enjoys our couplings."

"Everyone enjoys the coupling."

"I think he admires some things about me. And being a warm and compassionate man, he feels for me. That is not love."

"Nei, so it is not."

"Love, as I have learned by knowing him, is heedless. It cares far less for itself than for the object of its affection. It will—will sacrifice itself, if necessary."

"Well, listen to you, Sostir! Making such bold and sweeping declarations."

"I would do anything for him, whether he asked me or nay."

Runi stared. "This? From my strong and flint-hearted sister?"

"Flint-hearted?"

He began to laugh. "Never mind."

"Who calls me that?"

"Everyone. Men gave up long ago on catching your interest. I have never seen you look at any man as you do the seafarer."

"I've never known anyone like him."

"Then win him, Sostir. Win his heart. At least you know he has one."

"I do not know how to win his heart."

"You are a clever woman. I am sure you will think of a way."

Ach, at least one of them was sure.

Embra thought about going out into the settlement, back into the fray, and understood suddenly why Runi stayed away with his elven lover. Being here, well, it just hurt too much.

"Runi, what will happen now?"

"I have persuaded Borlika to calm the land and keep the fire from the sky. That way, all Husavik will think the gods approve of your marriage and of you holding the place of jarl, which should keep Asger at bay. If that is what you want." He shot her a look. "Is that what you want?"

"Ja."

"Then do you mean to persuade your seafarer to stay here with you?"

"Ja, or convince him to return to me, if he must sail."

"And if he refuses?"

"Then I shall have to put his welfare and wishes ahead of my own."

Runi snorted. "Forgive me, Sostir, for scoffing. But you, like me, are born of two of the most selfish people ever to walk this world. You expect me to believe you capable of such sacrifice?"

She widened her eyes at him. "I expect nothing. I venture—I venture to hope."

Chapter Thirty-Six

Apsel returned to the longboat the next morning looking sheepish and chastened. The others of the men who had gone philandering were already back on board. Apsel made the last to rejoin their company.

He came with his dark hair shining and a measure of rueful wonder in his eyes, and stood looking at Magnus bemusedly.

"So you are back, then," Magnus observed.

"Ja."

"Spent?" Magnus could not help but ask.

Apsel made a face. "Wrung out dry." He glanced over his shoulder at the settlement on the shore. "This place—is there some enchantment at work here? It is like being in a dream."

"An evil one, perhaps."

"I tell you, Magnus, now that I have awakened, I cannot wait to be gone. How soon do we leave?"

Magnus considered it, his own gaze straying to the shore. With Apsel returned, he had no excuse not to sail. All Mistress Catrin's belongings, pitifully few, were aboard. He must consider her welfare, keep his promise, and take her to Lodvar.

"Today," he told Apsel.

"Ja? What about your wife?" Apsel cocked an eye at Magnus. "Was wedding her not a bit hasty?"

"It is complicated."

"Ja, so I would say. Do you love her?"

A hint of challenge in the question returned Magnus's glance to Apsel's face.

"Only," Apsel went on when Magnus did not answer, "I have never seen you like this with any other woman."

"There was only ever Astrid."

"Astrid, ja, and you never looked at her the way you look at Embra."

He'd never felt toward Astrid what he felt for Embra.

"And I know how you like to keep your promises."

"So I do."

"Is a marriage vow not a promise?"

"I made a promise to Lodvar first." Yet he would have to go and tell Embra fairly that he was set to leave. It would not go easily for either of them.

He gazed out over the bay toward the open sea. Clouds hung heavy as a blanket above the water, promising rain. But the land had quieted. Perhaps it was the proper time to go.

He told Apsel, "Ready us to sail. I will go make my farewells."

"To your wife."

"My wife, ja."

Apsel nodded and moved off.

Feeling a tingle that crept up his spine and filled his head, Magnus called after him. "Should anything happen while I am away, guard Mistress Catrin well."

"What will happen?"

Magnus shrugged. He gathered his weapons and took up his shield before making his way ashore through the soft morning.

As he went, he wondered about the nature of love. He could not deny he felt a connection to Embra when they coupled. Tenderness and caring. That was just the product of coupling though, was it not? A powerful thing that fogged the mind. Just look at Apsel.

Yet—there must be a reason he'd never spoken for Astrid, back in Sorvagur. He'd been looking for something else, something more. Had he found that, in Embra?

He would speak with her now, set sail, and see what his feelings were once he was away from this place of guile and deception. If his heart demanded it, he would return for her. Return *to* her.

His bride.

The settlement, already well astir with the morning, bustled around him. Folks hurrying about their business stared at him, eyes sliding to him in a way that sent a wave of warning through his blood. Something was not right.

That conviction screamed loudly at him an instant before his step faltered. He turned. Warriors behind him. Closing in from the side, and encircling him. No more than a score of steps from Embra's door, he found himself surrounded.

The first face he recognized belonged to Asger. A score of other warriors, most of them aged, all of them armed, backed up the would-be jarl. Magnus's mouth went dry. He had sparred often enough with his father to know just how dangerous a man of this generation could be.

Ja, he himself fought well. He could easily take one or two of these men. Maybe five or six, if the battle madness returned. Not this many.

They had come for him armed not only with swords and axes but cudgels. It was the classic way to bring a berserker down—club him senseless, so the madness died.

Along, ofttimes, with the berserker.

So this was it, eh? He would die here, die for the sake of a woman he may or may not love. He would never see his home again.

He glared into Asger's eyes, which glowed with hate, and gripped his axe in his hand. Ja, and if so, he would go down fighting.

****

"Mistress Embra, Mistress Embra! They have attacked him."

Kennach crashed into Embra's quarters, eyes wild and hair flying. She started up from her place beside the hearth and felt all the blood drain from her head.

"Attacked—whom?" But she knew. *She knew*. She had felt this coming, the same way she felt the ground tremble beneath her feet or a storm build out to sea. *Magnus*.

"Where?" she gasped, not waiting for Kennach to answer, and ran to the door. There—she could see for herself. A battle took place on the slope just below her quarters. He must have been coming to her, coming to her when he was surrounded.

She pulled her knife from her boot and shouted at Kennach, "Go and find Runi. Quickly!"

Nearly all the folk of the settlement, or so it seemed, poured out from their dwellings, heading in the same direction as Embra. She had to shout and shove people aside to get through. Before she reached the pitched battle, she could tell it did not go well. The battle was, in fact, between a score of men and the one man who possessed her heart.

And he, in a berserker's rage.

They surrounded him exactly as hounds might a captured bear, attempting to attack from all sides. Like that bear, after which his affliction was named, he was dangerous. The crumpled forms of those he had already defeated lay in heaps. But as she ran, her eyes wide and her heart pounding, she also saw the wounds that marked him.

They baited him. One struck and when he spun, his bloodied axe at the ready, another hacked at him from behind.

He would die. Surely here before her eyes she would see him fall. No man—berserker or not—could withstand this for long.

"Nei!" She ran in screaming the word, her blade raised high. She held the place of jarl. They must listen to her. "Nei. Stop. Stop!"

They did not hear her, such was the racket of the fight, until she dashed in among them, pushing men aside and using the point of her blade when she had to. She inserted her body between Magnus and those who taunted him, still bellowing. "Stop. Stop this!"

The world screeched to a halt. Angry faces surrounded her, and reddened blades. She heard little beyond the pounding of her own heart.

A blade aimed at Magnus had stuttered off her arm. She barely felt the pain. Was this how it was for him? Did the madness take over so he did not mark the blows or the wounds, did not feel the blood flow? Yet she acted not from the berserker's fit but love.

She could feel him standing behind her where she

made her body a shield for his, feel the heat of him like a great fire burning. She heard, above the rattling of her heart, his breath.

She waved her blade and shouted, "What is the meaning of this?"

No one answered, but the attackers backed off a measure. Asger looked furious, his companions—many of whom bled freely—wary yet jubilant. They'd meant to torment Magnus as they might a captured animal, to the death.

She whirled and gazed into Magnus's eyes, but the man she loved wasn't there. The madness still possessed him fully, and his hazel eyes glowed with unholy light. When they met hers, they contained no recognition and no sanity.

For an instant, they stood so, she hanging on the edge of his madness, sharing it with him, feeling it all. For the first time in her life she forgot herself—the single person she had always cherished—for the pure love of him.

Against the wall of his madness and pain, she spoke into his mind. *My love. Ach, my love, return to me.*

As if she called to him across a great distance, as if her heart did, he came. She saw the madness clear from his eyes, like mist rolling away over the ocean, until his spirit—that she adored above any other—regained hold.

With a sob, she reached for him, laid her hands on his bloodied forearms. He parted his lips to speak and she heard his voice in her head before any word escaped him. *Embra.*

He did not in truth have a chance to speak aloud before someone behind him brought a cudgel down on his head, and along with him, Embra's world crashed into darkness.

Chapter Thirty-Seven

"This is a peaceful place. I often come here when I need some time alone." Magnus gave Embra his smile, the one that lit his gaze and her world along with it.

They sat on a clifftop, one clothed with brilliant green turf, overlooking the sea. Far below, looking small enough to be toys, two longboats floated in a harbor. Above, the sky—gray-blue and whirling with gulls—stretched forever.

"But you are not alone," she said. "I am here."

"Ah—ja." His smile deepened and carved dimples in his cheeks. "I am glad."

"Where are we?" Embra did not recognize this place.

"Home. We are home."

"Are we dead?" It seemed quite possible. The last she remembered, they'd both dripped blood. She had tried to defend him, but he had been struck down. This, though, looked nothing like Hel, or Valhalla.

Magnus searched her face with interest. "I do not think so. This is Sorvagur."

"Did we sail here? I do not remember."

He said nothing but reached for her hand. His fingers, marked by wounds, felt sticky with blood. Ja, and blood also marked his hairline. Why had she not noticed that at once?

Indeed, blood showed on her own left arm, the one

he held.

Was death like a return home? Yet Embra had never known a real home, and Sorvagur was his place of belonging, not hers. Certainly her parents had provided no place that felt safe to her, and she'd not found it in the quarters she called her own.

Was it that for which Runi had gone searching with Borlika? A home? He had found it with his elven lover.

Just as she'd found it in Magnus. Home was a feeling of trust, more than a place. Wherever Magnus might be, that was her home.

"How did we come here?"

Still he did not answer. But she could feel his strength flowing into her where his fingers clutched hers. She could sense the man he was and the depth of his heart. A home, in his heart.

"When I sit here," he said at last, "nothing else matters. I can feel the past—all my ancestors standing behind me—and the future also. The years stretch away from me. They carry magic."

Ja, Magnus was a place rather than just a man, a place where Norse met Gael. And the stronger for it.

Suddenly she felt humble—she who had been gifted by her parents with naught but privilege.

"We take what we are given," she told him. "The good with the bad. The strengths with the weaknesses. In the end, who can say which is which? Your berserker's rage—is it a curse or a blessing?"

"I am not that rage," he answered. "I am the light—there, on the water. I am the smile in my fadir's eyes. I am the chime of music in my modir's harp strings. I am here, forever. Embra, I love you." Suddenly he looked her full in the eyes. "And I will be with you always."

****

Embra woke to a wealth of pain. A seething stripe of fire blazed down one arm and a crippling cramping seized her muscles. The strength of the agony made her gasp and catch her breath.

How to endure? For an instant, she did not believe she could. Ach, let her lapse into senselessness. Away from this.

In the act of reaching for darkness, a thought broke upon her. *Magnus*. Where was he? They had been sitting together on the cliff, a place he told her was in Sorvagur. Only, had they been? Was he alive?

She pried her eyes open one eyelid at a time and tried to determine where she was—in her quarters, lying in her own nest of blankets. Her arm, the one that burned so terribly, lay atop the blanket, well-bandaged.

Alone?

Nei. A figure near the door stirred when she moved. She knew him even in the dim light. "Kennach?"

He hurried to her side and knelt down. "Mistress! I did not know whether you would wake. The healer said—" Kennach turned his head and the firelight caught his face. Immediately she saw that tears marked his cheeks. Never say he wept for her! "The healer said you were felled during the berserker's fit. How could that be?"

"Magnus. Where is he?"

"They prepare his funeral pyre."

"What?" Despite her pain, she shot up. She seized her man by the arms. "Dead? He is dead?"

"He lies in a state like stone, barely breathing. As

good as dead, the healer says. Only his heart keeps him here in the world."

Only his heart.

I will be with you always.

"Take me to him."

"Mistress—"

"Take me. Bring me my knife. His enemies…" She corrected carefully, for Magnus had not been attacked so much for who he was, as to strike at her. "*My* enemies may decide to finish him."

"He lies under guard. Master Runi came in time to prevent Master Asger's men beating him to death."

"Help me up."

Kennach tried. Together they gave it a valiant effort, but Embra proved too weak to stand. So this was the aftermath of the berserker's fit, was it? A terrible thing to bear.

She wept. "I must go to him."

Kennach's palm smoothed the hair at her brow as a father's might—the father she'd never had. "Do not weep."

Her man—her slave—gathered her into his arms as if she were a child. In all the years he'd served her, most her life, he'd touched her but rarely and only when strictly necessary. Tending a scraped knee when she fell. Offering a steadying hand.

Now in his touch she felt caring. "I will take you to him, Mistress. Let me carry you."

She hid her face against Kennach's chest as they went. She wondered what made him care about her, and if she'd ever cared enough about him, in the past. He'd had plenty to eat, always. A warm, dry place to sleep. She'd never mistreated him, though he'd been open to her father's discipline when Fadir lived, still, and Gunnar's vile desires for amusement.

What made Kennach care for her, in the face of all that?

She could not make a light burden, yet he carried her without complaint.

They went to the great hall, to the open area just in front of it, where torches flared and Runi was waiting. Her brother strode up and down, sword at his side, as if guarding the figure that lay stretched—

He did lie on a bier, the torches all around him. Like a hero. Like the berserker he was.

Runi spun to meet them when Kennach ran up, and the other men on guard stiffened until Runi waved his hand.

They protected Magnus. They protected her love.

Kennach set her on her feet, and her legs promptly gave way. Kennach and Runi both reached to uplift her.

Looking into Runi's face, she bleated, "Is he dead?"

Runi's expression, closed tight, did not change. "Difficult to say. He lives, yet he does not."

Embra stumbled to the bier. Magnus lay with his eyes closed. He looked like a carving, save for his wounds, which marked him in stark relief. Someone— the healer most likely—had made an attempt to wash away the blood and bandage the worst of those wounds, but they bled still.

If he bled still, that must mean his heart beat. He lived.

Bending over him, she spoke brokenly. "My love, my love. I am sorry! This is all my fault." If she'd loved him, she should have sent him from her. Bidden him sail at once to Sorvagur, the place he loved so well.

He made no response, gave no indication he heard her. His broad chest barely rose and fell.

It must have been a dream that they sat together and he told her he loved her, words he'd never gifted her in life. Just a dream.

She raised her face to Runi. "What does the healer say?"

He shook his head. "Sostir, I regret—"

"Nei!" To have love after starving for it so long, only to lose it. She sobbed. "Nei."

"Listen to me, Embra. I think you should order him taken onto his longboat and tell his men to set sail at once."

"He will never survive a voyage, not like this. He will die on the way."

"Quite likely." Runi flicked a glance at the near-motionless figure on the bier. "Better the seafarer should die at sea than here in this evil place. He is your husband and you are still jarl. If you give the order, it will be obeyed."

Send him away. To die.

"If you love him. Sostir, we were, ja, raised in selfishness. If you ever can reach beyond that, let it be now."

She nodded. It would break her to send Magnus away from her. Finish breaking her—for she felt already shattered.

"These are my men," Runi indicated the guards. "They will obey me. Let us now carry him down to his boat."

They went in a procession, Embra following the men who carried the bier, Kennach supporting her every step.

The folk of the settlement, many still astir, watched their progress. No doubt someone would run and tell Asger, and Vanja.

At the harbor, Runi sent one of his men out to signal Magnus's longboat.

Even before the *skupa* reached the longboat, Magnus's men hung over the side, shouting.

Runi's guard called back to them, explaining what was afoot. A furor broke out on board, Magnus's men taking up their weapons and threatening to go ashore, to their leader's rescue.

Once again, as she had before, Embra waded out through the water—above her knees, then her thighs and waist. When it lapped against her breasts, she called out.

"Master Apsel? Are you there?"

He leaned over the gunwale, his dark hair marking him, easily visible.

"You must take Magnus—take him away from here, or he will die." He might die anyway. On the bier behind her, he might already be gone. But, nei—she believed she could feel him yet, within her spirit.

Could she live in the future on but that hint of knowing?

"Take him," she told Apsel, a demand rather than a request. If she weakened now, she might never let Magnus go.

"Ja," Apsel called back. And to Runi's man in the *skupa*, "Bring him aboard. We will sail at once."

Chapter Thirty-Eight

Magnus came awake abruptly, on a wave of awareness that blasted all his senses. He must be lying on his back, because overhead he could see sails—familiar sails that told him he lay aboard his own longboat. Past the sails he glimpsed a night sky, just lightening toward dawn. The motion of the boat cradled him. They were asea.

And everything—everything felt wrong.

He hurt from head to toe with a ferocity that stole his breath. Wounds, ja. He tried to remember the battle in which he'd fought, but it refused to come to him. Beneath the pain lay a miasma that began to feel sickeningly familiar. The aftermath of the berserker's rage.

By all the gods, what had happened to him?

He stirred, only to be hit with another punch of agony. The weakness that followed on the heels of the rage covered a third and even deeper ache.

Something missing. Something missing—*his heart*.

With an act of will that astounded him, he forced his muscles to obey him and sat up. They sailed, ja, before a good wind, with a buoyancy that told him they rode the open sea.

Whence bound?

He needed to get up, to get to his feet and, as master of the boat, find out.

As soon as he sat up, two of his men were with him, one on either side. Apsel and Knut they were, full of concern.

With their help, he attained his feet and leaned against the mast. Beneath a near-full moon, he saw only open water around them. He swayed, and his aching stomach muscles heaved.

"What happened?" he gasped.

Knut, a look of concern heavy on his face, asked, "You do not remember?"

"Nei."

"You were attacked. Clubbed down."

That explained why his head hurt the way it did. About the berserker's fit, he did not have to ask.

Hastily, he shoved his friends away, limped to the side, and was heartily sick into the ocean. Knut's grip on the back of his tunic kept him from falling overboard.

"When did we leave Husavik?" His sluggish thoughts strove to make sense of it.

"Not long ago."

"Embra?"

Apsel pushed him down with his back against the side of the boat. "It was she begged us to take you away out of Husavik."

"She did?"

Apsel hunkered beside him. "Not because she does not care for you—the opposite, I think. She was beside herself, Magnus, frantic for your safety." Apsel made a face. "Hard to believe one of her breed could show concern for any but herself, but so it was."

She'd said she loved him. Perhaps she'd just proved it. And what of him?

Did he love Embra Fritisdottir?

He pressed the heels of his battered hands against his aching head. Before they sailed much farther, he needed to determine where lay his heart.

****

"Drink this." Runi thrust a cup of mead into Embra's hand. She brought it to her lips, but half choked on the contents. Runi had, rather surprisingly, been looking after her ever since Magnus's boat sailed out of the harbor. He'd brought her home, ordered her to change out of her sopping clothing, and stirred up her fire. More astounding yet, he showed no signs of leaving.

He eyed her as she gulped the mead, but she could not read his expression. Sitting beside the fire, she pressed her forehead to her raised knees. "What do I do now, Brodir? Tell me that."

He snorted. "You think I have answers?"

"Nei."

"We were never taught about love, were we? We had few examples of it. Ja, sure, Borlika has taught me some. It is not what I was led to believe."

"You are right, it is not. I never imagined caring for anyone the way I do for Magnus. And what I feel for him, Runi, is not love so much as need. I need to be with him. Failing that, I need to know he is somewhere in this world, safe and—and just being Magnus. Even if it tears the heart from me, seeing him go. Does that make any sense?"

"Ja. And nei." Runi shook his head. "The need, I understand. Over the years, it has taken me to Borlika time and again, even when I swore to keep away. Need. And—and tenderness."

279

That made her look at him. Runi, speaking of tenderness? "Sostir, perhaps you should have gone with him."

"How could I? Turn leadership, here, over to Vanja and Asger? You know what would happen. There would be no hope for innocents such as Ulla, if she is still innocent, or the slaves—"

"Ja, I know."

"There is no one else." Embra said it starkly, and half hoped Runi would contradict her, say he would take the leadership, the responsibility from her shoulders. But Runi was Runi, and anyway—

"He never said he loved me." She spoke the words that lodged in her throat.

"Nei?"

"Never once."

"Not even when you lay together?"

"Nei." She drew a breath against the pain in her chest. "So I must carry on here. Without—without a future. Without my heart."

"Embra—" Runi began to speak, but they were interrupted by Kennach, who came in the door. He shot a sharp look at Runi before he spoke to Embra.

"Mistress, they have cleared the harbor."

"Safely?"

"Safely, aye, Mistress."

"Good. It is well. Now the two of you may leave me."

"Mistress, are ye certain—"

"Go."

She did not want either of them to see her break down, could not bear for them to watch her cry.

****

Dawn flowed across the water, and with it came Magnus's vitality. Life returned to him softly, accompanied by memory.

He remembered his parents walking together on an autumn morning, his mother's hair like russet flame, and the scars on Fadir's face stark in the clear light. They moved in unconscious harmony, their steps in time as if their hearts kept one beat. Modir talked as they paced the green turf, and Fadir listened, as he so often did.

All his life he'd witnessed their love, set himself a standard by it. He'd always known that, in times of strife, they were able to travel to one another in spirit, even across great distances, to provide comfort and sustenance.

And Gyda and Lodvar—so entwined were their spirits, they spoke into one another's minds. Magic there was in it.

All this time he'd been searching for his share of such a magic. Had he failed to recognize it, when it came?

Perhaps so. For with every league of water gained between him and Husavik, he felt more desperate.

To be sure, he did not miss the place. But one woman there…

When had she become part of him? The first time she stood up for him? The first time they made love? What did it require to take an enemy and turn her into a lover? *Magic*.

Someone moved into place beside him, lit by the clear morning light. Mistress Catrin it was, wrapped tight in her shawl against the chill on the water, her face worn. She looked at him questioningly before lowering herself to the deck where he sat.

"Master Magnus, are you unwell?"

A mother's concern filled her voice. Ja, whatever else this woman had been in the past, she was a mother—one who doubtless knew a great deal about self-sacrifice.

"I fell victim to the berserker's fit, and still recover. I will be all right."

"You carry some terrible wounds. And your men say you were beaten down."

"It is, as all know, the best way to overwhelm a berserker."

"You inherited this—this ability from your father?"

"So it seems. Until a year ago, Mistress, I had no idea I carried the tendency, and had no true grasp of what it meant to suffer the berserker's curse. Fadir— Fadir always dreaded me inheriting it. We thought I had escaped. It turns out, for me and Gyda both, it takes much to spur it, and is brought about by a threat to what we love."

Catrin's eyes widened. "Gyda too? But she is a woman!"

"And a true woman, to her heart. She would fight the gods themselves for Lodvar."

Catrin gazed at her hands. "I am glad he has that. I was able to give him so little as he grew. Has he told you? How he was shunned, I mean—treated always by his father as an afterthought. When he decided to sail with Gunnar, serving as his shaman, I was against it. Gunnar always behaved most cruelly toward him."

"Gunnar," Magnus pronounced heavily, "was willing to use anything and anyone that came to his hand in order to further his own desires."

Catrin said softly, "The guiding principle of Husavik."

Staring over the side of the boat, Magnus narrowed his eyes. "Having been raised in such a midden, is it possible Embra should truly care for me? Love me?"

"Is that what she told you?"

"Ja, it is."

"Magnus, I have lived a long time in terrible circumstances. I learned long ago that one can live on crumbs, so long as one has a measure of love. Lodvar gave that to me, for a long while. His affection allowed me to walk through my days. Then I had to watch him sail away from me."

Magnus turned his head and looked into her pale, worn face and found her eyes. They glowed like those of a young girl. "Now, a miracle occurs for me, and I go to him."

"What are you saying, Mistress?"

She met his gaze. "That perhaps Embra is not meant to be your miracle. But you are meant to be hers."

Ah, ja, and why had he not seen that for himself? All this talk of selflessness, and he had been the selfish one. Waiting for the magic to come to him. Waiting for his dreams and expectations to manifest. When the woman who loved him fair starved for what only he could give her.

He fought his way to his feet and called to Knut, who manned the rudder. "Hie! We must turn about."

"Eh?" Knut called back to him. Many of the other men slept. They stirred at the sound of Magnus's voice and stared at him. "What did you say?"

"Turn the boat about. We must return to Husavik."

"Are you mad?" Jorg arose and came to him. "We are well away from that accursed place."

But Apsel gave Magnus a long look. "Best turn about. I do believe Magnus has forgotten something he cannot live without."

Chapter Thirty-Nine

The dream did not feel like a dream but real, immediate and vital. Everyone Embra knew was there, and that's what tipped her off, in the end, to the fact that it must be a dream. Populated by both those living and dead, it could be nothing else.

Fadir was there, wearing his customary self-satisfied, confident expression. And Gunnar, standing tall, his golden hair lit by the sun. Even though it had been a year since she'd seen them, since they'd set sail to, as they'd put it, wreak vengeance upon the berserker, their presence affected her the way it always had, prompting wariness and caution.

And Modir—Modir stood by, looking younger than she did now. Ach, and she was beautiful, her tumbled hair the same color as Gunnar's, her eyes wide. More, she did not appear mad, her mind not yet turned.

How could it be that Modir looked so young, when all her children stood around her fully grown? Not only Gunnar but Ulrik, returned to life, and even young Ulla standing and holding Modir's hand.

Holding Modir's hand. Something Embra could not remember ever having done in her life.

They all stood on the rise above the harbor, watching a longboat sail in.

A beautiful boat it was, riding low in the water, with graceful sides and a carved bow. The finest oak had been used to build it, bargained away from Erin, no doubt. And in the morning light it appeared to be chased in gold.

"He comes," said Runi, who stood beside her. She turned her head to look at him. He did not stand on his own. Next to him, Embra beheld a cloud of light. Even as she watched, it stirred and shifted and became Borlika, clasping hands with him.

The elven woman looked at Embra and winked.

"He is dangerous," Vanja pronounced.

Gunnar corrected, "He is death."

"He has come for me." Fadir stepped forward. "We must slay him before he kills us."

"Nei." Utterly certain, Embra held out her hands toward the harbor. "He has come for me. Only for me."

"Sostir, Sostir, wake." Runi's voice in her ear. "He is come."

"Eh?" With the remnants of the dream clinging to her like a spider's web, Embra raised her head from her blankets. She did not recall falling asleep. She had sent Runi from her. He must have returned. "Who?"

"Your lover, Magnus."

Runi's face, as so often, appeared emotionless.

"But," she objected stupidly, "I sent him away."

"He has returned. Word came from the harbor, and Kennach has confirmed the truth of it."

Returned? For her? Embra's heart expanded and rose, beating hard as if it would escape her chest, perhaps float to the harbor on its own into the possession of the man she loved.

"Nei," she breathed, scarcely daring to believe.

"Ja. Best get up. Gather your things."

"Why?"

"You do not suppose he has returned in order to stay here in Husavik, do you?"

With Runi's help, she stumbled to her feet. "I have nothing. Nothing I wish to take. Except—" she glanced at the door of her quarters where she now saw Kennach peering in. "Kennach? You will come with me?"

His somber face lit. "Aye, Mistress. If ye do want me."

"You cannot imagine, can you, that I would go without you? Hurry, get your belongings."

"I have naught either, Mistress." He blinked. "Save ye."

Embra looked at Runi. "If he has not come back for me—"

"Have faith, Sostir. Believe. The moment comes to each of our lives when we must believe in something. Your heart chose him, and it seems he does not disappoint."

"But—" As the remnants of the dream fell away, she began thinking more clearly. "I cannot leave here. If Asger takes leadership, what will happen to all I leave behind? Ulla—"

"You might take Ulla with you. Ask her if she wishes to go. Either way—" Runi drew himself up. To her astonishment, he caught her face between his hands and gazed into her eyes. "I will assume leadership here and try to muster some vestiges of decency."

"You? But you never wanted to be jarl."

"I still abhor the prospect. But I care for you, Sostir. And I perceive that some—some fineness in you, come from the gods only know where, will not allow you to abandon this place and follow your heart. So I free you, do you hear? Just as you free Kennach—

for the sake of love."

"Ach, Runi. Ach, Runi!" She began to weep, helpless against emotions she'd denied so long.

They stood clinging to one another while Embra's future sailed into the harbor, and a measure of healing came.

"Go," he whispered then. "Be happy."

"You—and Borlika."

"Borlika and I cannot break. We are too strong. Neither can I leave her, ever. I hope you understand."

For a moment longer they clung together before Embra uttered the words she'd spoken to so few. "I love you. I love you, Brodir."

"And I you, Sostir. Now go and seize your future."

****

She tripped over her own feet as she hurried down to the harbor with Kennach at her side. Runi had gone to wake Ulla and ask her if she wanted to go with Embra. If she did, he would bring her, and meet them below.

She reached the harbor just as Magnus's longboat came to a halt and dropped anchor. She was not the only one there. The guards, to be sure had given cry, and early risers hurried up. Exclamations filled the misty morning air.

Kennach strode out onto the pier, where he leaned forward, straining for freedom. And on board the longboat—

Magnus, covered with wounds, only half bandaged. He leaned over the side and stretched out a hand to Embra. *To her*.

All her doubt fled. She drew a breath that seemed her first in a lifetime.

"Ready the *skupa*," she told Kennach. "Are you sure you want to come with me?"

"Aye, Mistress."

"I must wait for Ulla." But her gaze reached for Magnus even as his hand reached for her.

She sent out desperate thoughts to him, speaking in her mind. *You returned.*

For you, for you, my love. But how could this be, that she heard his reply?

Runi and Ulla, both breathing hard, hurried down the slope behind her. Ulla carried a hastily-tied bundle.

"Take her," Runi said shortly. "She is willing to go."

"Are you, Ulla?" Embra looked into her youngest sister's face, and found it wet with tears.

Ulla nodded. "I am."

Embra laid her hands on Ulla's shoulders. "Are you perfectly certain? We go to a strange and foreign place, one founded by our father's enemies. Those who slew Fadir and Gunnar."

Ulla met her gaze. "If I stay here, I fear I will become—someone I do not wish to be."

"Get into the *skupa*."

Kennach already stood aboard. He offered Ulla his hand.

Embra turned back to Runi. "How can I ever thank you? This gift you are giving me—"

"No need for thanks. Go, before the others get here and make a scene. Be happy."

"I may never see you again."

"We must each cling to our own measure of happiness. Go."

She hugged him hard and climbed into the *skupa*.

The oars creaked as Kennach pulled on them. Behind Runi, lit by the radiance of the morning burning through the mist, she could see her sisters hurrying down, Vanja with Asger at her side.

She turned her back squarely upon them, fixed her gaze on Magnus, and embraced her future.

Chapter Forty

"A curious thing," Embra murmured as she burrowed in closer to Magnus, where they sat on the deck of the longboat. He tightened his arms, the better to embrace her. His pain and the last effects of his berserker's rage had started to ease from him the moment she'd come aboard, the instant they'd touched.

They had now cleared the harbor and moved far out to sea. The last of the morning mist was risen, revealing a silvery expanse of water as far as the eye could see. "When Kennach and I reached the harbor back there, I thought I heard you speak to me."

He glanced at her before consulting the tangled emotions that filled him. So many emotions, he could scarcely tell one from the other. Amazement that she had agreed to come away with him. Relief. Joy. *Love*.

"What did I say?" he asked with the peaceable calm of a man who held all he needed in his arms.

"That you had returned for me."

"Surely you knew I would." He nuzzled the soft hair over her ear.

"Hoped. I dared to hope. I thought it might be at the end of the summer. Or next year." Her gaze met his. "Not so soon."

Magnus's heart rose like a sail filling with the wind. "Well you see, as soon as I hit the open water, I realized the truth."

"And that is?"

"That I love you. I suppose I should have discovered it sooner."

"It might have been helpful."

"You are my bride. And you possess my heart. How could I sail away and leave you behind?"

She sighed and relaxed against him. For many long moments they remained so, listening to the shush of the waves along the bow. Magnus could smell the sea and feel the warmth of the sun on his own skin. It seemed to accelerate the healing begun by this woman at his side.

Strength she was. Strength to the bone. And endurance, wrapped in an astounding measure of self-sacrifice. What a fortunate man he was to be bringing home such a treasure from his voyage. Because it felt as if she'd saved up a lifetime of love, just to spend upon him.

After a few moments she murmured, "You do not mind that I brought Ulla? I could not leave her."

"I do not mind." Magnus stole a look at Ulla, where she sat at the rudder talking with Apsel. His charm, apparently, extended to females of all ages.

"Or Kennach? He has been with me most of my life."

"To be sure. Only look at that." Magnus nodded back to where Kennach and Catrin sat together, speaking softly. "They are looking very comfortable."

Embra tipped her head against his shoulder. "They have much in common. Magnus, I have been so thoughtless about so many things. I hope I can make up for it now."

He drew her still closer against his side.

"And I hope," her voice broke, "your family in

Sorvagur can accept me, the daughter of a man they must have hated full well."

Magnus thought about that. "My parents have learned a few truths over the years, about enemies, and forgiveness. As for Gyda and Lodvar, they understand full well the transformative power of love."

"Still." He felt her shiver and turned her toward him, so he might capture her face between his palms. He gazed deep into her eyes, which looked wide and blue, all her defenses crumbled.

How terrifying it must be for a woman like her, who'd fought all her life in order to protect herself, to hide her emotions lest they might be used against her, to open herself to him so completely.

"Trust me, Embra," he whispered just before he kissed her. "Trust me to hold you safe in my heart."

She gasped when his lips claimed hers, and her trembling ceased. He felt her then, the wealth of love, untapped, that filled her, and her spirit, eager to take flight.

Fear not, he spoke to her mind, to her heart.

Fear? How can I fear when you are with me? she returned.

Lips and spirits joined, the seafarer and his bride sailed on into a life as bright as the light on the water.

A word about the author…

Author Laura Strickland's books have won the prestigious RONE award, the N. N. Light book award, and placed second in the National Excellence in Storytelling contest. She delights in time traveling to the past and searching out settings for her books, be they Historical Romance, Steampunk or something in between.

Married and the parent of one grown daughter, Laura has also been privileged to mother a number of very special rescue dogs, and is intensely interested in animal welfare. Her love of dogs and her lifelong interest in Celtic history, magic, and music are all reflected in her writing. Laura's mantra is Lore, Legend, Love, and she wouldn't have it any other way.

Thank you for purchasing
this publication of The Wild Rose Press, Inc.

For questions or more information
contact us at
info@thewildrosepress.com.

The Wild Rose Press, Inc.